CRIMSON SPRING

Also by Navtej Sarna

Crimson Spring

A Novel

NAVTEJ SARNA

For Preeti

warm wishes

11.7.22

ALEPH

ALEPH

ALEPH BOOK COMPANY
An independent publishing firm
promoted by *Rupa Publications India*

First published in India in 2022
by Aleph Book Company
7/16 Ansari Road, Daryaganj
New Delhi 110 002

ISBN: 978-93-91047-41-2

3 5 7 9 10 8 6 4 2

For sale in the Indian subcontinent only.

Printed in India

'A people's memory is history; and as a man without a memory, so a people without a history cannot grow wiser, better.'

—I. L. Peretz

Dedicated to the heroic courage of
Bhagat Singh, Udham Singh, and Kartar Singh Sarabha,
martyrs for India's freedom

∿

Contents

Author's Note

Writers often carry several persistent aspirations in their hearts, not knowing quite what to do with them. In my case, some of the things I have long wished to write about included the Jallianwala Bagh massacre, early twentieth century Punjab, the Indian soldiers who fought in the Great War, and the revolutionaries who died for India's freedom. It is my hope that I have been able to do justice to these aspirations, individually and collectively, in *Crimson Spring*.

Once written, any novel should ideally be left to each reader to interpret according to his or her own lights. But in this case, as the novel is based, in considerable part, on historical fact, I feel a certain responsibility to point out a few things.

First, the protagonists, of which there are nine. The one whose portrayal is the closest to that of a real-life figure is Udham Singh, who assassinated Sir Michael O'Dwyer, the Lieutenant Governor of Punjab at the time of the massacre, in 1940. His broad biographical details, his footloose personality, his association with the Ghadar revolutionaries, his long chase of O'Dwyer and his final trial all hew as close to fact as possible; the portrayal however is literary and not literal. To create his character, voice, and the diary of his last few weeks, I have used his statements, letters, the transcript of his trial, the memories of his associates or their descendants, and my own visit to London's Pentonville Prison where he was imprisoned, hanged, and then lay buried for thirty-four years; fictional liberties have been taken to flesh out the scant details available of his early life and dramatize the other scenes where he appears. The most important decision I had to make was whether or not to show him to be present at

the Bagh during the shooting, a question on which there is no
clear agreement. I chose to place him in East Africa and not in
Amritsar on that fateful day. I was persuaded by his own statement
during the trial when he said: 'I did not know who was the
Governor at that time when the shooting took place because I
had gone to East Africa at that time. I was not in India at that
time.' I felt that even as unreliable a narrator as Udham Singh had
little reason to lie about this when facing certain death penalty;
on the contrary, an assertion that he had been present during
the massacre would only have added an even more dramatic
dimension to his act of revenge.

Some of the other protagonists, too, found their inspiration in
real persons but their stories, their emotional and psychological
journeys, their thoughts and dilemmas are all their own—and
fictional. Hugh J. Porter is inspired by the then Chief Secretary
of Punjab, J. P. Thompson, but the characters of the two men are
poles apart: Thompson felt none of the qualms and doubts about
colonial excesses that Porter does. Sergeant William J. Anderson,
personal bodyguard to Dyer and an eyewitness to the massacre left
behind a brief memory of the massacre, related by his family to
Alfred Draper, author of *Amritsar: The Massacre That Ended the Raj*.
This brief account gave birth to the story of Sergeant Nicholas
Williams in this book. Gurnam Singh Gambhir is inspired by the
Amritsar lawyer, Gurdial Singh Salaria, who gave evidence before
the Congress Punjab Inquiry (1919–20). Maya Dei's tribulations
reflect for a while the experience of Ratan Devi who too gave
evidence before the same committee and her early life is inspired
by my father Mohinder Singh Sarna's first Punjabi novel, *Peerhan
Malle Rah*.

The rank of the perpetrator of the massacre, R. E. H. Dyer, can
be a source of confusion. At the time of the massacre, Dyer held
the temporary rank of brigadier general but lost this rank when
he had to give up command after the Hunter Committee's report.

Post retirement, he made an attempt to retain brigadier general as his honorary rank but the matter, being a political hot potato, was tossed around between the War Office and the India Office and never resolved. Dyer's rank remained that of a colonel but he was usually referred to as General Dyer, both by his supporters and detractors. To avoid confusion, I have followed this colloquial usage where convenient in this book too.

A word on some other choices: Jalandhar and not Jullundur (except when used for the Jullundur Brigade), Simla and not Shimla, Bombay and not Mumbai. The Golden Temple is used interchangeably with Harmandir Sahib, as is the Holy Book with the Guru Granth Sahib.

A book of this nature relies on several sources—books, individual accounts, archival documents, letters and photographs— and they are too many to enumerate here. The sources to which I have turned repeatedly include the transcripts of the Hunter Committee (1919–20), the Congress Punjab Inquiry (1919–20), the Lahore Conspiracy Case 1915, the trial of Udham Singh, the diaries of J. P. Thompson, World War I diaries of several battalions, in particular the 47th Sikhs, and the regimental history of the London Cyclists Battalion. The books that were always at hand to provide valuable detail include *The Butcher of Amritsar: General Reginald Dyer* by Nigel Collet, *Amritsar 1919: An Empire of Fear and the Making of a Massacre* by Kim Wagner, *Jallianwala Bagh: A Groundbreaking History of the 1919 Massacre* by V. N. Datta, *Jallianwala Bagh, 1919: The Real Story* by Kishwar Desai, *The Patient Assassin: A True Tale of Massacre, Revenge and the Raj* by Anita Anand, *Letters of Udham Singh* by J. S. Grewal and H. K. Puri, *Indian Voices of the Great War: Soldiers' Letters, 1914-18* edited by David Omissi, *India, Empire, and First World War Culture: Writings, Images, and Songs* by Santanu Das, *The Construction of Religious Boundaries: Culture, Identity and Diversity in the Sikh Tradition* by Harjot Oberoi, *Punjabi Century: The Fascinating Story of a Virile*

People by Prakash Tandon, District Gazetteers and Punjab Canal Gazetteers of the time, and many others.

A large number of friends have given freely of their advice or opened doors to facilitate my research and I am grateful to all of them: Ramachandra Guha, Jeevan Deol, Santanu Das, Mahesh Rangarajan, Deepa Bhatnagar, Tony McClenaghan, Rana Chhina, Amarjit Chandan, Nilkanth Avhad, Ravi Murugan, and Namita Gokhale.

I am deeply grateful to David Davidar. His genius recognized the true intent of the manuscript and, with suggestions gentle and wise, helped fashion its final shape. My thanks too to the supreme artist Bena Sareen for the cover design, the meticulous Aienla Ozukum for going through the manuscript with a fine-tooth comb, and my patient agent Jessica Woollard.

My mother Surjit Sarna's presence has been a luminescent blessing. Satyajit and Nooreen, with their highly attuned literary and artistic sensibilities, have been perceptive advisers. A huge thanks to Avina who has long sustained the self-indulgent distractions of a writer with love and care. Her critical insights and forthright honesty as my first reader are invaluable, as is everything else she does for me.

Important Dates

15 July 1913: Formation of the Ghadar Party

28 July 1914: Outbreak of World War I

10 December 1917: Setting up of the Rowlatt Committee

11 November 1918: Armistice, end of World War I

18 March 1919: Passage of the Rowlatt Act

30 March and 6 April 1919: Hartals in Amritsar

10 April 1919: Shooting on the railway bridges in Amritsar

13 April 1919: Jallianwala Bagh massacre

15 April 1919: Proclamation of martial law

9 June 1919: Lifting of martial law

23 July 1927: Death of R. E. H. Dyer

23 March 1931: Execution of Bhagat Singh

13 March 1940: Assassination of Michael O'Dwyer by Udham Singh

31 July 1940: Execution of Udham Singh

Prologue
The Jallianwala Bagh Massacre

Let us begin, then, by stating the facts:

It was the thirteenth of April 1919, the harvest festival of Baisakhi. A large crowd of about twenty-five thousand had gathered in Jallianwala Bagh in Amritsar, Punjab. The Bagh, despite its name, was not a garden but an open area approximately two hundred yards square, enclosed by the high walls of flat-roofed houses and compounds. There were five narrow points of access and exit, some of them locked. On one side stood an old domed samadhi, or memorial, and, on the other, a large well with water twenty feet below its brow. A channel called the Hansli ran through the Bagh, carrying water to the sarovar surrounding the revered Harmandir Sahib or the Golden Temple of the Sikhs. There were a few trees but for the most part the dusty ground was bare.

The crowd was largely made up of men and children. Some people had wandered into the Bagh after the Baisakhi fair; others had paid obeisance at the Harmandir on this auspicious day and come to rest awhile in the open ground. Yet others were there to listen to an afternoon of speeches.

The drone of an aeroplane above distracted the crowd for a while. Then, shortly after five o'clock, a detachment of soldiers led by Brigadier General R. E. H. Dyer entered the Bagh through a lane so narrow that only two could walk abreast. Two armoured cars with mounted machine guns had to be left outside. The soldiers fell into firing positions on a raised bank of land near the entrance, twenty-five Gurkhas on the right and twenty-five Frontier Force men on the left.

On a rough platform about fifty yards away, a speaker was proposing a resolution opposing the Rowlatt Act, the draconian legislation that extended the government's extraordinary wartime powers to imprison people without trial, shut down newspapers and public debate, search homes without warrants and more, all without any regard to judicial process.

The crowd began to panic at the sight of the soldiers. Someone shouted that only blanks would be fired. No warning was given to the crowd to disperse. Dyer gave the order to open fire. The captain of the force repeated the order, whistles added to the confusion, and bullets sprayed instant death into the unarmed crowd. People began to run towards the exits; the bullets followed them, picking them off the walls as they tried to jump over. Dyer ordered the soldiers to reload their magazines and directed the fire to where the crowd was most dense. The soldiers picked their targets, including those who lay flat on the ground, their nails clawing at the earth. Several people jumped into the well to escape the bullets, only to die in it; many others died underfoot. The whistling of the bullets and the screams of the dying echoed back from the brick walls of the surrounding houses. At least 1,650 rounds were fired before Dyer gave the order for the firing to stop, almost fifteen minutes after it had begun. He then marched out through the narrow lane to his car and led his troops back to his camp amidst the old mango trees at Ram Bagh.

Hundreds died in those few minutes and hundreds more were wounded. The wounded were left to die as night came on, one body upon another piled up near the exits. No medical assistance was given and a curfew soon prevented people from coming out to search for their loved ones.

These, then, are the facts. Even a hundred years later, the facts speak for themselves. The before and the after is only history. Its recording and interpretation will differ from soldier to civilian, from brown to white, from ruler to the ruled, from historian to novelist. For every event in history is, at heart, made up of the acts of human beings and its telling is inevitably coloured with the differing shades of pride, regret, ambition, love, pain, courage, and longing that human beings carry within themselves.

PART I

Chapter 1

Nine Lives on
a Strange Baisakhi Day

Baisakhi Day. 13 April 1919. Amritsar was shut. Anger, hostility, and fear had strangled into sullen silence this bustling trading centre that stood on the Grand Trunk Road connecting Delhi to Lahore and Peshawar.

A persistent premonition that something terrible could happen any moment hovered over the city, on both sides of the railway line. On one side lay the crowded walled city with its twelve gates, its sinuous lanes becoming narrower and narrower as they snaked into its crowded interior. Its flat-roofed houses squeezed onto each other, their balconies almost touching, shutting out the light, until the sky was just a sliver above. The suffusion of strong smells, pleasant and not so pleasant, added to the sense of things closing in. At the heart of the old city was the Golden Temple. It sat in its gilded serenity in the sarovar, a pool of water in which the pilgrims bathed. On a normal Baisakhi day, the temple would be teeming with people; baptism with the doubled edged dagger on that day would be of special significance, for on that day the Khalsa, the brotherhood of Sikhs with a clear identity, had been born, two hundred and twenty years earlier.

Beyond the old walls and on the other side of the railway lines were the leafy green areas of the cantonment and the Civil Lines, the preserve of the British colonial rulers. Here there were lawns with flower beds, neat hedges, straight roads, the courts, the club, the church and even a golf course.

A two-lane carriage bridge and an iron footbridge over the

railway line connected these two worlds. It was on these bridges that three days earlier, on the tenth of April, the tension that had been building up in all of Punjab for months, had erupted. On that day, Dr Saifuddin Kitchlew and Dr Satyapal, leaders of the spreading protests against the Rowlatt Act, had been deported to Dharamsala under orders of Sir Michael O'Dwyer, the haughty Lieutenant Governor of Punjab. Crowds gathered on those bridges wanting to cross over to the Civil Lines and appeal to the DC, the Deputy Commissioner, to release their leaders. The authorities panicked and opened fire, killing several people. The angry crowd spilled back into the city's lanes, setting buildings on fire and killing five Europeans who fell into their hands. Marcella Sherwood, a supervisor of the city's mission schools was attacked in a side alley off the narrow lane, Kucha Kaurianwala. More soldiers were rushed to Amritsar. They marched through the lanes and set up pickets. Water and electricity to the city were cut off. Amritsar retreated into an uneasy silence. Its inhabitants were angry; this was no way to celebrate the Baisakhi festival of spring, the success of the harvest, the coming of the New Year.

❧

Maya Dei had managed to pray at the Golden Temple on Baisakhi morning, in the ambrosial hour before dawn. Every day, for the last fifteen days, she had woken up while it was still pitch dark, bathed, and walked barefoot to the gurudwara through the narrow lanes that led from the home of Lala Sunder Das, adjacent to Jallianwala Bagh, where she and her husband Joga Singh were staying. Each day, particularly after the firing and violence of the tenth, it had got more difficult; the police and military were everywhere, many lanes were barricaded. But Bisheshwar, the Lala's younger son, only fourteen years old, was her ally. He would guide her by a new route each morning; waif-like, he could dodge every barrier, criss-cross through private houses, find ways across roofs. No matter what the risk, the boy had got it into his head that he had to help her fulfil her vow to Waheguru that she would pray at the Golden Temple for forty days. And then He would grant her the only boon she wanted: a child to make her happiness complete; otherwise there was nothing lacking in the life she and Joga Singh had created for themselves in the village of Parhi, on the other side of the river Jhelum, over a hundred miles to the north-west of Amritsar.

For the last three years, without telling her husband, she had tried whatever the older women in the village had suggested, eating what they said, praying in the direction they pointed to, but nothing had worked. Then someone had told her the ancient story of Dani, the wife of a Sidhu peasant from Ferozepur who had been blessed with a son by Sakhi Sarwar Pir twelve years after marriage. Maya made the same pilgrimage that Dani had made in that legend, joining a group going from Sohawa to the Baisakhi mela at the pir's shrine at Nagaha. She bathed in the stream that ran below the shrine at the feet of the Sulaiman mountains and then climbed the steep steps to pray, breaking her overnight fast only when she came down. She tied sacred threads on the dead branches of the tree to which the Pir had tied his mare many centuries ago. The next year she had gone to the annual fair at Gujranwala and the next to the famous Jhanda Mela at Peshawar. Joga Singh did not go with her; he did not believe in these pilgrimages. But he didn't stand in her way.

But this year she had decided that she would not go to any of the Sakhi Sarwar shrines. Her husband's face had lit up when she told him first thing one morning: 'This year for Baisakhi we will go to Amritsar. I dreamt of Harmandir Sahib this morning and they say that if you dream of something just before you wake up then it means something special.'

That was why they had locked up the house with the red, yellow, and blue glass windowpanes and taken the lorry to Jhelum and then a train that helped them cross the Jhelum River on an incredibly long bridge and brought them first to Lahore and then to Amritsar, the Guru's own town. Lala Sunder Das had welcomed them warmly. He was a rich coal merchant and an old friend of Joga Singh who had moved from Rawalpindi to Amritsar in search of better business. That his business had prospered was obvious from his well-furnished three-storey house, the narrow back windows of which, with their painted iron bars, looked over Jallianwala Bagh.

Long after Maya Dei had returned from the Golden Temple and distributed the prasad to the entire household, Joga Singh stood looking down into the Bagh from those windows. Preparations were underway for some sort of event. Some men were hastily fashioning a platform with planks. Slowly, in ones and twos, people began to come through the only real entrance, from Queen's Bazaar. Several children were small enough to be carried on the shoulders of their fathers and grandfathers. Joga Singh's eye caught a strange sight: a smart, tall man of soldierly bearing wearing an army tunic and neat khaki turban was walking in with two bulls. He headed towards the large peepul tree near the samadhi and let the bulls loose to graze in the far part of the Bagh.

Someone tested a megaphone. There would be speeches, Joga Singh realized. Speeches no doubt against the Rowlatt Act and appeals for satyagraha. Gandhi's idea of hartals was catching on and Joga Singh was intrigued. On an impulse, he decided he would step down into the Bagh and listen.

∾

At the Golden Temple, Ralla Singh hadn't slept well at all; a strange disquiet had been gnawing at him all night. Finally, when the clock on the tower across had struck four, he had rolled up the light wool shawl with which he always covered himself, even during summer, and gone to sit cross-legged by the holy pool, eyes closed in meditation. By the time he finished reciting the Japji, the stars had begun to dim and the first gentle rays of light were making their way across the night sky and bowing their heads at the golden walls of the temple, as if seeking Waheguru's blessings for the day to come. The lamps were being extinguished one by one in the bungas around the sarovar and the pilgrims who came to stay in these hospices funded by the rich and powerful Sikh chieftains—the Majithias, the Attariwalas, the Sukerchekias, the Ramgharias, the Ahluwalias—were beginning their morning rituals. From the Harmandir, the strains of a rabab made a tentative foray into a classical raag.

Ralla feared that this disquiet was the harbinger of some bad fortune. All he could pray for was that he would still be able to meet his brother-in-law, Mehtab Singh, and nephew, Kirpal, later that day. Kirpal was back from the Great War; he had survived the bullets of the Germans and Turks.

'With Waheguru's blessing,' Mehtab Singh had written, 'we will meet in the gurudwara on Baisakhi. Kirpal will also come there. God willing, he will get leave from his regiment.'

The thought of meeting young Kirpu, the son of his sister Jindi, now dead so many years, warmed Ralla's heart. The boy had inherited Jindi's sunny smile and wide-open light eyes, their innocence heightened by a random pattern of tiny brown dots. He was a young man now, not a little child for whom Ralla used to get on all fours and pretend to be a horse. But this morning, the idea of just meeting up at the Golden Temple on Baisakhi no longer sounded so straightforward.

He tried to shake off his misgivings. Moving to the bathing area, he undressed down to his long breeches. With his dagger still worn across his chest, as indeed it had been since he had been baptized by the Sant of Alibegh, he stepped into the still cold water of the sarovar until it covered him to his shoulders. The dip made him hungry and he went to the hall where the early morning fires of the langar were being stoked. He took two rotis from the previous night's stock and ate them with a couple of pickled green chillies along with a glass of steaming hot sweet tea; at that moment it seemed to him a meal fit for a prince.

Then, just as the early magic of dawn was on the verge of descending into everyday ordinariness, he started walking towards the Baba Atal, the tallest tower in Amritsar. In his hand, he held his favourite cane with the silver lion head. He was very fond of that cane, its shiny black paint, its supple strength, the mystery of the foreign insignia on the lion head. He didn't know what it signified; nor had the shopkeeper, deep in a narrow Amritsar bazaar, who had sold him the cane.

Angrezi hai, is all that the shopkeeper had been able to tell him. But that applied to nearly everything in that shop, overflowing with second-hand goods discarded by the British— metal trunks, wooden cabinets, belts, boots, umbrellas.... For some reason, perhaps because of the lion head insignia, the cane had a reassuring feel for Ralla Singh.

He knew he was lucky to still have it. Pilgrims coming to the Golden Temple over the last two or three days had been searched by British soldiers at the pickets that had suddenly sprouted all over the city. Sticks and canes of any type were instantly taken away: they were seen as potential weapons in a protest.

He hurried up the nine floors of Baba Atal tower. Each floor, he knew, signified a year in the life of the child Atal—son of the sixth Sikh Guru, Guru Hargobind—who had renounced his life at that spot. It was a good place from where to look down into the lanes around the Temple complex. But even as he leaned over the parapet and looked around, his unease only deepened at what he saw.

∾

Though Ralla was not to know, by noon that day his brother-in-law, Mehtab Singh, was not too far away. He was standing in Hall Bazaar chowk, caught by surprise by a column of military officials headed towards Hall Gate. Instinctively he stepped aside, shrinking as far as he could under a tarpaulin awning outside a shop selling spices, even as the shopkeeper was trying to shut the folding doors. Mehtab had no desire to be part of any trouble.

At the head of the column were two Indian police officers on horseback, followed by a horse-drawn bambookat in which sat the naib tehsildar and the town crier with a drum on his knees. Behind them came troops on a slow double, rifles in hand and then a motor car with two British sahibs in it.

'That's the new jarnail, Dyer sahib, next to the Dipty Commissioner,' a young man standing close to him said to no one in particular, pointing with his eyes and a raised eyebrow to the ruddy faced military man who sat in the car. 'Came from Jalandhar night before last and brought all those soldiers with him.'

Behind that motor car was another with two police officers followed by two armoured cars with machine guns fixed on them. Mehtab had never seen guns like that before.

Deputy Commissioner Miles Irving raised a hand and the procession stopped at the chowk. The town crier stood up in the bambookat and beat his drum. The naib tehsildar then read out the proclamation loudly, first in Urdu and then in Punjabi, pausing after each sentence and looking around: 'No inhabitant of the city is permitted to go out of his house after 8 p.m. Persons going out into the street after 8 p.m. will be liable to be shot. No procession is permitted at any time in the bazaars or in any part of the city or at any place outside the city. Any such procession or gathering will be considered illegal, and will be dealt with accordingly and, if necessary, will be dispersed by means of arms.'

There weren't too many people listening—only those who, like Mehtab, had been caught by surprise in the lane. The others

had moved back into their homes or shops and even away from
the windows and the balconies. The shooting on the railway
bridges, just three days ago, had brought fear to every doorstep.
The charred building of the National Bank, not far from where
Mehtab stood, was a grim reminder of how the crowd, angry at
being fired upon had set it on fire and killed the English manager
and assistant manager.

Instinctively Mehtab's hand went to the small kirpan that hung
around his waist, its thick black cloth strap stretched across his
chest. It had always been part of his person ever since he could
remember, a sign of his baptized belief. Would they take it away
now? But no, he had already been permitted to keep it: Sikhs were
permitted to keep kirpans. And he was very obviously a Sikh, a
most proper Sikh with his neatly tied black turban, its careful folds
each equidistant from the other, and rising out from a pinpoint
in the exact centre of his forehead, showing the deliberate nature
of the man. There was not a careless flourish, not a loose end
in his appearance or his thought. His beard, now flecked with
grey at forty-six, was open but not untidy. It covered his jaws
and chin in regular curls that stayed neatly in place during the
day, having been oiled and pressed down with a tight cloth band
for half an hour every morning. His spectacles with their round
metal frames gave him a serious, thoughtful look; his well-ironed
black cotton waistcoat, the crisp white long shirt under it, its
sleeves folded to the elbow, and the English fountain pen tucked
into his breast pocket heightened that look. His gaze was clear
and determined, that of a man who knew his mind; however,
every once in a while, a troubled shadow flitted furtively across
his eyes, as if he feared that everything that he had, all he had
worked for, could be taken away in a minute.

∽

One of the British soldiers sitting behind Brigadier General

Reginald Dyer in the column was Sergeant Nicholas Williams, his bodyguard and ADC. His thin face was red from the heat, his light hair plastered on his forehead with sweat. He hadn't had time to breathe ever since they had driven in from Jalandhar two days ago. Dyer drove everybody hard, especially when, as now, he was possessed by a sense of mission. He had no patience for any trouble by the Indians; all protests had to be crushed with a hard hand. Dyer had been itching to get to the scene of the action and now that he was here, he had quickly taken matters into his own hands and Williams had been kept busy. Two marches through the old city of Amritsar in two days through sullen, silent streets with barred windows and shuttered shops. Past the burnt-out skeletons of the National Bank and Alliance Bank, past the places where five Europeans had been killed, past the railway bridges from which the soldiers had opened fire. Then, the setting up of a military headquarters at Ram Bagh while the rumours swirled around like sticky summer flies: railway lines had been uprooted somewhere; a huge, mutinous mob was headed to Amritsar; Lahore Fort had been taken; the Lieutenant Governor was dead. Each rumour was scotched by a counter rumour as soon as it was heard.

Williams had spent a tense night, not even taking off his boots, his rifle next to him. The orders were that equipment was not to be removed at all; anything could happen at any time. Whenever the buzzing of mosquitoes had awakened him, he had glanced towards Dyer's sleeping quarters where the lamp had burnt late into the night; he worried that this would be the second night that the boss would go without a good night's sleep. And now, they were out again this morning for the announcement with the town crier.

Williams saw people ducking away into side alleys. The few who stood in the lanes tried hard to keep their faces free of anger and scorn. A wine-seller who wanted to keep his shop

open came up to Dyer's car with folded hands and the police
dragged him away. Then another man who pleaded repeatedly
that he had come to meet his soldier son was also taken away.

Soon Dyer turned back towards Ram Bagh, his face burnt
red from the sharp sun. Williams knew they hadn't covered the
entire city, been nowhere near the Golden Temple. But in that
yellow burning heat, it didn't seem to matter. All he wanted, like
Dyer, was to take the shortest route back to the shade of the
mango trees and get out of the sun that was searing the back
of his neck.

Just then a CID man stepped forward to the column and
whispered something to Superintendent of Police J. F. Rehill as
the police officer's car turned a corner. Rehill jumped out of his
car and, catching up with Dyer's car, told him that a big gathering
was to be held in Jallianwala Bagh at four-thirty that afternoon.

Sitting behind Dyer, Williams felt the General stiffen.

༄

Lance Naik Kirpal Singh had not come to Jallianwala Bagh to
listen to any political speeches. On the other hand, he was keen
to get to the Golden Temple, meet his father and uncle, and go
home. The prospect of ever seeing home again had been so distant
all these years of the Great War that it had become part of a fairy
tale, the kind that one thinks of before falling asleep, the kind that
one embellishes and breathes life into, the kind that one knows
all along will never come true, at least not in the shape that it
has been imagined. He had kept that impossible thought alive in
the rat-infested, water-logged trenches of Europe, through the
devastating shriek and thud of shells, amidst the burning heat of
distant desert sands. He had fought enemies he did not know
he had; he had won and lost territory that was never, and would
never be, his; he had saved, and been saved by, strangers. All that
since he had been recruited while wrestling. Wrestling, ah yes.

He would never have learnt to wrestle if it had not been for his maternal uncle, his Ralla mama, taking him to Bhima Pehelwan, and that would not have happened if his father, Mehtab, had not taken him to Tibba, his late mother's home, in the first place. So many things were connected and one had to respect these connections, thought Kirpal. These were cosmic connections. One began to believe in them when one lived a door away from death for so long; the only thing you could rely on was your destiny, on what was written. Otherwise, men were just playthings of the gods.

It was just such an unexpected connection that had brought him here, to keep an eye on the two bulls that belonged to the farmer Kahan Singh. When the train that Kirpal had been travelling on could go no further since the tracks had been uprooted by protestors, the farmer had given him a ride in his bullock cart. For a day they had travelled together to the Baisakhi cattle fair, along with the two spare bulls that Kahan Singh needed to sell. But the fair had been shut down unexpectedly early at two in the afternoon and nobody had bought those bulls. Kahan Singh needed to go to meet some traders who owed him money for several months and Kirpal had offered to look after the bulls while he conducted his business. The bulls could graze or rest in the Bagh peacefully. There was nowhere for them to go; the place was enclosed by brick walls and the exits were too narrow or shut. Kirpal could keep an eye on the narrow passage that came in from Queen's Bazaar as he rested against the peepul tree. He would wait here for Kahan Singh; he owed him that much. Only after that would he head to the Golden Temple.

Slowly, the Bagh began to fill up with people. Evidently there was going to be a meeting. A picture had been put up on a wooden platform. Someone pointed it out as a portrait of Dr Kitchlew. A few boys were arranging drinking water for the crowd. Many young children were rushing around, excited to be part of the activity. Hawkers and peddlers were setting up their cane baskets for an afternoon of business. Kirpal looked around at the crowd. It was obvious that many knew about the meeting and occupied spots as near the platform as they could. Many others, like him, just happened to be there. If there was some tamasha happening, then a lot of people liked to be part of it. There were some suspicious looking men too, asking questions, making notes, drifting away. That did not surprise him: informers and detectives in plain clothes were everywhere these days. Then, the speeches began. Kirpal could only hear snatches; the crowd had grown very large. Somebody was recalling the events of the tenth which had led to violence and killings; another man recited a poem. Yet another man started introducing resolutions. Then Kirpal heard the unmistakeable drone of an aeroplane overhead.

૭

Sucha stayed back in the shadows as General Dyer's column passed through Hall Bazaar after making the announcement. Then he continued quickly on his way to Kucha Peshawrian to the home of the young Vakil sahib, Gurnam Singh Gambhir, the limp from his bad right ankle scarcely noticeable. He slipped quickly through the lanes, sensing the presence of soldiers and avoiding them; it would not do to be detained on any pretext. What Bisheshwar, the Lala's son, had learnt by growing up in these lanes, Sucha had learnt by hard work during his few months with the Ghadar revolutionaries, those impassioned men who had come from America to sow rebellion against the British government.

In his kurta pocket were a few doses of powdered medicine rolled up in rectangular pieces of paper and a small corked glass bottle with a dark red liquid, all of which he had prepared himself. He had always been a fast learner and in the time that he had been with Dr Hardit Singh, he had learnt to grind and mix medicinal compounds with the same dexterity that he had displayed in mixing chemicals for bombs four years earlier. He could stitch and bandage wounds with the same clean hand that he had shown in snipping wires and fixing charges. The doctor was happy with him; he was as good as any trained nurse. Largely confined to his home on account of his own weak health, the doctor found Sucha useful for other reasons too: the times were troubled, the talk of political reforms had faded, protest was in the air, and Sucha always had valuable political information. He kept his nose close to the ground and sensed coming events as if he could read the wind; his time with the Ghadar revolutionaries had not been wasted. Their conspiracy to overthrow the colonial masters may well have been betrayed and many of them were now in prison or had been sent to the gallows but Sucha, their faithful foot soldier, was still waiting for the revolution.

Three days ago, Sucha had seen with his own eyes how Gurnam had risked his life, rushing on a white horse between the unarmed crowd on the bridge and the police pickets. From that moment on, Gurnam was a fellow fighter in Sucha's revolution. When word had reached the doctor that the pleader was down with high fever, Sucha had quickly prepared the medicines that he was now carrying. He would hand them over to Bhagwan Singh, the vakil's old, loyal retainer who took care of the young man with the same devotion that he had given for years to Bishen Singh Gambhir, Gurnam's father. There was no one else in the house: the old man had died in Bhagwan's hands, very soon after his retirement as an inspector in the police, as if heartbroken by the separation from his uniform, the thana, the salutes; Gurnam's mother had died years ago after delivering a still-born baby girl, when Gurnam had been only five.

∾

For three days Gurnam Singh Gambhir burnt with fever and the dreams came with a vengeance. Scalding dreams, flaming at the edges, threatening to drown him in incendiary waves. At times, as he tossed and shivered, he knew they were dreams and he a helpless observer; at other times he was part of the horror. He dreamt of the big snake again, the snake that had haunted him for thirty years, whenever he was at his most vulnerable—like in the days after his father's death. In this dream, the shimmering black snake would go down a long lane, turning several times to look at him, accusing him of causing its untimely death. Gurnam would try to explain that he had not killed the snake, only pointed it out as it came out of an old crumbling mud brick wall and it had been someone else, someone with a long lathi who had killed it, and then the bigger boys of the lane had covered its shining body with old rags and set fire to it right there. But the words stuck in his throat and the effort to make himself heard woke him up, sweating.

Bhagwan Singh had not left his side. When the fever rose to a burning pitch, he sat by his bed, dipping a thick cloth in iced water, and placing it on Gurnam's forehead, then wiping his hands and feet with another cold cloth. Patiently, gently, the old man watched over him day and night, sleeping beside the cot on a mattress he had thrown on the floor, getting up if Gurnam so much as coughed or turned on his side.

On Baisakhi, too, the fever that had smouldered all night rose again at dawn. The bones of Gurnam's skull throbbed. He feared the touch of the cold compress on his forehead even as he knew it was good for him.

'Baisakhi today,' he heard Bhagwan say faintly, as if from a mile away. 'Strange Baisakhi....'

Then, in the half sleep, the dreams returned. The familiar dream born of a faint memory of his mother. Her hair open, freshly washed and oiled, and combed back, a wooden clip holding back the curls, a slight puff over the forehead. And the smile, warm and forgiving, understanding without a word being said, happy despite the unfair life she had lived. He held on to that dream, not wanting her to go away into the dark void again.

When next he woke up, it was midday. A slight wind was stirring the long maroon curtain that hung in the door that opened into the inner quadrangle of the house. A sharp sun reflected off the grey cement floor outside; soon that floor would be too hot to step on with a naked foot.

He could hear voices, Bhagwan's and another. With the clarity that comes sometimes when we are most debilitated, Gurnam recognized that it was Sucha, the medical assistant at Dr Hardit Singh's clinic who had once been involved with the Ghadari babas. He could hear snatches of their conversation.

'Announcement...help this man...Ram Bagh....'

∾

Hugh J. Porter, Esq., sat at his desk in Lahore, just thirty miles away from Amritsar. Usually, he had much time for the pleasant view from his office, particularly in the mornings. The sunlit lawn with its glorious beds of pansies and agapanthuses smiling benignly in the gentle breeze was a soothing sight. On the right was the classical portico to which the buggies and garis carrying visitors rode up. He had the advantage of seeing the visitors even before they were announced; he could then prepare his face and mind accordingly.

The mornings were also his favourite time to muse. On what had happened yesterday, or even on what had happened ten or twenty years earlier. The years between leaving Trinity College and reaching this station in Lahore where his name was inscribed in white paint on a long wooden board above his chair, the last in the list of illustrious men who had governed Punjab as Chief Secretary, always of course under the guidance of the Lieutenant Governor of the time.

Hugh J. Porter, Esq., Mar 7, 1919

His name appeared now on several such boards across Punjab. Sub-divisional Officer, Gurdaspur; Assistant Commissioner and Sub-judge, Rawalpindi; Deputy Commissioner, Montgomery; Deputy Commissioner, Rohtak...and now he was and he would only ever say it to himself—the master of all Punjab but for Sir Michael O'Dwyer, the Lieutenant Governor.

This Baisakhi morning there wasn't much time for musing. Bad news was coming in from different parts of Punjab. In fact, there had been no good news since Gandhi had launched his charade of satyagraha. Passive resistance, Porter arched an imperial eyebrow at the thought: a unique way indeed to fight the Crown. Now India was a mess. Almost daily protests with speeches and resolutions against the Rowlatt Act and disturbances in Delhi, Lahore, and Amritsar.

Gandhi had been kept away from Punjab but not without considerable effort; the chief agitators, Satyapal and Kitchlew, had been deported to Dharamsala. That had brought about more agitation. In Amritsar, the military, under General Dyer, had taken over.

Porter took off his new glasses and cleaned them carefully with the soft cloth that he kept in the top drawer of his desk for this purpose. He did not like these glasses; the bad tidings had started with their arrival. Besides, they left a red ridge on his nose and gave him an annoyingly persistent headache if he wore them for too long. He didn't want to change them immediately; that would appear an unseemly indulgence. But discard them he must; to his mind they had brought bad luck.

༉

Three months before Baisakhi and soon after returning from Basra and Baghdad after his stint in the Great War, Udham Singh had slipped out of Sucha's room with the banned copies of *Ghadar-ki-Goonj* hidden safely under his big brown shawl, with the feeling that he was finally doing something worthwhile. All he had managed to do in the war was lowly carpentry work and odd mechanical jobs with the Pioneers. There had been no glory to be had in that, no medals to be won. Nothing that would make the Central Khalsa Orphanage proud of the Kamboj boy who had lived there since he was five. But distributing those speeches, poems, and fiery articles by the Ghadar leaders in Punjab's villages, even though their conspiracy to sow rebellion among Punjab's soldiers had fizzled out, was still work with a large enough objective: the freedom of the country. This could make him a revolutionary, enable him to live up to the orphanage's motto—*Be a Man. Make Your Way. Make Us Proud.*

But that assignment for the Ghadar had proved to be a solitary glimmer. Nothing more had turned up in the following weeks and once again he needed to get a job while he waited for his big chance; the two hundred rupees that he had from his days in the army would soon run out. Odd jobs at the Lahore railway junction kept him going for a while but the work was not steady—a couple of weeks at a time—and the wages were low. The feeling that had enveloped him in Basra was getting to him again—he was wasting his time, frittering away his life. If he had to achieve something big, then this was not the way. Daily, he tried to hold on to the conviction that something would turn up, something had to turn up.

A small signboard on the Mall Road in Lahore intrigued him. 'Uganda Railway Company' it said in black painted letters on a pale green background. An arrow below pointed towards an office up a short flight of wooden stairs.

An Anglo-Indian man with jet black hair brushed back, and a clipped moustache, sat at a small desk. The small wooden nameplate on his desk said: P. H. Andrews. He gave Udham Singh one long, appraising look.

'Job?'

'Yes,' Udham Singh replied. 'But not coolie. Carpenter, other railway work. Army experience.'

Mr Andrews asked him a few desultory questions.

'Where are you from?'

'I was born in Sunam, small town about a hundred miles away. I've grown up in Amritsar.'

Mr Andrews was not interested in details. He had already made up his mind; he wasn't going to miss a chance of hiring a strong, young man with army experience for the Uganda railway.

'You can come and sign the papers tomorrow. You have to work with us at least three years. Salary is good, very good—two hundred and forty rupees every month—you won't get that here even if you become a superintendent. A place to sleep, food allowance also. We can pay for your ticket but then no salary for three months. Better you pay. For the rest, it's Africa.' Mr Andrews ended with a shrug of one shoulder.

Udham knew what that shrug meant—Africa: jungle, wild animals, disease, and very hard work. You had to be tough to survive. Udham grabbed the offer. For him it was more than a job—it was a way out into the world, where destiny might have other plans for him. A month later, he had drawn his first salary from the Uganda Railway Company and sent much of it for safekeeping to Jiwa, a relative in Sunam. But mere distance would not save this dark-eyed gypsy spirit from the pain of that Baisakhi in Amritsar. And it would take a lifetime to discharge its bloody burden.

PART II

Chapter 2

The Pleader Gets Angry

Three days before Baisakhi, Gurnam Singh Gambhir, tall and upright in the saddle of a well-bred white horse, galloped towards a roiling crowd on the bridge over the railway line outside the walls of Amritsar.

'Wait! Wait!' a voice hoarse with effort, rose above the din for one victorious moment. 'Gunnu! On that horse, oye! Wait! Listen!'

Someone had recognized him. Someone who knew him well enough to call him by the nickname that had stuck to him through his childhood, through all the careless afternoons spent in the crowded winding lanes of old Amritsar, playing marbles, spinning tops, eating at street corners; it still surprised him that after wasting so many hours at play, he had done well in his studies at Mission School, well enough to get a law degree.

Even as he rode into the crowd on the carriage bridge, Gurnam recognized that voice. Crazy Bhola. Nobody knew his full name, or even that of his parents. He lived in Amritsar's galis and katras, eating in any home, sleeping on any porch. One day he would be roaming the crowded lanes of Katra Ahluwalian, another day he could be found across the city hanging around near Lahori Gate. Dressed only in a loose shirt that came down to his knees, he knew neither shame nor embarrassment, and thought nothing of lifting up his shirt to urinate against any wall or into the open drains that ran along the sides of the lanes. But he was unkind to nobody, and ran errands for everybody; it was difficult to imagine those lanes without Bhola. At that moment, Gurnam felt a strange bond with him; the boy was a symbol of this restless, heaving wave of fellow citizens who seemed helplessly lost, leaderless in the midday April heat. He feared for them, with the instinctive, unthinking fear that one feels for one's own. He needed to do all he could to save them; he was one of the few among the thousands who were out that day, the tenth of April, who could actually do something to help, something that might stop senseless killing.

∾

He had reached the courts early that morning. Normally he would have sat for an hour or two in his small home office meeting the villagers from surrounding areas, some from as far away as the outskirts of Tarn Taran. Even though he was just thirty-four, Gurnam had steadily built up a reputation among them as a patient and understanding pleader. They would spend the night stretched out in one of the sarais around the Golden Temple, say their prayers, and eat at the langar. Early next morning they would land up with their pleas and petitions at the young vakil's home about a quarter of a mile away in Kucha Peshawrian—the lane of those from Peshawar. This was his family house even though Gurnam had never heard of any ancestor who belonged to Peshawar. But that was how old Amritsar's lanes and bazaars were named—after communities and professions— Sunehrian di Gali—the lane of goldsmiths, Telli Mandi—the market of oil pressers, Patang Faroshan di Gali—the lane of kite-sellers, Mochian di Gali—the lane of cobblers, Nimak Bazaar— the salt bazaar, Kapda Bazaar—the cloth bazaar, Chudi Bazaar— the bangle bazaar....

But that day he had wanted to reach the courts early because these were not normal times. There had been two hartals in Amritsar in the last ten days. Hindus of all castes, Muslims, and Sikhs had joined hands and shut their shops and businesses. A resolute silence, rather than vociferous shouting, had echoed through the lanes. Dr Saifuddin Kitchlew, the charismatic Muslim barrister, had read out the message of Mahatma Gandhi, the message of satyagraha.

'All countrymen should become prepared for resistance. This does not mean this sacred town or country should be flooded with blood. The resistance should be passive. Be ready to act according to your conscience, though this may send you to jail.... Do not cause pain or distress to anyone. Go home peacefully. Take a walk in the garden. Do not use harsh words in respect of any policeman, or traitor, which might cause him pain or lead to the possibility of a breach of the peace or a riot. This is the soul force, the insistence on Truth. It is a process of purification and penance.'

Gurnam had watched with reluctant admiration as that message had gone home and gatherings several thousand strong passed off without incident. He had not been sure this method would work. But then nothing had worked so far—neither the politics of the Moderates, nor the Home Rule that some proposed nor, at the other end, the radical violence of the Ghadar movement. People were tired, frustrated, disappointed. The war had ended and the British, despite rumours of defeat on more than one occasion, had come up victorious.

'But what has that done for us?' was the question that he heard wherever people gathered. In courts, in bazaars, in the gurudwara.

'Just see the price of dal, wheat, jowar...we cannot even think of ghee and gur...how is one to feed the family? And the taxes...the shopkeepers pass them on to us. We were to get more freedom after the war. We were to get more power in our hands. That's why our young men shed their blood. All we got was the Kaala Qanoon.'

Kaala Qanoon—the Black Law. Named after the president of the Sedition Committee, Mr Justice Sidney Rowlatt, the bill was now an Act, steamrolled through the Imperial Legislative Council.

It mattered little to the ordinary person that only one of the two bills had become an Act, and the other had been dropped.

The lawyers had all read the Act threadbare.

'What was the need for this?' Lala Duni Chand had asked, polishing his round spectacles for the hundredth time. 'I can understand they needed the Defence of India Act. Those days there was some Ghadar activity and not enough British soldiers around—they were away fighting in Mesopotamia and France. But now? When the war is over? And when you can't find a revolutionary worth the name in all of India? This is just repression—martial law without the name.'

Lala Todar Mal, Bar-at-law, was sardonic. 'The British system needs repressive legislation, you see. They need it. We Indians are so dangerous. They need laws that ensure that we stay quiet, no meetings, no demands, not even thought. Just stay in our homes, mumble our prayers and if we so much as see an Englishman, we should lower our eyes and salaam, salaam, salaam.'

'And we pleaders,' Gurnam had added 'will be out of our jobs. Na daleel, na vakil, na appeal. Trials will be rushed through without proper procedure, the laws of evidence will go out of the window, dead men will be witnesses, and juries will no longer be needed! And, of course, no appeal of any judgement will be allowed. One section says specifically that the person charged will not be represented by a pleader. I'm going back to farming in Tarn Taran.'

'Not to the farm, my friend,' Badr-ud-din Islam of the English Bar chipped in, 'prepare to go to the Andamans. For the rest of your life. If you don't reach the gallows first, that is. Someone like you will definitely be termed a dangerous anarchist. Tall, strapping Sardar—the very picture of a revolutionary. Ripe to be picked up without a warrant, kept in solitary cell, and not heard from ever again.'

'And yet,' Todar Mal continued, 'blessed is this country that responds only by fasting and prayer. I have become a devotee of this Gandhi. His satyagraha is lighting a fire under the British and they will not know how to deal with it. Hindus being welcomed in mosques! Muslims entering temples! How will Rowlatt handle that?'

~

In the office that Gurnam had left earlier than usual that morning, an invitation card signed by no less that Hugh J. Porter, Chief Secretary of Punjab, still lay under a half-spherical glass paperweight, even though the event was over. Gurnam had still not decided what to do with the invitation card. One option had been to have it framed and hung prominently on the wall behind him, though he might need one or two more to make a good arrangement. He had seen such documents in the offices of many senior Indian vakils. Invitations to durbars, to public addresses by the Lieutenant Governor, to investiture functions. Cards with insignias and letters with thick signatures finished off with a flourish. These were all signs of recognition by the government and would impress some clients. There were two certificates for good service in the police given to his own father, one on his promotion to the rank of inspector and the second on his retirement. They adorned an inner room, next to the garlanded photo of his father in which Bishen Singh still reflected all the authority he had wielded in life: khaki turban, smartly tied beard, piercing eyes that could identify a criminal at a glance. Gurnam could not remove those certificates, but he had begun to feel ambivalent about others seeing them; hence, the inner room. So he had hesitated about Porter's card; at a time when there was increasing anger with the government, displaying that invitation card might not help his practice at all, could even make him seem a toady of the sarkar.

The card had been an invitation to the opening of the High

Court of Judicature at Lahore on the first of April by the Lieutenant
Governor, Sir Michael O'Dwyer. Gurnam had been keen to attend
despite the mounting protests: if one was a pleader for life, he
thought, then he wanted to be a part of this big moment. The
new High Court would replace the Chief Court of Punjab. It
would have wider powers, as laid out in the Letters Patent issued
by His Majesty George V. He had manoeuvred to get that invitation,
and as directed by Mr Porter in the fine print on the card, had
been in his seat at 8.15 a.m., wearing patent leather shoes, the
requirement for Indian gentlemen who were not in morning dress.

There had been some back and forth about where the
gentlemen of the Bar would sit in the large ceremonial tent
outside the court building. They had objected to the lowest section
of the tent on the ground that they would then be below the
municipal commissioners. The Lieutenant Governor had then
allotted them the middle sections on both sides. This, too, was
not acceptable as the munsiffs would still be ahead of them. Finally,
it was decided that they would have the entire left side of the
tent. Gurnam could not be bothered too much about where he
sat; his height—a towering six foot three not counting his white
starched turban—ensured him a good view.

O'Dwyer had arrived sharp at 8.30 a.m., escorted by a
detachment of the 5th Punjab Light Horse. He was greeted by
the Chief Justice, Sir Henry Rattigan, Porter, and others. The 3rd
Punjab Rifles presented arms and a band played 'Rule Britannia'.
The morning shook with the salute of fifteen guns. The procession
that began with trumpets was led by the judges, with the chief
justice bringing up the rear. The registrar handed the keys of
the new building to the Lieutenant Governor who duly opened
the door. The judges escorted him inside and the door was shut
behind them. Gurnam took a deep breath and loosened the round
collar of his achkan, damp with sweat. It was with a sense of relief
that he counted the last of the fifteen guns; it meant that the

Lieutenant Governor had departed, and they were all free to go.

∽

The tension had built up quickly in Amritsar since then, even though the two hartals of 30 March and 6 April had been peaceful. People had followed Gandhi's directive—hartals meant suspension of work and the observance of fasts and prayers. Kitchlew and Satyapal, being the most prominent leaders, had been banned from speaking by orders issued in Lahore but the other lawyers had carried their message to the crowds. Gurnam, too, had been one of the speakers who had addressed the crowd of fifty thousand on 6 April at Jallianwala Bagh. He had spoken from his heart, putting aside his notes.

'One way to react to oppression is through violence and I can understand why people find it easier to follow that way. Instead of being rewarded for our sacrifices in the war we are being treated like traitors. Each one of us, even those who lost sons in faraway lands, or gave their gold to the war fund, or suffered in the trenches in foreign snows is today suspect. But yet I say to you, there is another way. I believe violence and force will not get us anywhere. The sarkar is too powerful. My friends, let us follow Mahatma Gandhi. Be patient, be true, be non-violent. Let the sarkar see the unfairness of the Rowlatt Act.'

He had spoken once more that afternoon: to second the resolution calling for the repeal of the Rowlatt Act and then watched with amazement as the thousands who had gathered there left the ground without any loud protest or violence. This was a force he had never seen before. Gandhi's words were working magic.

Nor had he seen a Ram Navami festival like the one on the ninth. Muslims had joined Hindus in the celebration and walked through the narrow bazaars arm in arm. Young Muslim boys formed cordons to enable Hindu girls to pass safely through the crowd. At various places on that hot day, and particularly at the chowk where the Munariwala Bazaar meets the Ghantaghar Bazaar, they stopped to make a big show of communal amity. Hindu boys wearing Muslim taqiyahs and Muslims proudly wearing saffron tikas on their foreheads drank water from shared earthen cups. Together they shouted the slogans: 'Ramachandra ji ki Jai', 'Mahatma Gandhi ki Jai', 'Hindu–Mussalman ki Jai'. When they passed Deputy Commissioner Irving as he watched the procession from the veranda of the Allahabad Bank in Hall Bazaar, the bands struck up a tune that should have pleased him—'God Save the King'. Again, there had been no violence, no damage to public property, no harm to any Englishman or woman.

Yet, a deep restlessness had hung heavy over the city. People knew that O'Dwyer would be smarting after these hartals and processions, even if they had been peaceful. Silent shows of protest, even demonstrations of Hindu–Muslim unity, would get under his skin. He would see in all this a grave provocation, an insurrection, a rebellion, an insidious effort to undermine all his success in crushing the Ghadar conspiracy. And he would do something.

∾

That morning Gurnam had picked up his black leather satchel which contained his day's briefs and the tiffin box in which Bhagwan had packed his lunch of three aloo parathas and mango pickle and stepped quickly through the lanes, past the familiar overhanging buildings with their porticoed balconies, their carved balustrades, ornate pillars, and painted brackets, dodging hand-pulled rickshaws, carts, and bicycles, each with three large donas— the bulbous brass pots for carrying milk—tied on their carriers. With his long strides, he hastened through Bartan Bazaar—the bazaar of pots and pans—and past the ancient sacred banyan tree whose hoary trunk arched over the lane like a protective arm of God itself. He folded his hands and bent his head in a hurried obeisance towards the Golden Temple; the strains of the morning's kirtan were floating out into the lanes. By the time he had walked past the pearl-like structure of the Saragarhi gurudwara and turned into Hall Bazaar, he knew that he had been right to leave home early. A sense of confusion and tension was palpable already, though nobody knew exactly what had happened. To save time, he hailed a tonga as he went through Hall Gate. That morning it seemed too far to walk across the bridge over the railway line and down the long leafy road that led to the courts on the other side.

But the news, confirmed by now, had beaten him to the courts.

'Kitchlew and Satyapal have been deported. There is a crowd in the city and there has been firing by police and military.'

The lawyers looked at each other. Their decision was instantaneous.

'Let's go,' said one of them, voicing everyone's thoughts. 'Otherwise, there will be carnage and killing.'

'Let's go and ask the DC if we can help.'

'We do not need his permission but let's ask. Maqbool Mahmood sahib, you please go to him with the proposal.'

Gurnam joined Maqbool and some others and they went to the DC's office. At such moments, Gurnam was thankful for the fact that his father had been in the police under British officers; it gave him some confidence that at times he too could work with the authorities.

'Yes, go and do what you can,' Deputy Commissioner Miles Irving said, relieved at the offer of help. He had been in the post only a couple of months and was not a man who relished crises. His face was flushed and tense and he was mounting his horse even as he spoke.

Four of them clambered into a car. Gurnam had already hurried off in a passing tonga, taking with him barrister Bihari Lal and the pleader, Qureishi.

The tonga met the DC again near the Octroi Post.

'Go straight to the railway bridges,' the DC directed.

The tonga reached the bridges at a trot and stopped on the Civil Lines side near Madan's shop. A group of dismounted British soldiers and some Indian policemen still on their mounts waited there, restive and unsure. They were all looking at the huge crowd on the footbridge. There would be chaos if the crowd crossed over.

A group from the crowd surrounded the car as it came up with the rest of the lawyers.

'Huzoor,' a man spoke up. 'The police fired on unarmed men. We only wanted to meet the DC to ask for the release of our leaders.'

'They have been taken away, huzoor. God knows where.'

Maqbool Mahmood was trying to placate the crowd.

'Stay calm, stay calm. The leaders are safe and taken care of. We'll talk to the sarkar. Everything will be all right.'

Gurnam saw that there were at least three officers there— Extra Assistant Commissioner F. A. Connor, the Eurasian Deputy Superintendent of Police, R. Plomer, and the Assistant Commissioner, R. B. Beckett, all waiting in a line on horseback at the foot of the iron footbridge, which was packed with people.

He stepped up to Plomer.

'DC sahib asked us to help you. We can try and get the crowd to back off.'

'Then, for God's sake, do,' said Plomer. 'And some of you go to the Telegraph Office.'

Gurnam rushed up to the footbridge and soon stood facing the crowd.

'I request you all with folded hands,' he said. 'Go back, there is no point trying to get across the bridge. There are armed policemen and soldiers. Let's all go back. I will come with you.'

A sullen silence greeted him at first. Then someone said: 'We will go back only if they give us the dead bodies of our brothers whom they have shot down.'

'Yes,' another took up the argument, 'not without the bodies. We have to take them home, cremate them.'

'Yes, we will make sure we get the bodies back but let us go back into the city,' Gurnam felt emboldened; some of the others had joined him.

'Come on, let us go back to the city,' he tried to persuade the people again. 'Let us not lose any more lives.'

The crowd seemed to hesitate. He tried to push home his advantage.

'Listen to me, I am one of you. Let us go back now.'

Slowly the bridge began to clear.

But just then there was more commotion near the carriage bridge on which a military picket consisting of several British and Indian soldiers on horseback had appeared. A vociferous crowd was moving towards the picket. It was a huge crowd. He needed a horse to establish authority. He rushed back to Plomer to ask for one. Plomer told one of the troopers to get off a white horse and gestured to Gurnam to take it.

'Can you ride?' he asked, as an afterthought.

Gurnam did not reply. He had ridden police horses before; his father had been one of the best trainers of horses and dogs that the Amritsar police had ever seen. Jumping into the saddle he dug his heels into the sides of the horse and galloped towards the carriage bridge.

This was when the urchin Bhola saw him and shouted: 'Wait! Wait! Gunnu!...'

Gurnam rushed between the crowd and the military picket. The soldiers seemed all set to fire. The Deputy Commissioner and some officers stood beside them, one of them waving a sword.

'Hold your fire,' Gurnam shouted. 'Give us some time to push the crowd back.'

The DC nodded. Gurnam and Maqbool Mahmood who had now joined him turned to try again.

Just then someone from the crowd threw a stick at the soldiers and they opened fire. The bullets whistled past Gurnam and Maqbool Mahmood, on their left and on their right, barely missing them. In a manner of minutes about thirty persons were on the ground, dead or wounded.

Gurnam dismounted and turned to the DC in anger.

'You could've given a warning before firing.'

But nobody was listening.

Maqbool Mahmood was pleading with the soldiers: 'Do you have any ambulance cars or first aid kits?'

The soldiers shook their heads.

'Then let me go to the hospital to get some assistance.'

'No, you cannot go.'

Finally, Mahmood was allowed to leave the bridge and soon returned from the hospital with Dr Dhanpat Rai, followed by an assistant and a few stretchers.

But Plomer would have none of that. He waved them away.

'No need for hospital stretchers. Let them make their own arrangements.'

People were bringing charpais from Hall Bazaar. Gurnam and the others began to help to put the dead bodies and the wounded on these charpais, sometimes two on the same one. There were enough hands to carry the charpais shoulder-high back to the city.

'To Dr Kedar Nath's clinic,' someone said.

'Or to Hardit Singh Vaid…' shouted Gurnam. He knew Dr Hardit Singh and his assistant, Sucha.

Gurnam's hands were covered with blood from picking up the wounded. His stomach turned and he was about to throw up when he saw a young boy, not more than fifteen or sixteen, lying on his side below the carriage bridge. He rushed to pick him up and then stopped short. The bullets had ripped open the boy's middle and his entrails were hanging out. He looked at Gurnam with faraway eyes.

'Don't bother, Vakil sahib…I've already said my sat sri akal to this world. Look after my brothers. Hindu–Mussalman ki Jai!' With that the boy slumped to one side. Gurnam fell on his knees and gently shut the boy's eyes, not even trying to hold back his angry tears.

Slowly the crowd receded from the railway line, carrying their dead and wounded. But the anger went with them. Gurnam stared vacantly at the spirals of smoke that began to rise from burning buildings.

The Deputy Commissioner and Plomer were on their horses just behind him. They were speaking to Maqbool Mahmood.

'Take this horse and see what's happening in the city,' the DC told him. 'Let us know the condition of the Europeans in the Bank buildings. Mr Gambhir, you too should go. Thank you for what you did here.'

Gurnam turned to meet the DC's gaze. 'You nearly killed us. There was no need to open fire. The crowd was going back on its own. We just needed some more time. You continued to fire even when they were running away. You could have aimed at their legs, if you had to fire at all. Most of them have been hit in the back or in the head or face. Look at that.'

He pointed to a corpse that lay not far away, with an eyeball blown out and the brains spread in the dust behind the shattered skull.

Before the British officers could react, Gurnam walked away. He did not want to see any more. The whirlpool of agitation that the wise had predicted when debating the Rowlatt Bills was now a reality and Amritsar was its very centre. He walked home quickly through the lanes to Kucha Peshawrian, ignoring even friends who wanted to talk to him about the shooting. Going straight to his office room, he pulled out the invitation card signed by Chief Secretary Hugh J. Porter and tore it into tiny, angry shreds.

Chapter 3

Our Name Is Ghadar

When Sucha reached Chartu halwai's shop that same day for his usual midday meal of poori-chhole and milky, sweet tea he knew that something had happened. He saw men running towards Hall Gate, barefoot and bareheaded. Shops were being shut even as he watched. This was the new method of protest: shut the shops, stop business, empty the lanes, go on a fast, don't raise a hand.

'What's the matter?' he asked the halwai. 'Hartal again?' Chartu, heavy, bare-chested, and sweating in the midday heat, was blowing on the coals in his cooking fire. He turned towards Sucha, his cheeks red with effort, and replied angrily.

'Hartal? Who's left to call a hartal? They've taken away Satyapal and Kitchlew.'

'Taken away? Where to?'

'Only they know. Where've you been?'

'I was with Doctor sahib.'

'Eat and quickly go back to Doctor sahib. You'll be needed.'

But Sucha was reluctant to disturb Dr Hardit Singh. The doctor's heart was weak and he kept his routine light. That had been his way since his retirement from government service. A few patients in the forenoon, a light lunch of dal and the vegetable of the season, that Prem, his old servant, only one month younger than the doctor, would have prepared and then to bed for two hours. Sucha would usually return at four to open the clinic again for about two hours before the doctor went to the Harmandir for the rehras prayers. The doctor did not need the money; he had no one to leave it to if his heart gave up on him. His wife had died childless, twenty years ago. His pension was enough to pay Prem's modest salary and Sucha provided whatever assistance he needed in exchange for a room.

'But what happened?' Sucha's curiosity was mixed with his desire to buy some time for the doctor.

'Only God knows—or that tyrant governor in Lahore. He sees our leaders as Gandhi's agents. People are going to Civil Lines to make a faryad to the DC to release them or take us all to them.'

'Will the DC meet them?'

'Who knows what he'll do? They fear everything nowadays, even people appealing with folded hands, without a single lathi among them all. And all bare-headed and barefoot, in mourning. I'll go too.'

The bazaar was emptying even as Sucha quickly swallowed his food. He wondered for a moment whether he too should follow the crowd or go back and tell the doctor. Just then a group of men came running into the city from the direction of the railway line and Hall Gate.

'Firing!' someone shouted. 'They are firing on unarmed people.'

'The DSP and his men were ready and waiting with bayonets on their rifles. I saw them myself.'

'Where?'

'Over the bridge, near Madan's shop. Also, at Thandi Khui. I don't know how many are lying dead by now. I saw at least three, maybe four, fall.'

'They are bringing the bodies.... To the masjid.'

'Take the wounded to Farid Chowk. Bashir doctor sahib is waiting....'

Sucha saw three bodies being brought through Hall Bazaar, limbs flung out in the disarray of sudden death, carried on mattresses covered hastily with dry grass.

Suddenly, the city was aflame. Men ran out of their homes as they heard the news, their anger giving them courage. Someone shouted 'Hindu–Mussalman ki Jai' and others took up the chant. One or two were carrying black flags. In twos, fours, and tens they rushed towards Hall Gate. Others headed for the railway line through Hathi Gate and Lohgarh Gate.

Sucha gulped down his tea and ran towards Hall Gate. An agitated crowd had gathered on the iron footbridge that stretched across the railway line. Some lawyers were trying to calm them down. He recognized the pleader on the white horse: Gurnam Singh Gambhir. Another crowd had collected below the carriage bridge and many were pointing to the picket on the bridge. Some British officers, one with a sword in his hand, and a handful of soldiers with rifles aimed at the crowd could be seen there. Even as people came slowly off the footbridge, the other crowd started moving up towards the picket. Then Sucha saw Gurnam gallop up the carriage bridge. He rode to the picket and then towards the crowd. From his gestures it was clear that he was trying to persuade them to go back into the city and avoid a confrontation with the soldiers. Even as he was speaking, the soldiers opened fire from behind him. Sucha could see the smoke rising from the barrels of their rifles and screams rang out from the crowd.

Sucha did not wait to see any more. His first thought was for the doctor; it wouldn't be good for the old man's heart to be woken up by a noisy crowd. He reached the clinic just in time. A small group was rushing to the house, their eyes wide in panic.

'Oye, Sucheya!' someone shouted. 'Where's Doctor sahib? Quick, he must hurry. There has been firing. Oye, goliyan! They are bringing the injured here. Get ready.'

As Sucha entered, he saw that the doctor was already up and was hurriedly tying his turban, the colour of amaltas flowers. His hands trembled with nervous excitement, but his tone was calm.

'Doctorji,' Sucha began.

'I know, I know…boil the water, quick. And take out the bandages and tincture.'

Sucha felt again the throb of blood in his temples. It had been four years since the Ghadar rebellion had been betrayed and crushed but he still yearned for the time when he had been a small part of that movement, when he had felt he was doing more with his days than just living! Once again, he readied himself for the fight, the fight that he had been drawn to ever since he had first heard mention of it at Bhima's akhara in the village of Tibba.

∿

Three or four years after the new century had started on the angrezi calendar, a wandering village minstrel, his trademark ektara in one hand, was walking towards the village of Tibba. A small boy, about five years old, tried to keep up with him but kept falling back; both seemed tired, as if from days of walking. There was no reason for them to be going to Tibba: they didn't belong there, nor was there a wedding or celebration coming up there to which this mirasi could have been invited to come and sing. On reaching the village, they stopped at the first large hut. A look around—the loamy pit, the wooden weights lined up against the hut, the posters of muscular men—showed the mirasi that they had reached a wrestling akhara. The wrestler himself, the gentle giant, Bhima, gave them food to eat, lassi to drink.

Only then did he ask: 'Mirasi bhai, how come this way?'

'Honestly, I am not sure why. Bas, we were walking. I had thought that we should reach Sarhali before the wedding season begins. Then we saw this village. From far this land looked bright and golden as the sun fell on it and I thought we could spend a night here.'

'And your boy?' Bhima asked looking at the child who had already fallen asleep, intrigued by the child's clear complexion and fine features.

'Not mine. His parents—a Sikh farmer and his wife—had been
kind to me. They let me stay on their land for a few months.
Then they both died in the influenza epidemic last year and I
could not just leave him alone. He has no one.'

'You think that those who lose their parents have no one?'
asked Bhima, pointing skywards with his finger. 'Leave him with
me here. It seems that is why God has put you on this path
today. This boy might or might not become a wrestler but at
least he will not be singing at weddings all his life. And I am
alone anyway.'

At first Sucha was unable to pick up the weights, the mugdar
and the wooden dumb-bells, that lay strewn around the akhara.
The bigger boys who came to learn wrestling would do their
bit to put them away, but Sucha too wanted to be counted. He
would try to roll, push, slide, at least one big mugdar inside before
the akhara went to sleep. By the time he was ten, a bit taller
and a bit stronger, it had become easier. He was soon also doing
the exercises that Bhima advised him to do—pull-ups on the
low-hanging keekar branch, push-ups on a low rock close by to
begin with and then flat on the sandy ground. But both he and
Bhima knew that Sucha was not built to be a wrestler; he was
muscular but not in a squat, powerful, heaving way. Instead, he
reminded Bhima of a dancing swordsman, the kind of boy who
could perform gatka at the Hola Mohalla—wiry, quicksilver-fast,
electric; he gave him the nickname Churi, a sharp knife.

It was only natural—and inevitable—that a mind and body
as quick as a knife would be curious too. By the time he was
fifteen, Sucha was finding it difficult to sleep. At least not the way
he used to, lost to the world, flat on his stomach on the string
cot, his grey khes covering his head and tired limbs against the
early morning cold.

'Sleeps like one who has just sold his horses, without a worry in the world,' Bhima would remark, head nodding in paternal indulgence. 'And why not? He works all day. Only the honest and the hardworking sleep like that.'

But in that summer of 1914, Sucha lay awake night after night, his eyes fixed on the flickering flame on the pir's grave at the edge of the village. His mind had begun a strange voyage. Everything around him—the endless dark plain around Tibba, the relentless buzzing of the insects from the thorny thicket, and above, in the inky blue sky, the stars that shone steadily and the stars that wavered in distant worlds—all added to this restlessness. They spelt a world beyond the akhara, a world of cities and towns, distances and deserts, seas and skies. All night his mind would grapple with uncertain shadows as he wondered if he would ever get away from Tibba.

During the days, while he worked, the restlessness took on a practical shape. It became, quite simply, a question of walking away from Tibba, but in the right way, for the right purpose. Even Ralla, who had grown up in Tibba, and had been the most regular of clients at Chaila's theka of country liquor, had gone away one morning with the Sant of Alibegh, chanting in the dawn. Many others passed through Tibba without even staying a night. Some would have a drink or two at Chaila's theka. Others would gossip with Bhima and share news of the outbreak of the Great War, of soldiers going away, of rising prices. They all took the path that curved away from the pir's grave towards the undulating horizon through the small patches of wheat and barley. Many a time during the day, Sucha found himself staring at the point where the path disappeared, as if he was waiting for a signal.

It was on one of those autumn afternoons that Sucha overheard Bhima speaking to a tall and lithe traveller.

'Who's this Baba that you are going to see?' Bhima was asking him.

'He is one of the first who started to talk of revolution.
Ghadar,' the man replied, his tone low and conspiratorial. Sucha
marvelled at how the veins in the man's strong forearms throbbed
and bulged.

'The famous one, the one from Sarhali who took the ship
to Canada?'

'No, that's Gurdit Singh. No one knows where he is. The
CID are looking for him everywhere. He wasn't among those
killed at Budge Budge. But this man, Baba Wasakha Singh, is also
important. He's a leader for those who've come to Hindustan
during the last year to drive the angrez out of India. I'm going
to meet him'.

Sucha's look pleaded with Bhima. He knew that he could
get his way with the wrestler. Bhima came close to whatever
Sucha would ever know of a parent; before that there was only
a warm feeling and the hazy memory of a woman in a dark
green salwar-kameez threshing wheat.

Bhima instantly understood Sucha's look.

'Maybe we could go with you to Sarhali and meet this Baba?'
he asked the traveller.

'Make haste, then,' said Umrao Singh, for that was the traveller's
name. 'He may not stay long. These men are always on the move,
wary of their own shadow. We will leave at daybreak.'

∾

In Sarhali, the smell of wood fire and fresh rotis being made in the
low white building behind the gurudwara spelt a warm welcome.
They ate a sumptuous lunch of rotis with black and yellow mixed
dal and chopped radish dipped in lemon juice. And afterwards,
as he sat on a patch of grass, Sucha forgot why they had walked
all those miles. It was still afternoon, and the warm sun was
comforting. He lay back, a pleasant laziness rose up in his limbs,
and the white dome of the gurudwara swayed gently against the

clear blue sky and he drifted inevitably into sleep.

'He dreams and lives only one thing—Ghadar, Ghadar, Ghadar....' Umrao Singh's voice drifted into Sucha's half sleep.

His eyes opened wide. Ghadar. Revolution. Sucha felt the blood rushing to his fingertips, and he sat up. Bhima and a couple of others were sitting around Umrao. One was an older man, wearing a black and white tehmat and a rough safa on his head. His face had been gouged by smallpox and a few wisps of white hair passed off as his beard. The other was a boy a few years older than Sucha; he looked like he could be Umrao's younger brother.

'Tell us more Umrao Singh, before the Baba comes,' Bhima urged gently, 'will he come? Or should we wait somewhere else?'

'No, wait here…he comes when it is safe,' Umrao Singh glanced towards the low sun.

'His ancestors were great warriors. One fought with the brave Nalwa at Jamrud. Another saw the end of Khalsa Raj, when the British took the Punjab throne and the Kohinoor from young Duleep Singh. The man saw it all with his own eyes and lived on to be a hundred and eleven.'

Sucha was now wide awake. He could see the battles being fought against the barren brown backdrop of the Khyber, hear the roar of the guns and the clash of sword on sword, see the pyres burning by the river at sunset, imagine Lahore Fort with its walls touching the skies. His eyes beseeched Umrao Singh to carry on.

'And he himself? He has come from very far? Amreeka?' Sucha heard himself ask, the words breaking through him involuntarily.

Umrao Singh looked at him, his indulgent smile barely hidden by his thick black beard. 'Oye, I thought you were fast asleep. Haan, Amreeka. Across the seven seas. But not only. He served in the British army for seven years and earned a good name for himself. And when his time in the army was over, he could not rest at home. So, he went off to China.'

'China? Is that as far as Amreeka?'

'Not as far…he mentioned strange towns and islands…Pelang, Shanghai, Hunko…. Bas, the rest you ask him yourself. Here he comes.'

❧

Baba Wasakha Singh had the faraway look of one who has seen distant shores, has lived as an outsider among strangers. Often, while speaking, he would look away, as if some distant scene from the past was being played out beyond the group that sat around him, its colours visible only to him. Sucha followed his gaze into the dusk that had slowly settled down in the gurudwara compound but saw nothing. He turned gratefully back to the circle of light: someone had brought a bottle with some kerosene oil and lit a thick wick in it.

The Baba's words flowed like a placid river of the plains. He told them about those who had set up the Ghadar party, quite simply—the Revolution party, in America. They had lacked for nothing—these farmers who had worked hard in lumber mills and farms, the students who had gone to study, the former soldiers of the Empire. But they could not be free as long as their motherland was enslaved. Now, they were coming back to fight for freedom—it was a sin to earn abroad if one's own country was in chains.

'We have now declared war on the British empire,' Wasakha Singh concluded. 'Only four crore Britishers and thirty crore Indians! Where is the comparison? We need to wake up our soldiers, farmers, peasants. If China, that nation of opium addicts, can be free then why not us? So far, we have been led by jackals, clever men like Gokhale seeking their own prominence and always ready to compromise. Tilak is the only brave one—follow him. Follow Hardyal and Parmanand. Think of Rani of Jhansi. Her name still gives high fever to the white man. Remember Mangal

Pandey, Aurobindo Ghosh, Ajit Singh. Read the Ghadar paper every month. Pass it on to others in your villages. The British empire is hollow, one strong push from our side will topple it. The Germans are going for them, others will follow. You don't need money, you have your blood. The rest will come to you— guns and bombs, tactics and plans. Men like Umrao Singh here will show the way. There are others coming on ships over the seas, others who have sworn to sacrifice their lives for freedom.'

Sucha shifted his gaze to Umrao Singh's face. It shone in the dark with an inner glow. His eyes were shut and he seemed to have fallen into a trance listening to Wasakha Singh. He began to sing, swaying gently, tapping his hand on his left knee.

Mulk wich macha deo ghadar jaldi!
Hun lok bhi rang wata chale!
Ugar gia firanghi da paj sara,
German fateh England te pa chale.

Revolt! Revolt! Time to make haste!
Back home, our countrymen await!
The Brits, they are now on the run,
Battles galore the Germans have won.

These words would buzz uninvited many mornings in Sucha's head.

The next day Sucha wondered if he had actually seen the Baba, or had it all just been some magical flickering image in the twilight? A year later, he would hear that Wasakha Singh had been tried in the Lahore Conspiracy case and sent to the Cellular Jail in the Andamans across the dark waters—and he would know that all that he had seen and heard that evening had been very real. That meeting had made another thing very clear to Sucha: there was no going back to Bhima's akhara. A rope to a wider world had

been slung in front of him and he had no intention of letting go
of it, no matter where it led.

⤳

It was the beginning of October. The early pleasant light had the
promise of winter. The trees that stood in clumps in the fields and
on the outskirts of villages were glistening in the sun. The blue
sky, airy and light, seemed to lift with a ballooning happiness. The
sunshine rippled joyfully on the streams they crossed, walking
knee-deep through the water or on a tree trunk thrown across the
water. Sucha's soul rejoiced in that early winter as he tried, even
skipping once in a while, to keep the pace set by Umrao Singh.

Bhima's parting words had tried to hide his sadness: 'Come
back once in a while, at least on Baisakhi. It'll be nice to go to
the mela together. Theek hai, Churi?' And then, when nobody
else was listening: 'All this is very good, this talk of freedom and
love of our country. But be careful, don't become gun fodder
for these revolutionaries.'

Umrao walked as if he had a map in his mind's eye. He
always knew where to step off the path and go across the fields
and where to rest, eat, and sleep. It was difficult to believe that
he had not always been walking these paths, speaking in long
bursts and then falling silent as if thinking over all he had said,
or perhaps simply looking at the map that only he could see.

'I must have been your age or perhaps a year older when I
left Punjab. Bas, there was a man who returned to our village
and talked about a whole new world across the oceans. He was a
havildar who had gone for Malka Victoria's celebrations to vilayat
and travelled further from there, to the far end of the Empire,
Canada. He talked of fertile lands waiting for strong hands to
till them, fed by rivers so big that you could not see their other
bank. Of endless forests to be cut and sawmills to be run so that
railway lines could be laid out across the vast plains. There was

money to be made from that land, money of a kind that our small villages have never seen. So we went, I and several others from Punjab. We sold all we had and bought passages on boats to Canada. Those days they were letting us in, unlike now. Just recently they stopped a ship—the *Komagata Maru*—with hundreds of our brothers, starved them and then shot them down like ducks when they came back to India. The truth is that those lands are meant for the whites, not for us. They consider us dirty and low, only good enough to be their coolies and slaves. But now they will be at our mercy. That is why our name is Ghadar, our work is Ghadar.'

As he walked with this restless man with the long stride, the boy who had known no other place beyond Tibba in his fifteen years heard of strange places: the sawmills of Oregon, the gurudwaras in Fresno and Stockton, and of men like Lala Hardyal, Bhai Parmanand, and Sohan Singh Bhakna. A picture began to form in his mind. There would be a sudden revolt in which soldiers of the native regiments in cantonments from Benares to Bannu would rise and kill their British masters, would open the treasuries and the armouries, and release the prisoners. The telegraph lines would be cut, the railway lines uprooted, so that the British could get no help. He could not believe that he was suddenly part of this picture. Someone had heard his prayers. His mind kept going back to Bhima. It was that man's love and affection and his devotion to the Devi that was making all this happen.

'We need to awaken India, we need the youth, young men like you, ready to shed their blood for freedom,' Umrao said.

Sucha swelled with pride even as he remembered Bhima's warning—do not become gun fodder for these revolutionaries.

He felt he had to say something.

'But what can I do? I don't even have a gun.'

Umrao Singh smiled and patted the boy on the shoulder.

'You will have more than a gun…we will teach you all that you need to know.'

A slow fever began to wrap itself around Sucha's head and heart. In this fever he saw himself with a gun in hand, a gun that he found in the false bottom of a bucket that had been carried down from a huge ship even while its Japanese captain watched, unaware. He imagined rushing through dark nights targeting white officials while his admiring countrymen, mostly young boys his own age, took his name in hushed whispers. The fever persisted through the cold, crisp days and during the nights when he lay under the luminescent sky and a declining moon.

Until finally it was Amavasya, the night when the moon was so new that one could not see it at all, and they headed towards the Amavasya fair at Tarn Taran. When they arrived, the celebrations were dying with the day. There was still a crowd but it was a tired, thin crowd; its earlier boundless enthusiasm which had embraced the merry-go-round, a row of astrologers, three cotton candy sellers, and a bioscope stand now lay like a garment discarded at nightfall. Some vendors, having finished their stock of chaat, churan, and gulgullas were sitting on their haunches around a small fire, sharing an early meal and desultory gossip. Tired, but excited by what he saw around him, Sucha sat where Umrao had asked him to wait, his back resting against the broad trunk of a tali tree, relishing the kulhad of very sweet milk that had been handed to him. The evening sank around him, darkening with each passing minute.

The men came with the dark; they seemed part of the night. Each man was a mysterious shadow and the mystery only deepened when the lantern in the circle lit up their faces. Bearded faces and determined eyes glanced towards him questioningly. Each time that happened, a cold shiver went through Sucha. Who were these men? And why was he here? But then Umrao put a quiet reassuring hand on his shoulder.

'He is all right. He will be with us. He has the fire inside him.'

He heard the low whispers, though he wouldn't understand them fully till much later.

'The guns are still not here. The ships were to arrive many days ago. We would have succeeded last week, we were ready.'

'Not until we can talk to the soldiers in the units....'

'We cannot depend...we have our own work cut out. Get the bombs going. We know what it takes, inkpots and chemicals. Nanak Singh's terrace in Amritsar is a good hide-out.'

'Kartar Singh Sarabha will also...what a man, eighteen years old with scarcely a moustache on his lip but what courage.'

'Punjab is strewn with targets. Every police station, every railway station is a target. We will also find guns and bullets there. On Diwali, it has been decided, we have to flood Punjab with propaganda.'

'Beware of the CID. Be careful to whom you speak. Our own people are informers. Just a turban and beard is not enough for a man to be one of us.'

'If we hit Mian Mir magazine, we'll get sufficient weapons. We have the word of the havildar that he will give us the keys. Let's fix a date and time now.'

'But it should not be like Chaukiman railway station. There were no guns in the guard room and instead we took away fifty rupees. Like ordinary robbers. Shameful.'

Behind these men, the merry-go-around still turned, but slowly and painfully, like an old man going uphill. At the far end of the ground, the Amavasya puja was about to begin. All of a sudden, a whisper snaked through the fairground. A policeman in plain clothes had been spotted. The men vanished as quickly as they had appeared, back into the dark, tarrying only to fix their next meeting. It would be at the small gurudwara of Jhar Sahib, in a jungle in Amritsar district. Sucha found himself running

headlong into the night with Umrao and a couple of others.
When he failed to see a ditch and fell into it, he twisted his
right ankle and the pain blinded him till Umrao could get him
to where it could be bandaged. It was only a fine crack in the
bone but the pain seemed to seal the fact that from that night
of the unborn moon, he had become part of something larger
and his life was no longer his own.

When they met at the small gurudwara hidden in the forest
a few weeks later, Sucha could sense the angry disappointment
that had settled on the men like the sultry heat that weighs
on an afternoon when the promised rain doesn't come. The
havildar who was to have handed over the keys of the Mian Mir
magazine to the revolutionaries never turned up. He had come
under suspicion and been transferred to another post. The plans
now became more desperate: they would infiltrate the cavalry,
beginning with the sowars posted in Lahore. Many were ready but
more would be needed to be contacted—in Lahore, Rawalpindi,
Ambala, and further east in Meerut, Lucknow, Faizabad, Benares,
and on the other side as far as Bannu and Peshawar. Wherever
there were Sikh units, cavalry or infantry, there was hope of
revolution. The message of revolt had to be spread, copies of the
Ghadar newspapers had to be made, even if they had to be made
by hand in Gurmukhi or Urdu and distributed to soldiers. The
revenue officials, the lambardars, too, had to be won over so that
they would stop collecting revenue for the sarkar.

And that winter, there was to be no sleep in the frosty
crystal nights. The gangs roamed the plains, shrouded in blankets,
precious pistols in some hands, lathis—some with sickles grafted
on them—in others. They attacked police stations and prepared
to cut telegraph wires and uproot railway lines so that when the
time came, and the units rose in revolt, and encircled the British
in their cantonments, there would be no reinforcements available
for the besieged and reviled firanghis.

Sucha had been with Umrao when six of them attacked the railway guard on the bridge. They chose the moment when a goods train was crossing. The noise from the train, echoing loudly in the night from the stones on the almost dry riverbed, drowned out the sound of the shot that killed the sentry and the screams of the other two sepoys who were cut down with sickles. That night they ran away with four guns and six bayonets and about two hundred rounds of ammunition. He knew that he had done more that night than many grown men could have, and got away, too; in another attack on a police party the same night, all the revolutionaries of another band had been killed, even those who had hidden in the long reeds.

The reward was not long in coming in the shape of a new responsibility. An arrangement was made with an elderly doctor in Amritsar: Sucha would get a room in the house and would assist the doctor in return. But he would also work with the revolutionaries. Amritsar was becoming the headquarters of the Ghadarites; the crowded lanes hid them better. Gulab Singh's dharamsala, deep in the old city, was where they usually met. But one could not go there directly. They had to first check in with a trusted man to find out the whereabouts of a particular person and to get a 'no danger' signal before they moved towards the dharamsala. Sucha was one such person entrusted with keeping the information up to date.

In his small windowless room in the home of Dr Hardit Singh, Sucha would often press his face close to the smudged mirror that hung in a carved wooden frame. He would stare at his moustache, the soft wispy wave of fine hair that had broken out on his upper lip, and touching it softly with his fingertips, attempt to shape it. He would look for signs of a beard. For several days now, he had been taking some of the butter served on top of his gobi paratha at the local dhaba and rubbing it on his cheeks when no one was looking; he had heard that beards grew faster and thicker if you did that. His voice had broken, thankfully, but he knew that not until he had a beard would he be counted as a true revolutionary.

Meanwhile he scurried through the lanes all day. His ankle had healed unevenly, it would ache whenever it was cold or rainy. But he had adjusted his walk to hide the limp and he kept his eyes and ears wide open, watching for any sign of danger or unusual activity. In just three weeks he knew the lanes of the old city better than anyone else. It was always a matter of secret pride for him that he could follow a route blindfolded if he had been on it once. Lives depended on his finding routes that were secure, at times that were safe. He had learnt to sense unusual activity, recognize informers from their body language, and make out a spy from the tone of his voice.

Towards the end of January of 1915, there was real excitement. It had taken many men travelling between Punjab and Bengal to convince Rash Behari Bose, the famed anarchist who had nearly killed the Viceroy in Delhi that the Punjab revolt was worth his time. He was finally ensconced on the upper storey of the Gulab Singh dharamsala and everything began to buzz. Nobody could use his name; he was known to all only as the Fat Bengali.

'There's simply nothing that he doesn't know about making bombs,' Umrao told Sucha. 'We'll do better now than the lotas we've been making with inkpots and splinters and stolen chemicals. Maybe he'll be able to organize a bomb factory.'

The number of visitors to the doctor's clinic suddenly increased. A constant stream headed towards the dharamsala, wanting to meet Bose. They were being summoned, they said, to be selected for different assignments or to head particular teams.

But then, about ten days later, without ever having been seen by anybody outside the dharamsala, as suddenly as he had come, Bose left Amritsar. Too many people came to the headquarters in this city, he had said. He needed a more secret place. The real reason, as Sucha learnt later, was that it was easier to get bomb-making materials in Lahore.

Sucha had felt the excitement drain out of the narrow lanes of the city and a sense of despair began to replace it. But Umrao knew better. 'Don't be a fool. Now the real game is afoot. The Fat Bengali is a genius, just that he is not like us Punjabis who talk too much and get caught. He has a method to everything, even to causing chaos. He wants to work quietly. I've seen the house which he has chosen near Mochi Gate in Lahore. Detailed plans are being made but we should not talk about them. I know that there are spies among us.'

'But then what do we do? Just stay here in Amritsar?'

'There'll be enough work for you.'

'Can I help make bombs?' Sucha had heard about the new techniques that were being used. He yearned to be able to help with strange yellow powders, glass phials, iron cases.

Umrao smiled.

'In due time, my young friend. But believe me, you will not be bored here. I will give you a new machine tomorrow and tell you how to use it.'

As he fell asleep on the flat terrace under the open sky, Sucha dreamt of machines being handed over to him—pistols, a very large surai full of iron splinters, a long rifle like the one the guard at the Imperial Bank carried.

The actual machine that Umrao unveiled a couple of days later from under a thick woollen blanket looked much more innocent. Reading Sucha's thoughts, he explained: 'This is much more dangerous than any bomb. Once you learn to use this you will be causing not one but several explosions. This is a duplicator. We want you to use it to make copies of the Ghadar newspapers so that they can be sent to more villages, to the cantonments. So that more and more of our brothers will be ready to join us when the moment comes.'

The papers would arrive at all hours. Sometimes a single issue, at other times a whole bunch. Almost always a different man would drop them off and after Sucha had worked the duplicator over a couple of nights, someone else would come to collect them. Always at night, under the light of a grimy lantern, Sucha printed six, eight, ten copies and hid them under a thick pile of old clothes until someone came for them. And, in the morning, the duplicator would be wrapped up in a blanket and rolled under his bed. No one, not even those who came to the back room to pick up or pass messages, or take the copies, saw the machine. He didn't know what happened to the copies he made, but he surmised that others like him were taking them across Punjab, and even further, that the message of revolution, the evils of the British Raj, the exhortations to rise, the inspiring poems were being read by soldiers and villagers with thumping hearts. He felt again at the centre of things, even though Bose had left for Lahore.

'It's all done,' whispered Umrao, when he returned to Amritsar in early February. 'Just after Basant, the country will rise. The sowars of the 23rd Cavalry are ready. Once the Mian Mir men rise, other soldiers in units all over Punjab will begin to kill their British superiors.'

'When?'

'The exact date will be decided by the Fat Bengali. Meanwhile you need to recognize this flag, the flag of the Ghadar.'

Sucha looked with interest at the red, yellow, and blue flag that Umrao pulled out of a pocket in his inner vest.

'Red for the Hindus, yellow for the Sikhs, and blue for the Muslims. I have just given the order to Navrang Singh, the tailor. You collect them from him when they are ready and keep them safe here. Our boys will pick them up and distribute them in the cantonments at the right time. Now give me your hand and say Maro Firanghi Ko—Death to the foreigner—that is our salute to each other now.'

Sucha took Umrao's extended hand and looked into the blazing eyes of the older man.

'Maro Firanghi Ko!' he repeated. His whole body was on fire long after he had shut the door and Umrao had vanished into the crowded bazaar.

He hadn't seen him since that day.

∿

Bit by bit over the ensuing months, Sucha had pieced together the events of that heady winter, from the time of that last meeting with Umrao.

Bose and his coterie had worked out the uprising to the last detail in the house near Mochi Gate in old Lahore. The Ghadar flags had been distributed widely. Wire-cutters, bombs, files to cut the prison bars were in the right hands. The sowars of 23rd Cavalry had been prepared to rise, kill, break open the magazine at Mian Mir and distribute the rifles. The date had been set: the twenty-first of February. But there had been snakes in their midst: their own people, people with brown skin and Indian blood, who were ready to betray.

One of them, a man who had returned from Shanghai, was spotted where he shouldn't have been. Before the man could leak the information, Bose brought the date of the uprising forward by two days. But the traitor signalled to the police from the rooftop of the house where the conspirators were gathered, and it was raided. Several men were caught and bombs, daggers, guns taken away. Somehow, Bose escaped.

The line of visitors who used to come to the back room of the doctor's clinic petered out and the duplicator went quiet. Sucha started spending more and more of his time helping Dr Hardit Singh, mixing medicines and elixirs. But a part of his mind was always waiting for the knock on the door and for that tall and wiry fighter, Umrao, to come in, hand extended and their salute, Maro Firanghi Ko, on his lips.

∾

Now, as the victims of the shooting on the railway bridges were brought in, Sucha helped clean the wounds—a shattered arm, a bleeding wound in the thigh, a deep graze of a bullet in a skull. Each wounded man was supported by five or six others, who looked on closely. Everyone was speaking at the same time. Soon the air in the small room was fetid with the smell of tincture benzene and stale breath. The doctor's hands were steady now; it seemed his long years of discipline and work under the civil surgeon had all been a preparation for this one April moment. Deftly he pulled out a bullet and let it drop with a mesmerizing clang into the steel tray held by Sucha. Then he made neat, minute stitches with the heated needle, deaf to the screams of the patient held down by two men.

Soon there was no place left in the clinic, but the crowd still kept coming down the lane, looking for the doctor.

'They are shooting unarmed people!'

'The vakils—Gambhir and Maqboolji—said there would be no shooting, that's why we turned our backs. And then they started!'

'Today we will burn and kill....'

'We weren't violent. We were faryadis...bareheaded, barefoot, our turbans and caps in our hands, without lathis.'

Sucha shouted above the din. 'There is no more place here. Put some charpais in the lane. We will come out. Send some patients ahead to Dr Bashir—he is also working.'

The next round of patients had to be treated in the lane near the entrance to the zenana hospital. Two women stood on its terrace, their elbows resting on the parapet, watching the commotion. The people in the lane were oblivious of them until one of the women, a white nurse, called out.

'Who's wounded these men?'

Someone replied: 'Soldiers. Angrez soldiers fired on these unarmed men.'

The nurse laughed out loud.

'Good! Achcha hua! You people get what you deserve, wretched natives. Now you will learn your lesson—this is the only way you learn.'

'Who's this woman?' someone in the crowd asked.

'Don't you know? She is Easdon memsahib and the other one is called Nelly, Nelly Benjamin—they work in the zenana hospital.'

'We are dying and she is laughing! Let's get her!'

'No, ignore her! Let's take care of the dying first.'

Sucha's mind was on the man lying before them, writhing in agony as the doctor tried to extract the bullet from his thigh. But the woman's next words rang out loud and clear and every face in the crowd looked up towards the parapet.

'Look what the fool is doing. That leg ought to be cut off. That man should be lame all his life.'

A whirl of anger whipped through the lane. A few men rushed towards the entrance to the zenana hospital. Someone banged on the door, shouting violently. Sucha looked up at the parapet. The two women were gone.

A boy jumped over the wall of the hospital and opened the door from the inside. A group rushed in, a couple of the men with sticks in their hands. But they came back empty handed; the woman had disappeared.

As the afternoon wore on, the stream of the wounded eased. A thin veil of perspiration shone on the doctor's forehead. His own breath was coming in gasps and he looked weak and faint. Sucha held him by the elbow and took him inside the house and asked him to lie down for a while. As he turned to shut the door, he could see smoke rising over the roofs of the houses across the lane. The National Bank had been set on fire by the angry crowd. He knew then that the doctor would not get much rest over the next few days.

Chapter 4

An Imperialist with a Weak Heart

India was a mess, Chief Secretary Hugh Porter thought to himself for the umpteenth time, shaking his head. He glanced at his desk calendar on which 30 March and 6 April were circled in red ink. There had been calls for hartals on both days not just in Lahore, but also in Amritsar and Delhi.

Fortunately, the Lahore hartal called for 30 March had been postponed so he had been able to keep his routine, so important ever since the doctor had detected an enlargement of the heart and an occasional reduplication in the sound which could not quite be classified as a murmur. It had been put down to a weakness in his kidneys as indicated by the albumen levels and he had been advised to knock off meat and alcohol and to take mild regular exercise, do less work, and to eat slowly, chewing well. He did all of that, including a gentle set or two of tennis three times a week at the club, but always in the evenings, avoiding the sun.

And he rode every morning. That had been his old habit, ever since his first district posting in Gurdaspur. He had decided early that he would not be the kind of civilian who governed by writing long, tedious, well-argued notes on file but rather one who was out among the people, resolving disputes, inspecting canal embankments, watching over the building of a school or a bridge. He loved the dew on the fields, the sharp morning air, the early mist. Then there had been long rides from village to village in the summer when typhoid had ravaged the district. Many young men had succumbed, and the villagers were convinced that the typhoid was the spirit of a spurned maiden who had died waiting for her

marriage and now took all the young men one by one. In the
evenings, by the flickering light of the lantern that hung low in
his tent, smelling faintly of kerosene oil, he had read Cunningham's
History of the Sikhs. The book had been written fifty years earlier,
but Porter felt it was an honest narrative, so honest that the
author—a captain in the Company's army—had been demoted
to a desk job and had died within two years of a broken heart,
aged thirty-eight. He also felt a closeness to the book for another
reason: his uncle, a soldier in the Punjab 14 Light Dragoon, had
fought the Sikhs at Ramnagar, Chillianwala, and Gujrat and had
been present when they surrendered, throwing down their guns.
It pleased him to know that he was now riding the same land as
an ancestor of not long ago, as if it were all ordained by destiny.

It was in Gurdaspur, too, that he had first lived through
Punjab's blazing summers and frosty winters. He had seen the
dust storms rise on the horizon, like those raised by the hordes
of yore riding down from Samarkand and Isfahan and Kabul
and been fascinated by the duck and geese flying low over the
stretches of water that would suddenly appear between villages.
One morning, when he caught sight of the Himalayas through
the thin mist, he had fallen in love with his career. He knew
then that coming out to India had been the right decision. That
whole thing about becoming a parson back home had just been
self-deception. Maybe he had thought he could save souls and,
in the process, save his own, or perhaps he had thought it would
be easier to stand out among priests than amongst civil service
officers. Anyway, he had been glad to have the matter behind him.

He had been invited to stay at the Deputy Commissioner's
bungalow in Gurdaspur, unless he was touring the district. This in
itself was an honour, particularly as the DC was a man of wide-
ranging tastes, a great reader and thinker and, not surprisingly,
regarded as somewhat impractical and non-pragmatic. He did not

bother to impress his seniors; instead, he made little effort to hide his view that he thought most of them to be semi-literate and not worthy of a serious conversation. He had been passed over for a commissionership but that had little impact on his behaviour or outlook.

'It isn't that we have inferior men coming here. You just have to see their university records to know that,' he told young Porter one evening. 'But it's the keeping up that matters. You'll be surprised by how few times you will hear a sentence about a book, or science, or art…. But I can assure you, young man, you will hear a lot of tattle in clubs about appointments and postings, gossip about anybody—man or woman—who is not in the present company, but rarely anything that will make you think.'

Through the years, these remarks had often come back to Porter. It was true: British–Indian society was a swirl through gymkhanas and dances and a race for this appointment or that. Routine work took up most of the time and the rest was spent in nursing rivalries. Perhaps that was why even he had stopped writing poetry after the first few years; it had become vacuous and forced. There had been nothing to feed it, no literary discussions, no encouragement.

And now he was nearing the end of the line. A senior civilian had once told him: you know the nice thing about the civil service is that the day you join it you already know the day that you will leave, unless you die of malaria, or the heat, or snakebite before that. But even knowing that, Porter couldn't entirely dismiss curiosity about the future. What after Lahore? What after being Chief Secretary, Punjab? Not too many places left.

Just a day after taking charge as Chief Secretary, he had celebrated his forty-sixth birthday in his usual way, underplayed on the surface but determined to make it a special day in every way, from the perfect chota hazri in the morning to the quiet brandy after a sumptuous dinner at the club. Sobered by having reached a certain age, he had even gone to church after a full twenty-one years. Things seemed to have changed in church too, and not all for the better. The service began only after the Lord's Prayer and just one psalm was sung, not three as he recalled it used to be. But soon he had been lulled by the perfect harmony of the moment as he knelt with the congregation and listened to the hymn echoing out of the vestry. A long-forgotten faint yearning for peace and quiet and detachment had stirred within him. And then it was gone. He tried to recapture it by shutting his eyes tight but it had evaporated, just showed itself through a diaphanous veil and vanished.

He knew he was too young to retire quietly, to go back to England to a cottage in Shropshire, with an occasional trip down to London, and a visit to the smoking room of the Athenaeum—his membership had finally come through after a twenty-year wait—a copy of *The Times* on his knees. Too early for all that.

∾

Riding out on 6 April, he had seen for himself what a hartal meant. The lanes of Lahore lay deserted, not a single tonga was to be seen, the locks on shop doors glared back in silent resentment. The processions began later in the day but there was no violence. When the mounted police units intercepted them, on the Mall and near Anarkali, they turned back towards Bradlaugh Hall.

At Bradlaugh Hall, there had been fiery speeches against the Rowlatt Act. Nobody understood the Act it seemed, and the rumours were wild: weddings and funerals would need police permission, if someone did not salaam a policeman he would be arrested, four people if seen together would be put in jail, if police saw smoke coming out of any home, they would raid that house and so on. And the black bands that the protestors wore gave rise to the question—Kya badshah mar gaya? (Is the king dead?) And then the new slogan: Hai Hai George mar gaya!

Another exchange between students and some soldiers of the 14th Cavalry in Gol Bagh was reported:

Students: 'You will fire on us? We are like you, Hindustani, dark-skinned?'
Soldiers: 'Don't worry. If they order us to fire, you watch in which direction we fire.'

All very disturbing. Perhaps, Porter mused, some of it was inevitable. You cannot educate a populace, let them enter the civil service, the police, the judiciary, the Bar and send them to Europe to fight for you in the Great War without opening their eyes and putting ideas in their heads. Some of the problems at least, and of that Porter was convinced, were self-inflicted. An after-dinner conversation at the home of the Bombay Governor, Lord Lloyd, a few months earlier, often came to his mind.

It had been his last night in Bombay, almost at the end of a tour undertaken as a special assignment to help the government decide what to do with the Montagu–Chelmsford Report, which advocated gradual political reform. A small group of civilians had been put together by the Governor, with whom Porter shared a Trinity College bond.

'I think meeting these people will help you with your report,' Lord Lloyd had said, 'give you the feel from the street, as it were.'

Over dinner, the Governor, utilizing the privilege of the host, had held forth, over generously flowing claret, about his days in the Hejaz where he had known T. E. Lawrence and of his times behind Turkish lines. All of it had been very amusing if a little incongruous: it was difficult to imagine the arch conservative in formal black tie, with his brilliantined hair receding in two perfectly symmetrical half-moons, as an agile commando slithering around in the dark desert blowing up rail tracks.

But, over brandy, the talk had turned closer home.

'I don't know how Montagu could imagine that this policy can succeed,' the Governor had pointed out, making sure that his cigar was out of the way of the conversation. 'How can we ever expect these people, even the best, the most educated, among them, to rise above being Hindu, or Mohammedan, or Sikh and run their own administrative institutions? It's all very well to sit in Whitehall and pronounce that India should gradually develop self-governing institutions and move progressively towards responsible government. It's another thing to actually put this into practice; we are only fuelling the political ambitions of small men. The millions in dark India can't even understand reform. Western democratic methods of governance are utterly unsuitable for Oriental people. Change must come, but it should come gradually over decades.'

Surprisingly, one of the officers, a man named Johnson, had put in a contrary thought. He was known in the service to be a pure district man who had scoffed at judicial or secretariat appointments and had spent his entire India career in the field.

'We've had a great run, Lord Lloyd, and I will be as sorry as the next man when these days are over, but I think it would be absurd to think that we can continue endlessly on these patriarchal lines. The only way to make the people fit for responsibility is to place responsibility upon them.'

This was blunt talk and it hung in the air until an editor of one of the newspapers, a gaunt, tall man with a neatly clipped moustache, decided to take it further.

'The mood has changed. We are no longer seen as kind benefactors. While not everyone may call for blood and violence like Tilak, there is an impatience in the air. If Canada and Australia can have Dominion Status, it is being asked, then why not India?'

'You cannot compare India to Australia and Canada,' Lord Lloyd's tone was dismissive.

'Perhaps you are right,' the editor responded patiently, and it was difficult to discern if he was being sarcastic. 'India did contribute much more in terms of men for the war. You would have seen for yourself the Indian soldiers entering Jerusalem with Allenby. They are proud of the battles they have fought and won, of their eleven Victoria Crosses. And since Mr Porter is here, he will surely agree that the contribution of the Punjab to the Indian army is something that has affected every village in Punjab and though it does not sound like a very polite word, somewhere there has to be a pay-off.'

Porter had kept his silence during the post-dinner conversation, not wanting to spoil the warm mood created by good food and wine. He was glad when the Governor proposed one more toast to His Majesty's health and he could retire for the night, after spending a few minutes making notes of what he had heard. He no longer trusted his memory a hundred per cent.

~

On 9 April, Porter had watched Sir Michael O'Dwyer make long phone calls to Delhi and Simla to make sure that the orders preventing Gandhi from entering Punjab, which had been sent earlier, were given effect. Delhi had, in addition, decided to confine Gandhi to the Bombay Presidency. O'Dwyer had tried pushing the envelope. He wanted Gandhi deported—to Burma or the Andamans. But he could not get agreement: the Viceroy had given O'Dwyer carte blanche for handling Punjab, not the entire country. Banging down the telephone in disgust, O'Dwyer turned to Porter.

'Government of India won't go that far. They don't know what's good for them.'

Then he began to walk around the room, his face clenched, the muscles in his cheek twitching, his hands clasped behind his back.

'I know these nationalists. We have plenty of them in Ireland. They only sow chaos. Gandhi's passive resistance is nothing but a clever invitation to violence and disorder. Anyway, let them handle him wherever they want as long as he doesn't become our problem.'

Porter knew what O'Dwyer meant, and agreed with him. Till last year, Gandhi had been manageable. To the consternation of many Indians, he had worked hard to help recruit men for the war, even claiming that he could become the government's 'Recruiting Agent-in-Chief'. But the Rowlatt Bills had disillusioned him and he had changed tactics; he was now set on the path of confrontation. People were following him and taking his satyagraha vow by the thousands as if he had assumed supernatural powers—he was their new messiah. In the process, he had become O'Dwyer's worst nightmare. If he were allowed to enter Punjab, he would break the law because that was his way of protest, and an arrest would have to follow. That would inevitably result in more disorder, violence, and riots.

'And also send instructions to deport Kitchlew and Satyapal to Dharamsala tomorrow. Enough of their haranguing. Let's show them that there is only one way of governing Punjab. This is the same situation as 1907. We sorted that out by deporting Lajpat Rai and Ajit Singh.'

'Yes,' Porter agreed. 'That agitation collapsed at once.' It came to his mind that there had been riots in Amritsar after that deportation, but he thought it better not to mention it. O'Dwyer had already made up his mind.

After the deportation order was sent off, Porter had joined the others at a dance at Government House. It was a very successful evening with the Lieutenant Governor setting a high standard with his Irish spirit in full display. It ended with the singing of 'Auld Lang Syne'. As the carriages drew up, a wireless report was brought to Porter: Gandhi had been taken off the train at Palwal and sent back to Bombay under escort, there to be interned.

When the news of the deportations and Gandhi being turned back to Bombay had reached Lahore, the tension had boiled over. A large crowd protested at the Badshahi Mosque, just below the Fort. Then the Danda Fauj, as they called themselves—actually just hooligans carrying short sticks, Porter had concluded— had swept through the lanes and streets, smashing images of His Majesty on the way. People of different faiths drank water from the same vessel to prove their unity. Slogans wished death on King George and claimed the Emir of Afghanistan or the Kaiser as sovereign. This was sedition. As were the posters that had been put up over the last few days: 'English are monkeys...deceitful and cunning...faithless, ungrateful, tyrannous.... Kill or be killed.... Turn these mean monkeys out of your holy country.... Enlist in the Danda Fauj, brethren.... Kill the Kafirs.... Stop dealing with Englishmen, close offices and workshops...this is the command of Mahatma Gandhi....'

But, by the night of 11 April, things were under control. Aeroplanes stood ready to drop bombs. Reinforcements had been sent in. Dyer had reached Amritsar and was getting things in hand. Even if it meant the army getting the upper hand over the civil service, Porter felt it might be for the better this way. He had never felt very confident about Irving, the DC in Amritsar; the man showed a tendency to crack up under pressure.

Some of the town's notables, whose personal interests lay in currying favour with the government, came to offer their services.

'We can negotiate with the satyagraha leaders to end hartals but the troops must leave Lahore,' they said.

'Out of the question,' Mr Porter had responded. Sir Michael O'Dwyer's instructions had been clear: 'We must have the terms of the conqueror.'

Sir Michael was like that, the high priest of the Punjab School of Administration. He believed that law and order, strictly served, was good for the people. The government should be mai-baap for them since it knew best, but if the people started questioning authority, they must be crushed hard and quickly. Be that as it may, thought Porter, for the present, India was a mess.

Chapter 5

Ralla The Baptized

A deathly quiet had smothered the city ever since the shooting on the railway bridges. Beyond the city walls, the pyres of those who had been killed that day had barely cooled; British soldiers with guns stood at every street corner and the people huddled in their homes behind tightly shut doors.

From atop the Baba Atal tower, Ralla Singh could see a few pilgrims walking in ones and twos around the placid Kaulsar tank. A group of naga sadhus sat under a tree in Guru ka Bagh, the garden nearby, their bare bodies smeared with ash from the cremation ground—a constant reminder of their own mortality—their hair hanging in long, matted dreads, taking turns at pulling deeply from a smoking chillum. There were a few more people around the Golden Temple complex but certainly not what would have been expected on a Baisakhi morning. He could see the flower sellers in one corner of the marble walkway, their baskets loaded with rose petals, marigold, and jasmine, which the pilgrims would buy to use as offerings when they paid their respects to the Holy Book. Near the hospice of the Nirmala sadhus were the sellers of kadas and kirpans and small kangas. Further away, he could see an Akali churning the amrit in a large metal trough on the broad marble terrace of the Akal Bunga, preparing for those who would come to be baptized into the Khalsa on Baisakhi.

His eyes flickered for a moment over the Gothic clock tower across the sarovar. That clock tower tortured him like a persistent thorn. It was more a watch tower, a British sentinel keeping an eye on the Sikhs, making sure that they never got strong enough

to challenge the firanghi masters as they had at Pherushah and
Chillianwala seventy years earlier. For the same reason, they kept
control of the Golden Temple itself through their appointee, Arur
Singh, ostensibly the manager or sarbrah of the temple but, in
reality, just a creature of the Deputy Commissioner. And what
a strange place the Harmandir had become in the hands of the
mahant priests and British toadies: teeming with sadhus, charlatans,
astrologers, opium, images. He missed the simplicity and the purity
of his Sant's dera on the riverbank, where there was no ritual or
ceremony, only meditation and service and prayer.

He looked again at the haunted lanes of the old city below.
Baisakhi should have been a happy day, a day of celebration and
renewal. These lanes should have been crowded with farmers
coming in from the villages for thanksgiving at the Harmandir,
dressed in their best. This was the day they had been waiting
for, watching the wheat, barley, gram, and peas ripen through the
winter months. There would be time enough for work later—for
preparing the fields for sugarcane and maize, looking after the cattle,
the repairing of bunds and digging of ditches, the re-thatching
of the roof for the next winter, the wedding of a daughter, but
for the moment there would be the celebration of the harvest.
A time also to sell and buy cattle and horses and mules at the
biggest fair in all of Punjab.

Like the Baisakhi fairs of his youth on the high right bank
of the Beas. That memory was suffused with colour—the new,
richly coloured turbans of the men, the brightly dyed dupattas
of the bright-eyed girls. The evening before the fair the men
drank in groups and the double flute could be heard at dusk,
guiding the practice of the bhangra turns. Dozens of little stalls of
bamboo and sackcloth came up by the river. Mithai shops, many
coloured glass bottles of sherbet, glass bangles, combs and kohl,
toys, hair oils…. One year there was even a giant Ferris wheel
that was set up and Ralla could never figure out why it never

appeared again. But that year he went up in it thrice and got off only when he ran out of coins. Other times he hung around the wrestling pit, watching Bhima direct bout after bout, choosing opponents, deciding matches. He never went near the astrologers or the amulet sellers who promised a grand future made of gold and silver, shaped like a palace fit for kings, and peopled with an army of sons. And cures for all ills, from toothache to impotence. He was convinced that these men were charlatans.

Those were nice times to remember, those Baisakhi fairs, a two-day ride by bullock cart from Tibba.

❧

Tibba was a small, windy village, bare except for two peepul trees, a clump of berry bushes near the well, and far away a straight line of keekar. It was so named because it stood on a small plateau that jutted out without warning from the surrounding landscape about halfway between the tehsil headquarters at Tarn Taran and Harike, the town where the river Beas met the Sutlej. If you glanced towards it from the road that ran between these two towns it would hold your eye because the soil that ran down the ragged slopes of the plateau was of a peculiar hue, different from the loamy red soil of the surrounding plain. In the late afternoon, when the sun rays hit it at a sharp angle, it seemed that strips of golden sand had been painted on the earth with a thick broad brush.

Perhaps it was this mirage that had attracted a lone, tired traveller, known in village legend as Natha Jat, who came to Tibba two hundred years ago, tied up his six goats, built a squat mud hut and got down to cultivating what must surely be fertile soil. Only it didn't turn out to be so. A few couples drifted up to where he was and soon Tibba became a small village of hard-working men and women who would work harder than others on the soil just so they never had to admit that they had been

wrong. They also believed that God had sent them an important
indication affirming their choice: the surrounding area was known
as Khara Manjha for its khara or brackish wells but the well they
dug in Tibba had sweet water, and that was reward enough for
their hard work.

The descendants of Natha and his companions prided themselves
on their hard work, and on their simplicity and unpretentiousness.
Even the name of their village, they would say, showed how
unassuming they were. It was not named after its founder, like the
village of Talwandi Sobha Singh fifteen miles away, nor did it boast
that its young men had started going abroad, like the villages of
Pannun Jats at Nausheran, or their rivals, the Sandhus of Sarhali
Kalan a bit further on. They may not have named the village
after Natha Jat but when he died, they did bury a handful of his
ashes in a shrine just at the entrance to the village beyond the
well and let the rest float into the rushing rainwater of the Patti
nullah a day's walk away, which swept them away with a sudden
swift curve towards the Beas. That shrine with Natha's ashes was
the most revered place in Tibba and on most nights at least one
earthen lamp flickered at its base. On special days like Baisakhi,
or Diwali, there would be a full circle of diyas. Or on nights of
the full moon, or on the annual festival of Karva Chauth, when
the women fasted for the long life of their husbands.

For young Ralla, the first things to go when his sister, Jindi,
went away were the games that he had so loved to play with
her. They no longer made any sense, not alone and not with
anyone else. The stuffed cloth clown, with its peaked green cap
and red upturned shoes, that had somehow mysteriously made
its way from some Englishman's nursery to a brother and sister in
a Punjab village, now sat forlorn in the alcove above Ralla's bed,
its one leg stretched at an unnatural angle, the cotton wool inside
broken by being swung around too hard.

When she had lived there, she would lay the clown between them every night and he would watch fascinated as she covered it with a corner of her tasselled, hand-woven brown khes and put it to sleep with a story. She would only tell stories once they were in bed. Never tell stories in the day, she told him. If you do, then travellers will lose their way. He could not understand who these travellers were and why it was important that they not lose their way. He imagined them as big, turbaned, moustached men on camels riding in the night, a gun in one hand, a swinging lantern in the other, and with that image in mind he would fight onrushing sleep, not wanting to give in before the clown slept. But night after night he lost the battle. Sweet sleep would embrace his limbs, tired from a long day of play, and his sister's story would carry him away to the clouds from where it was easier to count the stars.

Along with the clown went the five pebbles which they played with in the courtyard around the tulsi plant, while fireflies buzzed incessantly in the twilight. He had never paid attention to the ditties she sang as she threw a pebble in the air and then gathered first one, then two, three, four before the first one hit the ground, catching it even as it fell. He had been so busy watching the pebbles in the air that he forgot to concentrate on the words. If he had known the words, he thought later, he might have even tried to play the game alone.

But these were all excuses, he knew. He shut out the games because they reminded him too much of her; if he thought of those evenings, something began to choke his throat and a salty stream began to flow in his mouth from his smarting eyes and his gaze would go towards the two peepul trees beyond which lay the unending darkness of the fields. The last time he had seen her was on the path that curled away beyond those trees. He hadn't even seen her properly then, just the swaying doli, the bridal palanquin, in which she sat, sobbing. He had no idea how far she had gone. Though everybody told him otherwise, he had never really believed that she would come back some day. The three-day long presence of the bridegroom and about twenty members of his family and some friends had seemed too final.

They had been a serious bunch, unlike one or two other wedding parties that Ralla had seen. There was no outward show of celebration, no drinking, no session with a dancing girl. Nor any boasting and loud claims of being better than the girl's side. Their no-nonsense behaviour, their black turbans, and the short kirpans that they wore on broad straps stretched across their chests were imprinted on his mind forever. There had been some tension too, and it took a long conversation between the elders on both sides, with the bridegroom, Mehtab Singh, taking active part in the discussions, to sort things out. Only later did Ralla learn that the discussions had been about the kind of wedding ceremony that would be held—in the end there had been a strange compromise: two ceremonies, one in which the couple went around the fire and another—seen for the first time in Tibba—in which they went around the holy book of the Sikhs, the Guru Granth Sahib.

◦

The stuffed clown and the five pebbles were replaced by the games the boys played in the village square. Marbles and gulli-danda and spinning tops....

Ralla watched mesmerized as Des Raj wound a string tightly around a shiny red top and pulling away the string viciously, whipped the top onto a stony ledge on the side of the dusty lane. The top seemed to spin faster and ever faster until it became absolutely still.

'It's not spinning,' said Des Raj, 'its sleeping. You have to know how to put a latoo to sleep; that's the secret. I can go and run around the pathshala and the mandir and when I come back this top will still be sleeping like this. But everybody can't do it. It needs real talent.'

Ralla stared at the top as it slowed down. Its colours and serrated edges became visible again and just then Des Raj bent down and scooped it on to his palm, and there it stayed until it stopped spinning and toppled down, tired.

'I have a sackful of them, though this is one of my best,' Des Raj boasted. 'I am rich, oye...flat-topped ones, spherical ones. Some I bought, others I won in games, all fair and square. What do you know, Rallya? You know nothing, I say. That's what you know. Playing with dolls with your sister, you some wimpy girl or what? So, why didn't you also get married and go away?'

In that moment, all of Ralla's sadness, loneliness, and longing for his sister turned to white anger. His left fist crashed into Des Raj's chest while his right found the nose. Des Raj fell backward in the dust where even his spinning top had not deigned to go. He wiped the thin stream of blood from his nose with his hand and looked at it, incredulous. For a moment he was silent, and then he said.

'Why did you go and do that? Can't you take a joke? You have to learn to take a joke. We are friends after all, aren't we?'

Des Raj got up and dusted himself. When he spoke the arrogance in his voice had been replaced by a new respect for Ralla.

'I will take you to Jaggi Baba and help you choose a latoo and then teach you how to put it to sleep. Don't go without me, he will loot you'.

The next day they were on their way, through the fields and across the village stream. Ralla was, as yet, not tall enough to be able to jump across the stream. Inevitably, his pyjamas got wet as he landed in the water, a few inches short of the other bank. The clear, cold water and the smooth pebbles below felt good to the touch and he was happy for the first time in days. Soon,

he was sitting in front of Jaggi Baba, his precious one pice coin
held tightly in his sweaty left palm. Des Raj advised him to take
a flat-topped yellow spinner, a crimson line marking its widest
circumference, its iron pin gleaming.

'Take it, Rallya,' said Jaggi Baba, his long beard quivering
as he spoke. 'It's fresh from the lathe in the town and it's made
for great things. I can feel its balance with my hand. It will spin
longer than all the tops in the village. You will be the shahenshah
of latoos before you know.'

On the first day, Ralla was close to tears as he tried again and
again to make the top spin. Each time it just fell on its side in the
dust, dead, unmoving.

'Be patient, it will come,' said Des Raj, as the sun sank
beyond the keekar trees and the square turned cold and dark
and empty. Reluctantly, Ralla went home, frustration rising in
his throat in acrid waves.

But, finally, the yellow top with the crimson line was spinning
its magic through the afternoons. Ralla slept with it next to his
pillow and every time he stirred in his sleep his hand would reach
for it to make sure it was still there. It became a living thing, a
true friend. At times he found himself whispering to it, recalling
how it had outspun six other tops that afternoon and that too
not on the hard, stony ledge but in the dusty part of the lane.

But all magic, no matter how mesmerizing, fades and a year
or so later, Ralla was not to be found in the village square each
afternoon. His longer, stronger limbs yearned for something more.
He ended up where all the young men of the village ended up, at
least for a while. At Bhima Pehelwan's akhara, at the far edge of
Tibba village. It was the last but one establishment of the village;
just across the wrestling pit where the keekar began was Chaila
Ram's theka, the furnace for country liquor. Only the grave of
an unknown pir and the cremation ground lay beyond that.

'Oye, Chailaya, may thieves take your mother,' Bhima would curse the one-eyed liquor vendor. 'You had to come and start this factory of hell right next to my akhara! You couldn't find another place in this big, wide world? The youngsters whom I try to put on the path of health, you send the same boys to their destruction. One day, lightning will strike this place. An akhara and a theka cannot exist together.'

Ralla and the other youngsters went first to see the strong man himself, to see how he exercised and what he ate and to listen to his stories of the bouts that he had won. He was a true and undefeated champion of the akhara whom nobody had ever been able to pin flat on his back on the black soil of the pit, charon khane chit. He had wrestled for years at the district Dussehra mela or in dangals held in other districts during festivals and fairs. He had been challenged by, and had in turn challenged, wrestlers from far and wide, from Amritsar and Jalandhar, from Hafizabad and Pindi Bhattian, even Rawalpindi and Lahore. But the large, heavy, powerful men who could do thousands of dand-baithaks every day, men with muscles like rippling steel cords, their bodies glistening with oil, their foreheads anointed with saffron tikas, practised in a hundred dav-pech, a hundred wrestling gambits, had not been able to defeat Bhima. Whimpering and defeated, their egos humbled, they would go back to where they came from, shaking their heads in disbelief. It came to be believed that Bhima was surely the reincarnation of Sadika Gilgoo, the Rustam-e-Hind who had ruled the wrestling world under the one-eyed benevolence of Maharaja Ranjit Singh, and was known for feats of endurance, once even running from Lahore to Amritsar to warm up for a major fight. Others believed that Bhima was an incarnation of Bhim, the mighty second Pandav brother of the Mahabharata.

Amongst the tales that were repeated around the akhara in Tibba was that of the wrestler from Persia, a chela of the famous

Rustam himself, who had challenged Bhima. He was travelling through Hindustan and the posters all over, in towns and villages, on trees and walls, showed him with his monstrous muscles, his huge wooden mugdar over one shoulder, his peaked eyebrows under a bald, fearsome skull. 'I will fight Bhima of Hindustan with my left hand,' he had been known to say. For a while Bhima did not rise to the challenge. Even his most loyal supporters began to think that perhaps this Persian pehelwan was too much for Bhima, so best to lie low. In fact, Bhima vanished from the village. But, a week later, he emerged at the dangal in Patiala, doing dand-baithaks at the edge of the akhara. He stood with his hands on his hips, filled his massive chest with air and bellowed: Aan deo, let him come. And Chottu Ram, the village dholwallah who had accompanied him, began to sound the dhol. This was as loud a challenge as possible to the Persian.

And when word spread that the Persian's challenge had been accepted, shops, homes, workshops, and temples emptied out. On the day fixed for the fight, the field around the akhara was crowded like never before and those who could not see scrambled up on trees to get a view. Even British officials could be seen in the front row, their sola topis protecting them from the sun; some even said in hushed tones that the Deputy Commissioner and the Maharaja himself had turned up. Who wouldn't want to see the battle between Iran ka Badshah and Sher Bhima Punjabi? This would be the battle that would decide, if all the megaphones yelling throughout the district were to be believed, who the strongest man on earth was.

It all happened so fast that nobody ever quite knew what exactly happened that afternoon. The two wrestlers circled each other for a few minutes, setting out their opening gambits and testing feints, while Chottu Ram got into his rhythm on the dhol. Then Bhima went like lightning for his opponent's ankle and the Persian fell so hard on the soft, freshly churned dark earth

comfortable by two pillows. A woven dhurrie was spread across the floor and the villagers knew that they had to step on it barefoot. Despite its stark appearance, the room inspired awe, with its high ceilings and red registers. Whenever Bhaiyaji had to do business with the villagers beyond the mere buying and selling of things, he would call them into that room. They would stand or sit on the dhurrie while he himself sat on the bed, resting his back against a pillow. He would sharpen his reed pens with a small, sharp folding knife and make entries in the register that rested on a sloping, low wooden desk before him. Occasionally, he would blot the ink by sprinkling sand on it from a bottle with a perforated lid. These were the accounts of the money he lent to three villages, the interest due, the valuables—gold nose-rings, silver anklets, brass utensils—that had been left behind as collateral. The interest that he had earned over the years had enabled him to build the largest house in the village with a pucca room and a stable in which stood a horse and a bull. He had even acquired plots of land in other villages, the owners of which had been unable to return his loans.

'How long can you carry on like this, whiling away your time? Listening to that pehelwan's worn-out tales, half true, half made-up? He didn't achieve what he should have himself and now he is making sure that all the young men of this village end up as wastrels. You need to take over this shop from me soon. And all this hisab-kitab,' Bhaiyaji looked meaningfully towards Ralla and waved his hand towards the two piles of registers, each volume bound in crimson cloth with white embroidery on the spine.

But his tone was more resigned than angry. He could never be truly angry with his son, and Ralla knew that. Ever since smallpox had claimed Ralla's mother when the child had been just two, Bhaiya saw himself as both father and mother to the children. If one part of him wanted to be harsh, the other wanted to be protective. So Ralla did not react strongly. He merely said: 'Not whiling away time, Bhaiya, I am learning wrestling from him.'

'Learning wrestling? By listening to stories? Wrestlers are bhagats of the akhara, they worship it, swear by it, they are wedded to it. They think of nothing else but to train and exercise and eat the purest of things. It isn't something you learn sunning yourself on idle afternoons. Give up these dreams and get down to work. The shop is easy, but you need to sit and learn the art of moneylending. It's the most useful thing that I do: how many lives have been saved in these villages, from Talwandi to Sarhali, even up to Tarn Taran, with my money, how many weddings performed, houses built, cattle bought? Someone would think, the way people criticize moneylending, that I am a scavenger. But everyone comes to me when they fall on hard times.'

Ralla Ram did not respond; it was no use. Deep in his heart he knew, though he wouldn't have been able to give a reason, that he would never become a moneylender, not even a shopkeeper. He, in fact, had never understood how Bhaiya had got into this profession. You hardly ever heard of a moneylender in Sikh families. But somewhere along the way things had changed. One of Bhaiya's ancestors who ran a successful cloth shop in Ranjit Singh's Lahore had managed to put away a bit of money. Occasionally, he would loan it to other merchants in the bazaar. This trend carried on in the family when the sons and grandsons, unable to live off the shop alone, travelled out of Lahore in different directions. On one such journey, Bhaiya's father had seen, from afar, in the magic hour before sunset, the golden strips that seemed painted on the soil around Tibba and had decided to settle there. By then he was too far removed, both from Sikh traditions and from the heart of the Sikh kingdom, for anyone to wonder at his profession. He did in Tibba what three generations of his family had already done—set up shop and loan money on interest. Somewhere on the road from Lahore to Amritsar to Tarn Taran to Tibba, he had become a Devi-bhagat and like many others at that time, he saw no contradiction in believing in the Devi and in the Sikh gurus at the same time. Idols began to appear in the house, annual pilgrimages to the Devi shrine in the mountains became an essential ritual, and he did not think twice about giving his son—the one whom Tibba called Bhaiya—the Hindu name of Jagat Ram. And Jagat Ram had named his own son Ralla Ram.

As Bhaiya continued to harangue him, Ralla realized that he actually had a reason why he could not carry on his father's trade. He said: 'I cannot do this. With this we become part of what the angrez is doing. You don't know but you should see how the villagers, and the travellers who pass through Tibba, talk of moneylenders. Leeches they call us. We are blamed for being agents of the angrez, for feeding on the misery of those who are already suffering from famine and disease. How do people who don't have enough food for two meals for their children pay us interest, and interest on interest?' Ralla pointed accusingly at the red registers and then he fell silent, suddenly realizing that he had never spoken to his father in this manner.

Bhaiya too fell silent, his shoulders slumped in quiet defeat. He knew that his son was speaking the truth in a way only the young can. He watched Ralla get up and walk to the inner courtyard. The sky was darkening slowly and the evening was suffused with the smell of jasmine from the bush near the entrance. Ralla made a perfunctory, involuntary invocation to the tulsi plant that stood at the centre of the courtyard and went to his room to sleep, not even bothering to light the lantern.

૦૦

The telegraph office was in Talwandi Sobha Singh. From there, late at night, a runner brought a short telegram sent by Mehtab Singh. In stark words the brief message told them that Jindi had died after giving birth to a son. They would soon learn, through word of mouth that travelled from village to village and reached them even before Mehtab's detailed letter written in neat black Urdu letters, that she had bled to death after giving birth to a boy, that her husband had not left her just to the mercies of the midwife but had gone into town and brought a proper doctor, but nothing had helped.

If there was a moon the night that telegram came, Ralla could not see it. The entire village and all creation was shrouded in pitch darkness and nothing, not even a lonely flickering orphan diya at Natha Jat's shrine, broke that darkness. There would never be another dawn because everything that could bring light—the moon, the sun, the stars—had all gone away with that ready smile. Tears were slow in coming; a heavy rock of shock and grief stood in their way. But, slowly, they oozed out into the cracks of his heart and then came in a rush. Everything dissolved in that grey, swirling, choking flood which burst from his heart and ended in a long loud lament to the dark, unheeding sky.

When he came out of the house for the first time ten days later, he had entered the world of grown-ups, though he was not yet thirteen. In this world, Chaila's theka held more charm than Bhima's akhara. From that day onwards, if anybody came looking for Ralla they usually found him on the charpai that was stretched out under the keekar in the splattered shade of its thorny branches, right next to the furnace. The wrestling sagas were forgotten, the youthful attempts at bodybuilding abandoned. Life was a merciful haze that came on with the first glass of Chaila's orange special just before lunch—another glass would revive the haze just as it was beginning to pale. Chaila did not insist on payment. He would only twirl his moustache and give the next glassful to Ralla when he asked. The money would come, sooner or later. The dues were all being totted up and the village moneylender had enough cash to pay for his son's indulgence. When he caught the reproach in Bhima's eyes from where he sat in the neighbouring akhara, Chaila would simply say: 'I know this is not a good thing, this drink. But it has its uses. Keeps a man from worrying too much. Now look at our Ralla. He didn't know what to do after his sister died. This drink gives him some time to rest. He will soon be fine, once he understands that such things happen.'

Over the months and years that followed, Ralla would go to the akhara occasionally and somewhat shamefacedly, including when young Kirpu, Jindi's son, came to Tibba with his father and persuaded Ralla to take him to the wrestler. On one of these visits, Ralla had been surprised to see a five- or six-year-old boy helping Bhima, dragging heavy dumb-bells and mugdars nearly his size around the akhara.

'That's Sucha,' Bhima had explained. 'He was walking around with a mirasi from village to village after his parents died and I thought it better that he stayed with me.'

∿

Lying under the pleasant winter sun, Ralla had drifted off into a deep sleep. Into a summer sky full of stars, the stars under which he and Jindi had slept on charpais in their courtyard. Night after night they had stared at that sky until the stars were as familiar as close friends. They knew where each star lived, where it came from and where it went, as well as they knew the homes of other children in the village. That afternoon, drunk on the country brew, he travelled the skies with all his old friends among the stars. With Dhruv that shone with eternal light and whose steadfastness he always yearned for but never could manage. With the seven sages, the Saptarishi, which could be seen as a four-poster bed and a three-cornered hearth. This was the bed for the steady Dhruv star and on that hearth were cooked meals for all the bhagats of the universe, his grandmother had told him. That is why all who worshipped in the early hours of the morning, while the stars were still out, were fed on this heavenly bounty. At the far end of the sky was the celestial pen formed by the stars and the inkpot formed by a million smaller stars. It was with this pen that the destiny of all human beings was written. He panicked as one can panic only in a dream when he could not find Venus in the night sky. Venus was the star of all married women. His grandmother had said that Venus must be in the sky whenever a wedding was fixed or performed, otherwise the bride would never be happy— her husband would stray or she would, or become a widow. It is said that when Venus—Shukra—is not in the sky it adorns a human shape and possesses the women who are married on those days. But Venus had been in the sky when Jindi was married, the pandit had confirmed that, then why had she gone away, unhappy, unfulfilled....

'Santji has come, wake up, Rallya, we are all going,' Des Raj's voice broke the dream.

Ralla opened his eyes: the dark skies vanished; the stars faded instantly in the sunlight.

'What sant?'

'The one from Alibegh. The one who stays on the banks of the Chenab. The whole village has gone to see him. Get up!'

From the moment he set his eyes on the holy man who sat on a slightly raised platform, wearing a long white robe that came down to his knees and a flat white turban on his head, Ralla felt that the Sant was talking only to him. The few dozen villagers who sat on the grass were simply not there. The Sant's clear deep eyes that looked straight into Ralla's soul were full of mesmerizing, swirling shadows. Ralla was transfixed. The voice he heard seemed to be coming not from the person sitting a few feet away but from within himself.

'Man is lost today, lost in the dark night of superstition and ritual. Chasing a thousand gods, looking for salvation in stones and trees, the soul wanders aimlessly from door to door. A simple path lies before us but we refuse to see it: the path of meditation on the Name. This is the only path to salvation but you need to be pure to achieve progress on this path. The path our Gurus have shown has been forgotten; we are going back into the swamps of ignorance. To those who want to find the true path to the Creator, those who want to live a clean, righteous life and find God in such a life, I will administer the amrit. But it is not a simple path. It needs belief, discipline, sacrifice. Like the Guru said: "Jau tau prem khelan ka chau, sir dhar tali gali meri aao." If you wish to play the game of love, then step on to my path with your head on your palm.'

Just as quickly as Ralla had gone to Chaila's theka, he now wanted to run away from it. The Sant's words had sent the blood racing in his veins with a new energy and his mind wanted to hold on to that promised glimpse of another world. He spent the night in a pleasant restlessness and, while the stars were still visible in the sky, he began to prepare for the initiation ceremony that was to take place at the first touch of dawn.

The rope uncoiled quickly, and the pail fell headlong into the dark well and cracked the thin sheet of ice that had formed on the water's surface. Without a moment's hesitation, he bathed with water that still had fine splinters of ice in it, washed his hair, and combed it carefully, aware that once he was initiated as a Sikh, he would never cut it again. He wore fresh clothes—a homespun long shirt, a washed pair of drawers, a tehmat. He took out a new safa and tied it around his head, like his father used to, and, wrapping his brown and white loyi around his shoulders, he quietly slipped away towards the Sant's camp where several others were already gathered in the brittle cold of the early morning.

A granthi—one of the Sant's followers—was reading passages from the Guru Granth Sahib in a soft undertone and a few others sat by, listening. As the Sant came in and bowed before the

Holy Book, the reading became louder. The granthi then gently closed and then opened the Granth Sahib at random; the verse at the top was the command, the direction, the blessing for the day. The ceremony of baptism could begin. One of the followers poured water into an iron vessel, another poured sugar, and the Sant began to stir the mixture with the double-edged dagger, the khanda, while reciting the Japji. The khanda passed between him and four followers and together they captured the spirit of the Beloved Five who had been baptized by Guru Gobind Singh. When the prayers had been recited, the waiting initiates were beckoned to come forth one by one.

Ralla was ready when his turn came. One of the disciples had already made sure he had all the required five Ks on him. His kes, or hair; his breeches, the kachch; a small kanga or comb to tuck into his safa; a small kirpan, or ceremonial sword, hung on a black strap across his chest and a new iron bangle, a kada, that glinted on his right wrist. Attired in all the accoutrements of the Khalsa, now he needed steel in his soul to fight the righteous war. He knelt in the pose of a warrior, his left knee up, his right touching the earth as he rested on his right toe. The Sant took some amrit in his cupped palm and brought it to Ralla's waiting lips to drink. Then, with his fingers, the Sant sprinkled Ralla's shut eyelids and said, 'Bol, Waheguruji ka khalsa, Waheguruji ki fateh.' Ralla responded—the Khalsa belongs to the true God, victory belongs to the true God. Then the Sant sprinkled some drops of the amrit on his head and repeated the call.

When Ralla opened his eyes and looked into the deep, gentle eyes of the Sant, he knew that his life had changed forever.

'From this moment,' the Sant said, 'you are a Sikh of the Guru, a member of the brotherhood of the pure, the Khalsa. You are Jagjit Singh, brave and fearless like a lion. You know no God but the true God, the one who is the true Creator, formless, without rancour, fearless, timeless…. You have given up the weaknesses, the divisions, the superstitions of your past.'

The new name—Jagjit—didn't stick; instead Ralla Ram simply became Ralla Singh. The next day he went to Chaila Ram's theka to pay his bills. Then he went across to the akhara to touch Bhima's feet. The wrestler looked at the young man with open admiration and detected a new clarity in his eyes, a new purpose in his walk, and he was happy for him. He looked towards the Devi's picture as if to say, yes, miracles do happen. Then, twirling his moustaches into sharp little points, his face even more florid than usual, and his voice heavy with pride, he said: 'You did well, Rallya, otherwise you would have spent your life in Chaila's cursed charpai. Go—now that you have taken this step, see it through to the end.' The young boy, Sucha, watched from where he sat at the edge of the akhara, and a strange yearning could be seen in his eyes.

Ten days later, on the auspicious day of Basant Panchami, when the waves of the mustard in the fields were at their yellowest and everything—the cotton flowers, the pea pods, the turbans of the men, the sweet rice cooking in the earthen pots—had become a bright, blazing yellow, the Sant and his followers lifted their dera and moved on, first to Jhelum and then back to Akhnoor. Ralla Singh left with them. Bhaiya made a half-hearted protest, but fell silent when he saw his son's radiant smile and uplifted spirit. He had rarely seen him like this before and certainly never since Jindi's marriage. He knew there was no way he could bind Ralla down to the moneylender's sloping desk or to the red registers with their record of bonded lives. Or to the bits of gold and rolled up land records that lay in his safe. He understood, that Ralla had been touched by a more powerful wand.

There was nothing to hold Bhaiya down to Tibba too, though it would take him another two years to realize that. Then, one day at dusk, he would see the faces of his ancestors hovering

over him in the shadows and he knew that the end was near.
It was time to square the balance sheet, to draw a line under
that hisab-kitab of the long registers. The next day he hired a
drum-beater who went to five villages and announced: 'Bhaiyaji,
the honourable friend of all the needy, wants to leave the village
of Tibba and go on his tirath-yatra, his pilgrimage to the holy
places. He is ready to wipe out all old accounts. Come and take
your valuables back from him.'

And when it was all settled, when the safe that lay encased
within a brick wall was empty and open, Bhaiya, too, took the
path out of the village that had been taken by Jindi and then by
Ralla, one to an early death and the other to a new life. Bhaiya
went to the tiraths of Haridwar and Kashi, to atone for the sins
of this life and to seek a better one next time. He left the keys
of the house with the sarpanch, saying 'Kaka, if my son comes
back, give these to him; otherwise make it a dharamsal.'

∾

The Sant and his followers wandered through villages and towns
on their way to Jhelum, stopping wherever the holy man felt a
sense of peace and calm. At one such camp near Amritsar, they
met a group of itinerant sadhus. During the evening hour of
prayer and discourse, the Sant's eye fell on two small Sikh boys
who were travelling with the sadhus.

'Their father died recently,' explained the leading sadhu, 'and
we happened to be passing at that moment. They've been with us
since but, if you permit, they may be better off with you, Santji.
You can guide them better, otherwise they will only wander
aimlessly all their lives with us.'

The Sant looked at each of the boys carefully.

'What are your names?' he asked.

'Sadhu Singh,' said the elder one.

'Sher Singh,' replied the younger one, looking the Sant straight in the eye. The Sant smiled at the younger boy's defiant tone and direct gaze.

'These are good boys. Jagjit,' said the Sant turning to Ralla. 'Prepare to baptize both of them early morning. Take care of them till Amritsar.'

The next morning the two received baptism at the hands of the Sant. He also gave new names to them—Mukta Singh to the elder one and Udham Singh to the younger one. They travelled with the group till Amritsar where, on the Sant's instructions, Ralla took them to the Central Khalsa Orphanage.

'They are too young to be wandering with us,' the Sant had said. 'In the orphanage they will grow up with other children,

Ralla's years began to pass placidly on the banks of the Chenab, where he would often sit watching the river gurgle its way down from the hills. He learnt to meditate to the sound of the water in the early morning and to gather within himself a peace and silence that would help him go through the entire day with the name of the Creator on his lips. Whenever the Sant moved from Akhnoor to a different part of the country, Ralla would be at hand to serve him day and night. He knew that this was a pattern he would gladly follow for the rest of his days.

Once when the Sant travelled to Sandal Bar, Ralla took his permission to go for a few days to the village called Dharamsinghwala. He had suddenly been possessed with the desire to see where Jindi had gone as a bride when she had left Tibba in that palanquin. Where she had seen the joy of marriage and love, and where, suddenly and unexpectedly, she had died. He spent about ten days there and Mehtab Singh looked after him with deeply felt joy. The usually restrained man was overcome with emotion; it was almost as if some part of Jindi had come back. Ralla's laugh, his way of holding his chin between his thumb and forefinger, the way that he ate every speck of food on his thali, everything reminded Mehtab of his young wife and his grief at losing her was at some level transmuted into a deep affection for his brother-in-law. Every night, Ralla would tell Kirpu stories, the stories that Jindi had told him years ago and the stories that he had picked up since then. For hours they would walk to the canal embankment and back, the nephew holding the uncle by the forearm as the dusk settled on the green fields that had now replaced the thorny wastes of the Bar around the canal colony.

After that visit, Mehtab Singh ensured that Ralla got news regularly from him. The letters that drifted to Ralla at the Sant's dera in Akhnoor had unfamiliar postmarks—Rawalpindi, Sheikhupura, Sargodha. By then, Mehtab Singh had been with the irrigation department—the most powerful department of the day, building canals all over Punjab—for many years. His job now took him from one canal colony to the other for inspections. Thank God that Mehtab's mother was still alive and strong and could take care of Kirpal. Sometimes the letter he would receive would be written in angled Urdu which Ralla Singh had learned to read, though with some difficulty. On other days the letter would be written in neat Gurmukhi, which Ralla could not read at all; he would then have to seek out someone to read it out to him. In those letters, Mehtab Singh would tell him how Kirpu was growing up, how he was doing in school. That was Mehtab's way of saying that he knew how close Ralla had been to Jindi and for that reason had a very special bond with her son. Or perhaps that was his way of communicating with the long dead Jindi, explaining how he lived his life, what he worked for and believed in, why indeed he had never remarried, and had in no way neglected his son. Sometimes he would include a new address where he would be staying for a while and Ralla Singh too would respond, asking one of the literate disciples to write the letter. That was how it had been fixed that on Baisakhi that year, 1919, they would meet in Amritsar, not just Mehtab and

Ralla but also Kirpal, only recently returned from the treacherous war front, now a young man of twenty-two.

～

The day Ralla had reached Amritsar, four days before Baisakhi, the city seemed a quiet shadow of its usual bustling self. Not a tonga, not an ekka at the railway station. He didn't mind that. He was used to walking and he knew well the way to the Golden Temple from the station. There were few people to be seen in the lanes and many of the shops were shut. Even the hawkers seemed to have vanished. New police pickets were visible.

He had been half prepared for something like this from what he had heard on the train.

'Hartals are taking place in many places. There was one in Amritsar last week,' an important-looking man in an English summer suit with a watch hanging from a silver chain in his pocket had told fellow passengers.

'What is a hartal?' asked one of the listeners.

The important-looking man took a deep breath.

'Gandhi's tool to protest against the government. To protest against the Rowlatt Act. But peacefully. Satyagraha, he calls it.'

'Kala Qanoon,' echoed a listener. Even those who had not heard of the hartal had heard of the iniquity of the Rowlatt Act. 'The British will use their guns and horses, they will arrest whoever they want, no questions asked. No appeal, no newspapers…it will be worse than during the war.'

'I hear the government is preparing for another hartal. They are sending more soldiers to Amritsar.'

Ralla had found his way to the Golden Temple without incident. Once there, he forgot all about the talk of protests and the new law. After bathing in the sacred pool, he sat and listened to the magical melodies of the evening kirtan.

But word kept filtering in from the city. That evening, the

Nirmala sadhus came back energized from the Ram Navami celebrations.

'It was a very big, very peaceful procession,' one of them recounted. 'Kitchlew sahib was there and so was Satyapal. I heard, though I did not see him myself, the DC was watching. Today there were slogans too: "Hindu–Mussalman ki Jai", "Mahatma Gandhi ki Jai". Muslims marching with us—that will not be liked by the British sarkar. There has never been such harmony between the two communities.'

But the next day, on 10 April, at around eleven thirty in the morning the mood had turned. The news of the deportation of Kitchlew and Satyapal had flashed across the city, through the galis and katras and even penetrated the Golden Temple's precincts. Crowds had marched to appeal to the Deputy Commissioner. Bullets had been fired on the bridges near Hall Gate and several people had been killed or wounded. Some buildings—the banks, the Town Hall, and the railway station—had been set on fire, some angrez killed.

He did not leave the temple for the next two days. Once or twice when he looked out into the lanes, he could see small funeral processions hurrying towards Sultanwind Gate. Go and bury or burn your dead but be back by two in the afternoon had been the explicit orders of the Deputy Commissioner.

∾

Looking down from the Baba Atal on Baisakhi morning, he was no longer optimistic that he would be able to meet Mehtab and Kirpal. It would be a wonder if they had managed to get into the city safely or if they had even met each other. Too many trains had been cancelled, the military had taken over the city, communications had been cut. Every road into the city was blocked.

As the sun rose, and the day became warmer, Ralla Singh sat back against a wall away from the parapet to rest. The beating of a tin far below broke his reverie and brought him to the parapet again. He could see a young boy walking through the lane that led towards Guru ka Bagh, beating a ghee tin with two short, roughly fashioned drumsticks. Every fifty yards or so he would stop and beat the tin even harder and then stop, swelling with self-importance. When a few people had gathered around him, he would shout something at the top of his voice. At first Ralla could not make out what the boy was saying but when he came and shouted almost at the foot of the tower the words reached him: 'Hear! Hear! All of you listen carefully! Four thirty this afternoon. There will be a public meeting in Jallianwala Bagh. Lala Kanhaiya Lal will preside over the meeting. Four thirty this afternoon in Jallianwala Bagh.'

That announcement gave Ralla hope: if Mehtab and Kirpal could not make it to the gurudwara during the day, they might end up at that meeting at Jallianwala Bagh. It would be a good idea to go there, he decided.

Chapter 6

Mehtab Singh Makes a Mistake

The whispers began as soon as the announcement ended, and the military column began to move towards Hall Gate.

'How can they fire at the people? They're bluffing.'

'Why, did they not fire the other day? Killed people left and right. So many were shot in the back. They almost shot Gambhirji.'

'Haven't they heard of the other announcement? About this evening's meeting in Jallianwala Bagh. Hans Raj announced it at Dhab Khatikan yesterday.'

'And why are they going in the wrong direction? Why don't they go and make this announcement in the crowded part of the city, towards Katra Jaimal Singh or Harmandir Sahib?'

'They've also printed this announcement at Roz Bazaar press earlier today. Sheikh Karim told me himself—he did fifty copies for them. But what's the use? They aren't pasting those handbills in the city for people to see.'

A panic was beginning to grow inside Mehtab. He knew that as soon as the column passed, he should move towards the gurudwara. His plan of getting Kirpal and Ralla to Amritsar had been a bad mistake. He should have read the signs better. After all, he had followed all the debates about the Rowlatt Act, he was intelligent enough to have formed a sense of the mind of Sir Michael O'Dwyer. He had worked with this government; he knew how good they could be when they wanted to be—and how bad. Then why had he allowed his son to walk into the heart of danger? He should have asked him to go straight home to Dharamsinghwala. They could have come together to the Golden

Temple later, in better times. He had never worried so much about Kirpal's safety during the war as he did now in that moment of panic. It seemed to him then that if Kirpal came to any harm, all that he had cherished in life—his father's determined effort in settling the village of Dharamsinghwala across the Ravi, his own hard work to get a job in the irrigation department, his marriage to Jindi—would all have been in vain.

∾

A few dark weeks after Mehtab's grandfather died, his grandmother, too, did not wake up one morning. The villagers who came to condole with Mehtab's father, Dharam Singh, and his younger brother, Narain Singh, all said the same thing: 'They couldn't stay away from each other. Even if they didn't exchange a word for hours, they were always together, like two sparrows. How could she have let him go alone?' Those days Mehtab would not let his father out of his sight. The moment it became dark he would be tormented by the thought that his father, too, would die, and have to be taken to the cremation ground beyond the edge of the village—then Mehtab and his mother would be left to fend for themselves. Things were easier during the day: he simply stuck close to his father wherever he went. Whether it was the arrangements at the gurudwara run by the family, which so far had been left entirely to his grandfather, or whether it was to eke out whatever they could from the hard, unfriendly sandy wastes of Tibba, the fourteen-year-old Mehtab was always at his father's side. Ostensibly to help him, but equally to keep an eye on him so that he would not vanish all of a sudden.

Thus it was that he was at hand when excitement arrived in Tibba one morning in the shape of a drummer who announced that the British sahib was keen to meet the villagers at the dak bungalow in Khara, a day's journey away. He would be there for three days, and important announcements would be made every afternoon. The sarkar, it appeared, had land to give—fertile, fecund, free land.

The sahib stood on the veranda of the dak bungalow. A respectful semicircle of villagers listened to him from beyond the steps. The white man pitched it strong: 'The sarkar understands your difficulties. Your holdings are growing smaller and there are not enough wells. That is why the sarkar is building canals all over Punjab. For the people of Punjab…. For the villagers of this area, for all of you, we have reserved two hundred murabbas in Sandal Bar across the Ravi. The water will turn this wasteland between Ravi and the Chenab into green fields. You will not regret it. It's almost free….'

There was a bewildered silence and then some whispering among the villagers. Two hundred murabbas was a lot of land. Five thousand acres! Finally, the lambardar of Tibba, feeling the weight of his responsibility, spoke up.

'Huzoor, aap mai-baap hai. But Sandal Bar! It's very far, sahib, and it is all jungle with no means to cultivate it. How will we manage that distant wilderness? It's difficult to even look after the land we live on. And we cannot possibly leave the villages of our ancestors and go there, Ravi paar?'

'Look to the future, lambardar. Someone like you can get ten murabbas in Lyallpur district and here you have entire families fighting over half a murabba. The canals that are coming will wipe away the jungle and scrub; all the prosperity of Ravi and Chenab will be in your laps. Sandal Bar will not be wasteland for long.'

Dharam Singh was silent all the way back to Tibba. On reaching home he went straight to the gurudwara. When he opened the Granth Sahib at random and read the verse at the top of the page he was immediately at peace.

Santaa kay kaaraj aap khalo-i-aa har kamm karaavan aa-i-aa
raam
Dharat suhaavee taal suhaavaa vich amrit jal chhaa-i-aa raam

The Lord himself is there to resolve all the tasks of the saints
The land is beautiful, the pool is beautiful, and in it is the
ambrosial water

His decision was clear: he would go away, and leave the land in
Tibba for his younger brother.

In the village square the next day, Mehtab watched his father
announce his decision to the others. One by one several other
farmers moved to stand next to him in support. The lambardar
scoffed at them:

'You have fallen for the trickery of the gora sahib. You will
find nothing but snakes and scorpions waiting for you out there.'

A month later Dharam Singh, along with two other Sikh
farmers, left Tibba to board the train at Patti for Lyallpur. Along
with his bedroll, Dharam Singh was carrying the precious Granth
Sahib with which his father had started the Tibba gurudwara.
Mehtab went to the station to see him off. He had been left with
the responsibility of escorting his mother and younger siblings to
join their father when he was ready.

∾

The village of Dharamsinghwala was so named because it was
Dharam Singh who first walked on to the land allotted to the
group from Tibba by the English settlement officer. And, because
he was carrying the Granth Sahib with him. He also carried a map
given to them by the office in Lyallpur. The square plots drawn
on the map with straight lines were invisible in reality, hidden
by the thorny bush and bramble of the vast Sandal Bar. But the
hardy farmers had not left their homes on the other side of the

Ravi to be deterred by bleak landscape: they had come with their hoes and spades and ploughs. Buffaloes and bullocks and carts followed. The boundaries of individual plots soon appeared and then within them rose huts and houses. A stream came from the canal straight to the village and outlets were created every two or three murabbas to direct the water to individual fields. The farmers could only marvel at how well the English engineers had planned these things, and at their own good fortune.

Sandal Bar bewitched young Mehtab when he arrived with his mother three months later. Its vastness gave him a sense of unbounded freedom and he waited with joy for the early morning squawking of parrots and sudden screams of peacocks at dusk. He bathed in the stream coming from the canal and helped his father in the fields. But his father urged him to finish his schooling.

'I want you to learn not only Urdu and Gurmukhi but also some English. You, my son, are not going to plough fields or just look after the gurudwara,' Dharam Singh told him once they had settled in. 'You should get a permanent government job with the canal people.'

Mehtab did not need much urging. He had seen the Indian clerks of the irrigation department conversing with their English bosses, and marvelled at how they could understand the charts set up on easels in the camp offices. He knew that to be like them he would need to know not just some English, but also arithmetic and geometry. Only then would he qualify to work in that department, to go on tour with a bedroll, and stay in the rest houses that were being built wherever the canals went, to be able to calculate the amount of water that would flow from month to month, to know when to open the sluice gates and send more water and when to shut them, to tell the farmers about the amount of water they could draw and how much land it would irrigate.

It was this desire that accompanied him as he walked seven

miles in the damp dawn every morning along the raised bank of the new canal, to the next village and the simple school of three rooms with a roof of sloping tin sheets and a long veranda held up by wooden poles. It was there that he learnt to write his sharply angled English letters with the royal blue ink mixed from tablets and to pour sand on the wooden slate so that the ink would dry.

Dharamsinghwala grew bigger. After the first settlers came those who could serve the village—the shopkeepers, the tinkers, the ekkawallahs, the ironsmith. There was no dearth of space, the land stretched into the shimmering distance without end. Dharam Singh's gurudwara became the heart of the community, a brave new presence in this land across which Nadir Shah had once ridden his tyrannous hordes, where Dulla Bhatti had challenged Akbar. And where they said if one's love was true, one could see a proud Heer walking with the swagger of a graceful deer towards the Chenab or hear a Mirza singing for his Sahiban.

◈

Soon enough, Dharamsinghwala became a favourite destination for travellers, some of whom, Mehtab was convinced in his heart, had made the journey just for his benefit.

Like Charanjit Singh who arrived to speak to the congregation in the gurudwara on the night of the birth anniversary of Guru Nanak. A tall, thin man, a picture of dignified elegance, he seemed to belong to another world. It was not just his starched white, neatly tied turban with a light brown achkan and white churidar pyjamas which created that impression—but the way he spoke. Quietly and evenly, almost in an undertone, but with clarity and determination as if he were inscribing his words in the air and leaving them to hang there until they had been understood.

'Brothers and sisters, I speak to you as the representative of the Singh Sabha of Amritsar and Lahore. Soon, we hope that each town in Punjab will have its own Singh Sabha. You are here

because you believe in the true teachings of the Gurus. I feel
the energy here, I feel the potential of your young men to learn
and to teach, to carry our tradition forward. You are fortunate
you have Dharam Singh and this gurudwara.

'Education is the only way ahead for us. That is why our
leaders have started the Khalsa printing press for newspapers and
journals.These are our instruments for shaping the consciousness of
Sikhs today. In these you can read the thoughts of great thinkers,
men who have inspired dozens like me to go out and walk from
village to village and cleanse the poison of superstition and ritual
that is slowly eating away at our insides.'

The message went deep into Mehtab's heart and by the time
Charanjit Singh came back a year later, Mehtab had convinced his
father to put up a small board inscribed in Gurmukhi letters outside
the gurudwara: *Sri Guru Singh Sabha Gurudwara, Dharamsinghwala*.
What had been a family affair became a community institution
with clear-cut rules and practices, regular hours of worship, and
annual celebrations on designated holy days.

It was Charanjit Singh's clarity of thought and strong message
of education along with his own father's yearning for progress that
had moulded Mehtab. He was today a man with a strong sense of
community as well as a recognized hard worker—a superintendent
in the irrigation department who had been awarded a gold medal
for courageously handling a breach in the Lower Bari Doab
Canal. And yet, he could be naïve.

∿

The marching soldiers were only an arm's length away; Mehtab
involuntarily shrank back even more into the shadows.

A man across the lane could not control his agitation.

'What will happen to my business?' he asked loudly of nobody
in particular. 'I have a licence for selling liquor at Lohgarh Gate
after eight o'clock.'

He rushed off behind the inspector.

The panic that had been building up inside Mehtab got the better of him and for one moment he forgot his habit of deliberate, considered thought. What if he could not meet Kirpal before the curfew set in? What if Kirpal did not know of the curfew and came into town after eight o'clock and got into trouble with the authorities? He needed to tell them. He needed to get special permission. Surely the General would give it; Kirpal was *their* soldier. He was one of them.

He rushed after the wine-seller.

The English police officer had piercing blue eyes, eyes that could open a secret at ten yards.

'What is it?' was his curt question.

The wine-seller spoke with folded hands.

'Sahibji, I am Atma Ram. I sell wine. I have a liquor licence. No curfew for me sahib, please. Otherwise, I will be destroyed.'

The blue eyes threw a question towards Mehtab.

'Sahib, my son Lance Naik Kirpal Singh is coming on leave today. I have not met him for four years when he went away to fight alongside British soldiers in France, in Basra. Please allow me to meet him, sahibji. He has fought very bravely, sir, for the King.'

The police office gestured to both of them to move closer to the leading motor car. The motor car stopped. The police officer conveyed to General Dyer what the two men had said. Dyer glanced at them. His face had no expression, his eyes had no sympathy. Mehtab Singh knew then that he had made a mistake by speaking, but it was too late. Dyer gave a curt order to the police officer.

The next minute Mehtab was being dragged along the column; a soldier was pulling him by a red cloth looped around his upper arm. The wine-seller was being similarly dragged in front of him. A few other men were picked up at random as the column moved from Hall Gate to Hathi Gate and Lohgarh Gate and from there

to Dhab Khatikan and through several katras to Lakkar Mandi
and Bagh Jhanda Singh. These were not the most populated parts
of the city, and it was clear that the soldiers were keen to hurry
out of the midday heat. The pace did not slacken at all. If any of
them lagged for a moment, a thrust in the back with the butt of
a rifle would hurry him on. At Dhab Khatikan the wine-seller
asked a familiar person in the lane for water and when a boy ran
along with the procession to hand over a glass, a soldier snatched
it away, saying, 'Not allowed.' Finally, the procession reached the
military headquarters at Ram Bagh across the railway line. Here
the detained men, with their wrists tied behind their backs, were
roped to an old mango tree.

More than hunger or thirst or the pain from the rough
rope cutting into his wrists, it was the regret of having been in
the wrong place that was troubling Mehtab Singh. This was not
what it was meant to be: the plan had been to proceed to the
Golden Temple and meet up with his soldier son after four years
and, after giving thanks to God, to take him home. Instead, he
was sitting, along with several others, on his haunches under the
mango trees of Ram Bagh, his hands tied behind his back. Two
soldiers kept watch over the prisoners and periodically showered
them with desultory abuse.

Sometime in the afternoon, the tension that had been
concentrating itself in Ram Bagh dissolved into activity. Mehtab
saw General Dyer stride out of his tent, issue instructions, and get
into his car. A handful of other officers accompanied him. Two
armoured cars with machine guns fitted on them and dozens of
armed soldiers began to follow the officers' cars towards the city.
Mehtab overheard some mention of a gathering in Jallianwala
Bagh. He could not make out what exactly had happened, but
he knew that his chances of meeting his son and his brother-
in-law were now very remote and he had only himself to blame
for the way things had turned out.

Chapter 7

The Making of
Lance Naik Kirpal Singh

The Great War was over and in the days before his leave was sanctioned, Lance Naik Kirpal Singh found his mind going back to many things. To the battlefields that he had fought on, so far now that they seemed part of another world and yet were always part of a nightmare that just would not go away. To the friends who had fallen and had not even been cremated the right way; some had been buried, others just abandoned. To the laughing girl with dark, flashing eyes he had met in Basra, the daughter of an Indian Muslim sheikh living outside the mosque; she had made fresh lemonade for him and two other soldiers and then had turned back from the door and looked at him once before vanishing into the house, a look that he had never forgotten. To the time when he first became a soldier and went to war—because he was a champion wrestler.

∿

'Here, hold my leg. With both your arms, my young pehlwan. Here, just above the knee. And then lock your hands fast.'

The massive pillar of muscle that was the leg of this man-mountain barely came within his clasp but seven-year-old Kirpu was determined to try. After all, nobody had forced him to come to the wrestler's akhara. He had seen wrestlers before, but at a distance. Big men with brown bodies covered with sweat and oil, grappling with each other in a mud pit beyond the wheat fields of his father's village of Dharamsinghwala. But he had never gone

near them. In Tibba, the village where the mother he had never
seen had grown up, things were different. Ralla spoilt him with
toys and marbles and stories, and when he mentioned Bhima,
the village wrestler, Kirpu grabbed his chance. He pestered his
uncle to take him to Bhima to learn wrestling.

'Oye Kirpu, you have the limbs of a sparrow yet, what wrestling
are you going to learn?' Ralla tried to put him off. 'Drink milk
and eat ghee and butter for a few years, do at least one thousand
dand-baithak a day, swing from the high branches to build your
biceps, then you will be ready for wrestling.'

But Kirpu had persisted, and finally one afternoon, Ralla had
taken his nephew to the akhara.

Kirpu had never seen a man like Bhima. What a complexion!
Like gulal mixed in milk. What a voice! Like a lion in the deep
jungle. What moustaches! Pointing straight up towards his ears.

Bhima looked at him quizzically. The rolling laughter seemed
to gurgle in his deep belly and through his massive chest before
it reached his mouth.

'I hear that you are keen on wrestling. Balle, balle, oye mere
chote pehlwan!'

Suddenly, Kirpu was up in the air, swept up towards the sky
by the wrestler. Frozen with fear, he looked down on Bhima's
bald pate. For a moment he thought the wrestler would fling him
away, and he hoped he would fall on the charpai on which his
uncle was sitting, a glass of hooch from Chaila's liquor theka in
his hand. This was a mistake; he should never have come here,
he thought, even as the fear congealed into a salty trickle that
went down his throat.

But then, as swiftly as he had gone up, he was down, struggling
to stay on his feet.

'We'll teach you wrestling, my young friend. We'll turn you
into Gama.'

Then Kirpu was faced with the massive leg of the wrestler,

and he knew this was his chance to learn from a champion. 'Go on, grip my leg tight. Higher. That's right. Now lift it up. Yes, lift up my leg so I fall down. Go on, pehlwan, use your strength, all the breakfast you ate.'

The boy clasped Bhima's thigh just above the knee with both hands and held it close to his chest and tried to lift it up but Bhima wouldn't budge. Then, not wanting to break the boy's heart, Bhima lifted his leg himself and staggered back in mock defeat.

Kirpu turned up every day at the akhara for the next month. There were village boys who came to wrestle there and there were those like his uncle who came to drink near the well and then lie down in the sun. Another boy, perhaps younger by a year or two, who went by the name of Sucha, was a constant presence, helping Bhima in every way that he could.

Bhima indulged Kirpu, teaching him grips and gambits, showing him how to stand with his weight balanced on both feet, knees and hips flexed, his back low, and how to get the opponent flat out on the ground with the head touching the earth. Something in Kirpu's earnest eyes had touched Bhima's heart. He saw in him a lonely determination, a resolve wanting to be formed.

'A very good wrestler you will be too one day,' Bhima told him, a day or two before he was to leave Tibba with his father. 'Take care of your body, eat well, exercise. Don't go your uncle's way.'

Kirpu left with his father for Dharamsinghwala soon after that, a hired mare taking their bedroll to the railway station at Patti. But the memory of that first visit to his mother's village that would stay forever in Kirpu's mind would be of Bhima and his akhara. There had been nothing else in Tibba for him. He had no memories of his mother; all he knew was a name: Jindi. He didn't know what a mother was all about. Perhaps just a lonely, unanswered ache in the night.

∾

It was the middle of 1914, almost ten years after that visit to Tibba. The crowds had turned out in the pleasing sun of the northern autumn for the annual wrestling tournament of the entire tehsil of Toba Tek Singh. Only the best wrestlers reached here: for two days they pitted muscle and tactics against each other in the freshly churned cool earth of the akhara to the echoing beat of the dhol that hung around the bull neck of Peeru, the dholwallah, dressed in his special black kurta and green tehmat. That rhythmic beating of the dhol sent the blood racing not only in the veins of those who were crouching in the akhara circling each other but of the entire crowd, riven by ancient village rivalries.

Kirpal knew that once he got hold of his opponent's thigh and locked his strong, sinewy arms around it that would be the beginning of the end. He lunged but his opponent, no novice either, moved away. He lunged again. This time he got the grip he was looking for. He drove forward with all the strength of his upper body, forward and up. His opponent staggered back on one leg, fighting hard to keep his balance. Kirpal felt the rush of the crowd's roar in his ears, the dhol picked up rhythm, he was at the head of a victorious army and there was to be no looking back. With a heave he had his opponent on the ground and fell upon him, pushing down on the man's forehead. With teeth set and eyes narrowed, his opponent fought back, with all the strength of his muscular shoulders and neck and for an eternity they were locked without any movement, strength matching strength. And then it was over. His opponent's head touched the holy earth of the akhara, his shoulders sank into the soil and Kirpal, breathing hard and deep, fell over the man with the sudden release of tension. The dhol went into a fast riff, and then with three loud beats fell silent. The crowd's intense roar scattered into broken, spread-out comment.

Kirpal pulled up his opponent and with a quick hug they

left the akhara. He drained the brass bowl of water that someone handed him.

'Wah oye pehlwan, you are going to become Rustam-e-Hind one day.'

'Let him be Rustam-e-Rawalpindi for a while. Hind is not going anywhere.'

Kirpal revelled in the laughter and the friendly ribbing. The victory made him feel good and warm inside. He would sleep well tonight but before that he would go and bathe in the irrigation channel that branched off from the canal. And when he got home that evening, he would eat well of the pile of buttered tandoori rotis and saag and dal that Pritam Kaur, his grandmother, would have ready for him.

❦

A short, bald man, his moustache dyed a dark orange with henna, broke into the group. Everything about him spelt authority: his crisp kurta pyjama, his traditional embroidered Punjabi jutti with its curled toes, and the register in his hand.

'Kaka, you fought well. You are a strong boy, a real Punjabi boy,' he said and stretching to his full height patted Kirpal on the shoulder.

One of the boys recognized the man.

'Tehsildar sahib, a thousand salaams.'

'My sat sri akal, too, tehsildar saab.'

The tehsildar was rarely seen in the villages, appearing only on important occasions; someone had pointed him out once to Kirpal at a Baisakhi mela. Now, he felt a thrill that the tehsildar had been watching him wrestle.

'Come over there, near the peepul tree. All the winners, and even some who lost, as long as they are strong, are gathering there. You are indeed lucky. The sarkar wants to meet you all today.'

The sarkar! Kirpal's imagination exploded. Who was it who

waited for him under the peepul? The Deputy Commissioner or perhaps the Lieutenant Governor, whom he had heard occasionally speaking on the radio from Lahore? Surely it was not George Pancham himself, dressed in brocade and gold, who had come to meet the wrestlers of the tehsil.

As they neared the peepul tree, the tehsildar curved up in an obsequious posture that came to him naturally, ingrained by three generations of serving the British rulers. He began to step softly, as if walking on his toes, and signalled by a look and a downward gesture of his hand to the boys following him that they should quieten their steps.

The sarkar, the man who, at that moment, embodied the entire British Raj, sat behind a small table. The brass buttons of his military uniform glinted in the sun. He sat absolutely erect as if he had an iron rod in place of a spine and he looked each person directly in the eye. Kirpal could not look away from the eyes that bored into him. They were a strange mix of blue and green and seemed to have golden stars drifting in them.

When he did look away, his eyes fell on a poster that was pinned to the tree trunk just behind the officer: a uniformed soldier standing legs apart, a rifle with an attached bayonet in his left hand, a smart turban on his head; a cupped pair of hands in front of him offered a pile of gold coins. Superimposed on the soldier's features was a question mark in bold black. Written below it in bold Urdu script was this: *Who will take this money, this rifle, this uniform? He who enlists in the Army!*

The recruiting sergeant, for that is who the sarkar was, spoke in the Hindustani of a British soldier who had spent the last two decades in India.

'We have seen the wrestling. This is the way brave men test each other. I am not Colonel Rattray, otherwise I would have come into the akhara myself and tested each of you like he did. All the boys he wrestled with are proud soldiers in the Indian army, the backbone of the Sikh battalions.... His Majesty will be pleased to take you brave young men into the army. You are true representatives of your courageous race, the Sikhs of Punjab, whose valour and loyalty is well known to His Majesty. You will eat well and dress well, you will be taken care of, and you will be well rewarded, with pensions and jagirs. There is a war coming and this is the chance to write your name in golden letters and win medals that your coming generations will be proud of.'

Kirpal and the others gave the speaker their full attention. They knew that war had broken out in vilayat and the king emperor was facing a powerful enemy. But they also knew that British army regiments, like the ones housed in the cantonments of Jalandhar, Ambala, and Lahore, would take on the enemy, just as they had done in Swat and Baluchistan. It hadn't occurred to them that the sarkar would come looking in the villages for men to become soldiers. The poster on the tree made sense now. The uniform was inviting, it had so many pockets, and the buttons would shine just like the sergeant's, and it would be nice to hold a rifle. That pile of gold coins was a lot of money. It could do many things—repair the roof once and for all, pay the moneylender all that was due and the interest too, pay the aarhti in the village for the grain and the sugar for the entire winter.... But to Kirpal all these things meant less than the chance to get out of Dharamsinghwala. To meet men who had travelled to distant places and seen the world. Perhaps even talk to some British officers, then come home wearing his uniform and show his friends the medal that he would have won for bravery in the face of bullets.

It did not cross his mind that soldiers could also die. At his age, death only happened to other people. For a moment he thought that he should ask someone for advice. But who? He was not sure where his father was, somewhere on tour, in one of the dak bungalows of the irrigation department which had become his home. His grandmother would only cry if he told her. Even if he left the house for a day she would worry, standing in the doorway with her dupatta tucked under clenched teeth, her eyes misty with tears. She would never want him to go to the war. But if he went, and sent back money, and came back in a starched uniform with stripes and medals, there would be no one prouder than her. The minute he thought about that he didn't wait for another thought to come. He stepped forward towards the table.

'Name?'

'Kirpal Singh, son of Mehtab Singh.'

'Age?'

'Eighteen,' Kirpal did not hesitate to round off his age by a year and some.

'Sure?'

'Ji, eighteen'.

'Go and stand there. Height and chest measurements, that's all. The rest will be done at the depot'.

But Kirpal wanted to tell the recruiting sergeant something more.

'Huzoor, I can read and write. Gurmukhi and some angrezi.'

'Oh, good, you've been to school?'

'Huzoor, till class eight. Khalsa School.'

He didn't add that his father, who hadn't been able to do much else about his bringing up, had insisted on that.

'Good then, Kirpal Singh,' said the sergeant, making a note, 'I'm sure that you will do well in the army and one day you'll become a subedar sahib.'

༄

Now Kirpal was back, not quite a subedar but at least a lance naik, a veteran of Flanders and Basra, and he knew it was nothing short of a miracle that he was back. He had been protected by the Holy Book, the final form of the Guru, that the 47th Sikhs had always carried with them. Otherwise, it had been the devil's war, a war without end, in which the shells fell like monsoon rain and men dropped to the ground like jamuns fall from a tree in a storm. Fought first in a land of cold misery, rain, and snow, where death came screaming in the form of bullets from snipers hidden by the mist. Where bodies lay unburied and unburnt for months, preserved by the snow. In this war, one did not see the enemy face to face, sword did not clash gallantly with sword. Men did not stand up and do battle, instead they burrowed into the ground. Airships sailed the sky like kites and cannons shot fireballs that weighed twelve maunds each and destroyed the earth for five hundred paces around where they fell. Death leapt up from mines in the ground if you stepped on them and poison gas choked you to an unholy end. And then there had been the forgotten war in Mesopotamia where the heat announced itself from afar, like an angry God in the sky, and poured down in molten sheets. And the rain turned the land into a quagmire which rose to the ankles and mosquitoes swirled in thick clouds and it became difficult to walk in the endless desert. If one had to see the anger of the Almighty, this war had been it.

He promised himself that once his leave was sanctioned, he would go to the Golden Temple and give thanks to Waheguru for saving him and he would pray for all those who did not return.

Chapter 8

Another Way to Die

Around the time that Kirpal was born, the plague began to sweep through parts of Punjab. The people were used to pestilence, to famines, to police brutalities, to the stranglehold of moneylenders but not to a devilish wildfire that could not be seen. It went from house to house, emptying them of living beings until entire villages lay abandoned, fetid with random death. Some said that it was a devil that had returned from the grave after being buried for long decades. Others said it was a demon that had travelled in the form of a rat on a ship from China. In the end, it did not matter how it came or who brought it. For the people of Punjab, when it reached them around the turn of the century, it became just another terrible way to die.

When it invaded the village where eight-year-old Maya lived with her parents, the people said that someone—the village elders or the lambardar or the British officer who rode through the area on a white horse—should have warned them. The villagers knew how people usually fell sick: when the rains came and the river rose in a flood, swarms of mosquitoes brought a bad fever with chills and shivers. Or when people went to fairs and drank water from unclean wells and ate all sorts of thing they could not resist—churan and imli and freshly cut amrak that made the mouth water as soon as the eye fell on it, fried pakoras and gulgulas soaked in a spicy sweet mix of red chutney and thin slivers of radish and sucked on red and green and yellow ice lollies, they fell sick and vomited day and night till nothing was left in the stomach to vomit out and then they just shut their eyes and waited for the darkness. Or from the smallpox that came after many days of body-wrenching fever and formed painful, pus-filled ulcers all over the body and if you were not fortunate to be among the dead then you lived all your life with ugly marks on your face and body and were scared to glance at yourself in the village pool, even if you could still see. Only the Goddess Sitala Devi could save you from smallpox: she was the one who sent it and she could call it back. And Sakhi Sarwar Pir could save you from so many other diseases if you prayed hard enough at one of the khanqahs which bore his name, or went to the fair at Gujranwala, or were brave enough to go on the annual pilgrimage to his shrine.

But this disease was different. No one knew what to do with the rats that lived in village granaries and stores. There were no traditional ways, developed by village hakims through the ages, of fighting it, no boiled plant or root extract or blood of a pigeon that could cure it. And it gave you no time to pray to any devi or pir.

For Maya, the horror began when her father, the gentle Jeevan Singh, only thirty-eight and still hopeful of becoming a wholesale supplier of grain not only for his village but for the entire tehsil, went to his storehouse early one morning. This was usual for him; he liked to walk through the entire store before his two assistants came, casting a sharp eye on the sacks for any leaks. That day he found a dead rat, swollen and foul-smelling, in the far corner of the storehouse. Covering his nose with the loose end of his turban with one hand, Jeevan Singh picked up the rat by the tail.

'Sohri deya,' he cursed under his breath, 'good that you have chosen to die yourself, otherwise I would have killed you. You and your bastard brothers are the ones making holes in the sacks. Today, you got what you deserved.'

But even as he carried the dangling, swollen dead rat by the

tail to the stream across the abandoned field and swung it around
in angry little circles before letting it fly into the water, the rat
had passed on its merciless message of death.

The lambardar, who had recently attended a meeting with
the Deputy Commissioner about the epidemic, knew his duty
well. His chest bursting with self-importance he had rushed
immediately to the policeman in-charge at Pind Dadan Khan:

'Huzoor, Darogaji, rat, rat....' he could barely get the words out.

'What? What are you babbling about? A rat took your tongue
or what?'

'Huzoor, a dead rat...just like DC sahib had told us.'

'Where is the dead rat?'

'Jeevan Singh's store, huzoor, and he is now sick. He is dying.
The whole village will die now.'

'You know what has to be done. I will report this dead rat
but you have to vacate the village.'

'We have already been telling people, huzoor, but you know
how it is....'

'Meaning?'

'They won't leave, huzoor...none of them want to leave,
even if they die. The Muslims say it is wrong for them to leave
a village if there is an epidemic and the others think they will
never get their houses and things back and the thieves will take
it all. Especially the sahukars and moneylenders; they have the
gold and silver of the entire village hidden in their sandooks.
They would rather die than leave those sandooks. But it is true
that the thieves are biding their time.'

'Meaning?'

'They are waiting to raid any house where the family moves
out. You have to catch them, huzoor....'

'You get your villagers to catch the rats. As many as they
can. You know the reward? DC sahib has announced six pice

for each dead rat. But they have to prove it. They have to cut off the tail and bring it to you and you have to bring it to me. Only then will they get the six pice. I am not going to give it simply on anyone's word, otherwise our treasury will be empty in a day, liars that you all are.'

For years afterwards, the memories of the days that followed haunted Maya like thieves, like the men with oiled black bodies and tight loincloths who crept into the plague-ridden houses, their greed overcoming all fear of death. Her mother stayed with her father till the end; she would not leave him to die alone. And even while he still had breath in his body, she herself began to feel faint and feverish. Somebody in the village did the family a favour and sent a telegram to her masi, her mother's sister, Karam Kaur, and her husband, Makhan Singh, in Parhi. Three days later, they arrived and took Maya out of the house. They joined the other families who had moved out into the fields from where the village was a distant, smudged silhouette against the night sky. Silent, subdued, and scared, the villagers gathered on a gentle mound of earth that rose like a plateau in the fields, uncultivated and prickly with dry grass. For three nights they slept under a vast, fragile sky that shimmered like glass. Then the authorities put up tents and to some that seemed like a luxury. To Maya, it made no difference. The pyre of her father and then, just five days later, of her mother had put her beyond all pain or joy.

Two weeks later, the lambardar came to tell them that they could go back to their houses, that the plague had left the village, and the houses had been cleaned. The chamars had washed the walls and floors with the strong phenyl solution sent by the district headquarters in large cans and the windows had been left open to let in the sun. In a daze, Maya went back into the village. But it was by then no longer home, just a strange abandoned set of houses, smelling sharply of phenyl, the open windows looking uninviting and grotesque. The house in which she had lived with her parents was a yawning cave full of ghosts and she crumpled into a heap at the door and fainted. When she came to, she found that Masi Karmo had wrapped her up in a warm, soft shawl that had belonged to her mother, a cream shawl embroidered with small flowers in peach and rosy-red with bright green stems, a shawl so soft and fine that her mother had said it could pass through a ring.

'We will go away soon, my child, and we will take you with us, sitting on a mare, to your new home in Parhi.'

Chapter 9

The Trader in Half-truths

When Udham Singh returned to Amritsar from Basra and Baghdad after an uninspiring stint in the army where all he had been able to do was nail down planks and fix some trucks, it was early 1919. In a few months he would leave for East Africa to work for the Uganda Railway Company. But for those few months that he was in Punjab, he felt the thrill of a real battle building up.

The protests against the Kala Qanoon were rising. He did not fully understand all the arguments that the political leaders made against the Rowlatt Bills but his revolutionary's instinct told him that here was a cause that could unite people, incite them enough to shed blood. The Ghadar movement, that had seemed dead for four years, was beginning to breathe again. He had got a message that he could start work. The Ghadar newspapers, considered seditious by the government, needed to be distributed in Punjab. Men like him—he was a man, eighteen after all—were indispensable. For this cause, Udham Singh was willing to take risks. There wasn't much to lose, and a world to win; the big stakes were their own prize. If he were to be caught with these copies, he would be charged with sedition and sent across the kala pani for sure. That was where the great Ghadari baba, Sohan Singh Bhakna, had gone, as had many more who had not been strung up on the gallows. In that possible punishment itself lay a pot of glory, a low-caste orphan's way of becoming a real man. If there was one regret he had, it was that his dear brother, Sadhu Singh, had died without seeing what Udham was capable of.

Another message told him from where the copies of the newspaper had to be collected. From the house of the doctor, Hardit Singh Vaid, in Katra Ahluwalian. Udham smiled to himself; they always found great places to hide things.

The young man, roughly his own age, who opened the door for Udham at the doctor's house was watchful, trained. Only after an exchange of passwords did he allow Udham to step in. He could see the doctor sitting in his armchair, reading a newspaper in English, *The Tribune*, a pillow covering his arthritic knees. Sucha guided Udham into an inner room and shut the door behind him. The doctor had not looked towards them, nor acknowledged Udham's mumbled sat sri akal. He was clearly used to unknown men coming and going into the house as long as Sucha allowed them in.

Sucha raised the wick in the oil lantern in the small room.

'Haven't seen you before,' he commented, not looking up.

'Doesn't matter,' was Udham's reply.

Sucha looked up.

'I mean, are you from Amritsar?'

'As much as I am from anywhere at all.'

'Which lane?'

'No lane. From the orphanage.'

'Putlighar?'

'Yes.'

Sucha could not see through the mask of indifference on Udham's face; it seemed permanent. But under the indifference he sensed a determination. The man also exuded a rough brute strength. Something about the man's shoulders and bearing made him ask the next question.

'Been to the war?'

Udham was silent for a bit and then decided to answer him.

'Haan, Basra, Baghdad,' he was silent again and then carried on in a rush, 'could have done much more, fought wherever they needed men like me. But kismet made me pass my time as a carpenter. Also looked after military vehicles. That is also war. But…there will be more chances.'

'And now this?' Sucha asked, glancing at the bundle of copies tied by a string.

'This is my duty now. They will be all over five Majha villages by tomorrow night.'

Saying this, Udham took the bundle and whirling quickly was nearly out of the door before Sucha could ask.

'Bhai, your name?'

'People call me Udham Singh. Nowadays.'

Then he was gone, melting into the darkness in the lane, the copies hidden under his brown shawl.

Udham Singh was not deliberately dissembling in front of Sucha. It was difficult for him to say clearly where he belonged, or what his name was. He had no memories of the Pilbad mohalla of Sunam where he was born. And only shadowy recollections of the hut by the railway crossing at Upali, at the edge of the jungle, where his father, Tehal Singh, had raised and lowered the railway barrier for passing trains. If he belonged anywhere, it was to the Central Khalsa Orphanage at Putlighar, outside the walls of old Amritsar, as much as anyone can belong to an orphanage. Before that there had only been the road, first with the sadhus with whom he and his brother had travelled after their father's death and then with the Sant of Alibegh. Udham had a dim memory that one of the Sant's young followers, a kindly man called Ralla, had dropped them off at the orphanage. As to his name, he was born Sher Singh, baptized as Udham Singh, and referred to as Ude.… The man who slipped out of the doctor's home into the dark Amritsar lane was already training himself to be an elusive shadow, a trader in half-truths for whom changing identities would become second nature.

Chapter 10

The Destiny of Nicholas Williams

The telegram came to Sergeant Nicholas Williams in Jalandhar at 4 p.m. on 10 April. Captain J. W. Massey was asking for reinforcements to be sent to Amritsar. Then the line was cut and they lost direct contact. Another telegram followed, this time from Lahore. Major General William Benyon of the 16th Division ordered Brigadier General Dyer to send one hundred British and a hundred native Indian troops to Amritsar.

Dyer, accompanied by Captain F. C. Briggs and Williams, immediately rushed to the railway station.

'Stop the first train we can get. Convert it to a military train to Amritsar,' Dyer told the stationmaster.

'None, sir, till after midnight.'

'Blast! That one, then.'

They then rushed to the barracks of William's own batallion, the 25th London Cyclists—the battalion's name referred to their earlier cycling duties as part of the Territorial Army—and the 2nd/151st Infantry to order the troops to start packing for the journey. Dyer decided to add an additional hundred of a motley bunch of Indian troops from various Frontier Forces available at the Jalandhar depot to the reinforcements that were being dispatched.

Williams sat by the phone most of that evening while Dyer and his wife entertained at Flagstaff House. He reported in to Dyer when the troops, led by Major F. A. S. Clarke, marched off to the station at nine. They had to wait till one in the morning to entrain and would make slow progress past the burnt and looted stations of Bhagtanwala and Chheharta, getting off every few miles while the men of the Indian Defence Force in an armoured train ahead repaired the line wherever it had been uprooted.

Over the phone, Williams learnt of the shooting in Amritsar on the bridges earlier that day and the violence inflicted on the city by the angered crowd. British families had been moved from the Civil Lines to the Fort. The garrison was severely stretched but fortunately a party of more than two hundred Gurkhas from the 1st and 9th battalions on its way to Peshawar had been detrained in the city, along with their commanding officer Captain Gerry Crampton; being between depots they had to be issued rifles from the Fort. Another 125 Royal Sussex men and 175 Baluchis had arrived a few hours earlier from Lahore under Major Macdonald. As each bit of news came in, Williams would make a note of it and send it in to Dyer. He knew that his boss's mind was not on his guests.

The next morning Major Clarke returned to brief Dyer. The army had taken over Amritsar; the civil authorities had virtually abandoned control. Commissioner Kitchin had come down from Lahore but was not expected to stay long and the Deputy Commissioner, Miles Irving, was not much use. The troops had orders to use all necessary force. Two aeroplanes had flown over Amritsar even as Clarke had been planning to return and two armoured cars were expected to come in later in the day.

Williams had a gut feeling that Dyer would want to be at the heart of the trouble and, soon enough, they were in the car, the General and his bodyguard along with the two captains, Briggs and Southey.

It took them only three hours to reach Amritsar.

It was only destiny, thought Williams, that he was now in Amritsar as Dyer's ADC and bodyguard. It was only destiny that had put

him, a boy from London's cramped Admiral Mews, on board the
ocean liner SS *Ceramic* and dispatched him to India. He had been
transfixed by the ship's size, its four masts and huge funnel. All
around were signs of past luxury: it was easy to imagine languid
passengers lounging on its four decks, or dancing to swing and
jazz in its halls, as it sailed from England to Australia in better
times. But in early 1916 the liner had become a troopship, a
potential target for torpedoes and submarines. This did not worry
Williams and his fellows as much as the fact that they could not
smoke on deck after dark; no lights were to be shown on the ship
for fear of submarines.

They had sailed for three weeks, going past the Rock of
Gibraltar, and Port Said and through the Red Sea, until the
Ceramic entered Bombay port, becoming the largest vessel to
have done so until then. Williams had stared in amazement at
the Gateway of India rising above him against the inky Indian
sky; it was being built to commemorate a royal visit that had
taken place five years earlier.

Those were good memories. That landing and the first train
journey when they meandered towards Bangalore for thirty-six
hours. The barracks with the wide open maidan before them
and the fragrant breeze that blew past their balconies in the
early morning. The long marches in the equable temperature of
the Deccan plateau, the leisurely musket practice at the camp at
Hebbal, the luxury of your own 'boy'—always called 'boy' even
if he were seventy—to clean buttons, boots, topi.

Not all his memories were as pleasant: among the worst were of
the Waziristan campaign of 1917 when the fresh downcountry
soldiers had found themselves pitted against the murderous
Mahsud tribes of the north-western frontier. The silver-tongued
enemy was deceptive and the heat and sandfly fever had toyed
with them at will as they advanced slowly from the detrainment

point at Tank to the inner reaches of the Frontier fastness. The
Mahsud laid one ambush after another, slipped in every trick they
knew, while the Cyclists, used to scouting around the country
hedgerows of coastal England, struggled as dust whirlpools swirled
around them like maddened spirits. The rocks gathered the heat of
the day within them and exuded it all night. If an arm accidently
touched a boulder, as the men tossed and turned and tried to
sleep, it was enough to blister the skin.

On the first day itself, as he woke up in camp and stepped
out of the tent, Williams had seen a poisonous black krait, its
stripes milky white on shiny black skin, slither out of his tent
virtually between his feet. Before anybody could react, it had
vanished deep into the boulders above.

'Nothing can harm me now,' Williams had told himself. 'God
must be on my side, else I would've copped it.'

Doggedly, he had led his men up the valley, determined to
prove that the promotion to sergeant had been no mistake, through
boulder-strewn riverbeds where the clear water of the meagre
streams was unsafe to drink. The men, heat-crazed, would throw
themselves into the water, hoping that it would soak through
their skin and cool their insides.

For weeks, the torturous advance had continued as the
Cyclists played their role in the brigade, clearing pickets, building
perimeter walls, destroying tribal villages, or simply searching for
water supplies—all in anticipation of bringing an elusive enemy
down to a peace settlement.

But the mosquitoes got him before that. The night heat,
sticky and humid after a short spell of rain, was stifling. Unable
to breathe, he had pushed aside his mosquito net, and when
he woke up, he was burning with fever. There was no hospital
around to test his blood but the medical officer did not need
one. One look at Williams shivering in the heat under the canvas
cover was sufficient.

'You've got it, Sarge, malaria.'

For four days and nights, as the skirmishes continued in the surrounding hills, only an occasional burst of gunfire had managed to penetrate the burning darkness of his fever. He was lost in another world, a world of his earliest memories. The memory of a bright rose bush beyond the bars of the cottage window, a determined protest of beauty in an otherwise harsh, ugly collection of wooden slum tenements somewhere between the canal and the railway line. And of his father, a brusque, perpetually tired man who one day, after his evening meal, started to get up, pipe in hand, to go and sit in the late twilight and then slumped back in his chair, never to move again. And every time he shut his eyes, the smell of soap, its edgy freshness cleansing and overpowering, was all around him. His mother had smelt of soap; the small backyard had smelt of soap; the bundles of clothes that she brought in every evening and washed all morning, before returning them to the big houses around Kensington Palace, had all smelt of soap.

After four days of quinine and a 'no diet' that meant milk only, the medical officer had dispatched Williams to the casualty ward at Tank. Half delirious, he was transferred to a 'dhoolie', a stretcher carried by four runners. Their every step on the rocky earth was like a hammer blow to his burning head.

At Tank, further weakened by the journey, he had lain, virtually unconscious, for two days. By the time he had been strong enough to take the two-day train ride to Rawalpindi Hospital he was on a 'milk diet' of eggs, bread, and butter. When he finally reached Jalandhar, his classification had been changed to D III—unfit for any duty but likely to become fit within six months. But Williams was determined not to wait that long; prolonged absence from duty would only make him appear weak to his men, and to his superiors. He forced himself to eat as much of the chicken diet that he got, even though he hated the taste of Indian chicken: the boiling and then the frying of the meat made it tough and tasteless. By the time the rest of the battalion returned, worn out by fatigue and disease, he had made himself well enough to help out with decorating the bungalows and the officers' mess for Christmas.

By the spring of 1918, word had reached the 45th Brigade that soon Brigadier General R. E. H. Dyer, would be taking over the command of the brigade. The reputation of the new commanding officer, the CO, had walked in months before him.

'Doesn't listen to anyone,' it was whispered. 'But he's good to his men, not standoffish. Likes to mix.'

'Just back from the sarhad where he did stuff he wasn't supposed to. But then he knows the place and the bloody tribes. Fought in the Black Mountain and other places before we were born.'

'We'll see action with him if it's anywhere to be found.'

The stories about Dyer had accompanied the 25th London Cyclists into the Simla hills in summer. They left the train at Kalka and walked up the hills, with the loads following on mules. The pine needles made a soft, slippery bed under their boots as they climbed, halting at Kasauli and then Dagshahi. Solan spread out below them, unmistakable with the belching chimney stacks of its brewery. Dyer's father, Edward Dyer, once owned that brewery, the men had heard. He had made quite a fortune making beer, first in Simla, and then in Rawalpindi, and finally in Solan with its excellent spring water and nearby railhead at Kalka that made it convenient to get the coal. There had been a ready market too: it had been difficult to transport beer all the way from home—by the time it got to India, it was usually not fit to drink. Edward Dyer had finally sold the Solan brewery to his old rival Meakin and moved down country to Lucknow; Simla could get lonely for box-wallahs as the civil service men didn't mingle readily with them.

'Our CO grew up in these hills,' men remarked in the evenings, unwinding their puttees and checking their calves for any leeches that may have got through.

'He learnt Hindustani and all with his servants.'

'Boy, he had servants!'

'Heard him tell someone how he used to catch snakes and twirl them by the tail.'

'Went to a fancy school somewhere around here, then they shipped him off to Ireland.'

'Hear he doesn't see his parents any more. Some problems when he got married.'

The weeks in Jutogh outside Simla had been pleasant but then the Spanish flu got virtually every London regiment man in Jutogh. Somehow Williams, perhaps because he had already had his share of Indian illness with the malaria in Waziristan, escaped. Instead, he received orders to join the brigade at Jalandhar earlier than the rest. When he reported for duty, being allowed to take the train down the mountains, the adjutant dismissed him quickly.

'You have to report to the brigade staff now,' he said, and seeing the surprised look on the sergeant's face, carried on. 'They seem to have picked you for something special. They've been looking at your reports.'

The brigade major, when he met him, did not waste any time.

'Sergeant Nicholas Williams, right?'

'Yes, sir.'

'Of the Cyclists, I see.'

'Sir!'

'You are on the General's personal staff now. You will be one of his bodyguards. Travel with him. Watch over him. Protect him. Pretty straightforward.'

'Yes, sir.'

The day was made even more memorable when, within

twenty-four hours of his appointment, news of the Armistice came in. The war was over. He tried to keep up with Dyer and his son, Ivon, a lieutenant posted at Jalandhar, who rushed in a car around the brigade compound, personally passing the news to the officers and the men. Williams was instructed to get back to Flagstaff House to welcome the officers who had immediately rushed there. Everybody drank heavily and General Benyon, who was staying with Dyer, was woken up and he made a speech. Then they all cheered and drank some more.

Williams had been amused to hear later that his batallion, still in Jutogh, had drunk a lot too. They had presented the guard of honour to the Viceroy, Lord Chelmsford, who read out the terms of the Armistice. Then they were treated to unlimited drinks by the officers and so drunk were they that the commanding officer marched nearly alone back to the train leaving a trail of drunken men all the way up to the Ridge. He, too, could have been one of those men, Williams smiled to himself, having a good time on the Simla Ridge, but destiny had other plans for him.

PART III

Chapter 11

A Force Stronger than Soul Force

In Lahore, Chief Secretary Porter took off his glasses to rub the red ridge on his nose with his thumb and forefinger. Then, putting them on with a visible expression of distaste, he read carefully through the draft wireless message he had dictated, a blue pencil poised in his hand for corrections like a harpoon looking for a fish under the water's surface.

> Railway stations between Kasur and Amritsar looted. British soldier killed and two British officers injured at Kasur. Bands of rebels reported on the move—Kasur and Tarn Taran treasuries attacked. State of open rebellion exists in parts of districts of Lahore and Amritsar. Lieutenant Governor with concurrence of General Officer Commanding, 16th Division, and Chief Justice of the High Court, requests the Governor General in Council to suspend functions of ordinary Criminal Courts in Amritsar and Lahore Districts, to establish martial law therein, and to direct trials of offenders under section 22, Regulation X of 1804. Section 4 will be borne in mind. Situation is critical. Moveable column starts on march from Ferozepore to Amritsar through worst tract with guns tomorrow.

Satisfied, and congratulating himself for the hundredth time for the clarity of his mind, and the precision of his drafting, he left his office with the message and began to walk down the colonnaded corridor to Sir Michael O'Dwyer's office.

It was just past noon but the bamboo chiks had already been

lowered, so that the hot sun could only throw the occasional thin slit of light into the corridor. A sweet smell from the damp khus curtains that covered the office windows wafted through the corridor. The Indian peons sitting outside the rooms stood up and salaamed as the Chief Secretary walked ponderously past, hardly acknowledging their presence. His mind was on Sir Michael. The man was understandably irritated. The last thing he would have wanted just weeks before his retirement was this crisis. Not the best way to crown his long tenure in Punjab as Lieutenant Governor. It was beginning to tell on him too: Porter had been surprised by how badly the Lieutenant Governor had delivered his last speech to the Legislative Council on the seventh. He had fumbled his notes, mixed up sections. But the message had been strong and clear: those who were inciting the mobs would not be spared and would be among the first of O'Dwyer's targets in case of any serious disorder.

Porter had to admit that O'Dwyer had clear priorities and a tested strategy on how to deal with such a crisis, inconvenient though it may have been for his personal plans; there was no confusion in his mind. Confusion in an administrator was a weakness; quick, decisive action was his motto. He was known for his aggressive tactics, his way of crushing situations before they got out of hand, ever since his days in western Punjab. More than once, Porter had heard him quote the Persian poet Saadi:

Sar-i-chasma ba bayad giriftan ba mil
Chi pur shud na shayad guzashtan ba fil

A stream can be stopped at its source by a twig
Let it flow, and it will drown even an elephant

This time, too, O'Dwyer had concluded early that a storm was coming, convinced that a big revolt was brewing that could involve the army, police, Sikh peasants, and frontier tribes.

'Yes, martial law is what we need. Show these people that there is a force stronger than Mr Gandhi's soul force,' O'Dwyer hissed angrily as he perused the draft that Porter had prepared. 'Under martial law, it will be the troops and not just the police who will open fire on these rascals. And Simla has already cleared that if they fire, they should do so in a manner that sets an example.'

The Lieutenant Governor signed off the message with a flourish.

'I think we better send it off en clair to save time,' he instructed his staff officer as he and Porter rose for lunch.

Chapter 12

The Sun Was Shot to Smithereens

After the march through the city on the thirteenth with the town crier, General Dyer's military column returned to the shaded camp at Ram Bagh. The fountains around the summer palace of Maharaja Ranjit Singh had long since dried up and wild creepers now covered the ruins of the buildings but the fourteen-foot boundary wall and ramparts gave a sense of security to the camp.

Sergeant Williams glanced up gratefully at the dark green leaves of the huge mango trees that dominated the compound. In a few weeks, they would bear fruit and when the clouds gathered dark and heavy in the Indian sky, the fruit would ripen. He had been in India long enough to know that there was no fruit as sweet as a mango ripened in the Indian sun.

Some wretched men were chained to the broad tree trunks under a London Regiment guard. These men were supposed to have been behind the looting and killing that had taken place three days earlier. Dyer's party had given chase to them the previous day in the lanes while the natives had watched in sullen anger from the rooftops. The wine-seller and the other man that the police had detained in Hall Bazaar earlier today were also tied to a mango tree. But Williams scarcely threw a glance towards these men as they sat on their haunches, their heads wilting in the afternoon heat. He had a hundred details to look after; under pressure of work, his habit of moving his right shoulder sharply towards his chin had become even more pronounced.

Dyer got busy immediately in his camp office in the overgrown but airy pavilion, the baradari. The news brought to him by the CID man in the bazaar that a meeting was being held in Jallianwala Bagh that afternoon had energized him, and he began planning his response. It had been difficult to finish off the rebels in the narrow, twisted alleys of the old city. Now their foolish defiance had forced them out into the open in the Bagh. This was the big opportunity. As Williams rushed around trying to complete the tasks at hand, he caught snatches of Dyer's conversations with other officers.

'These are the same men who wreaked havoc three days ago. They are going ahead with this gathering against my specific orders, and I will disperse them by force.

'Any weakness will mean that we will face a major revolt. Thirty thousand Majha Sikhs are getting ready to loot Amritsar.

'They will be punished for violating our proclamation. This will be a lesson for all Punjab. The Lieutenant Governor has told me that these people must be taught that rebellion is a costly game.'

Several times during the afternoon Williams heard Dyer say, almost as if he was talking to himself: 'I've got to do it. I'll probably be cashiered for this but I have got to do it.'

An aeroplane ordered to fly over the Bagh reported back: the Bagh was an enclosed space surrounded by the high back walls of houses. There were four or five narrow exits, mostly barred. A huge crowd had gathered around a wooden platform to listen to the speeches.

'Twenty-five men from the Gurkhas and twenty-five from Frontier Forces and another forty Gurkhas with khukris only as escort,' Dyer ordered. 'They will do what I tell them without question and they don't care much for Punjabi natives. Captain Crampton will be in command of all of them. No need for British infantry. I don't need the company commanders either. Whatever has to be done, I will do myself.'

Five more detachments of troops, each of forty men, were

prepared to stand by. They would form pickets around the city walls.

As they waited, all ready for word from the Bagh, Deputy Commissioner Irving came forward.

'General,' he addressed Dyer, 'if you could excuse me from accompanying you, I intend to go to the Fort.'

Dyer shrugged his indifference.

Finally, the police received word that the meeting in Jallianwala Bagh had begun.

'Let's go,' said the General and climbed into his car. Williams waited for Colonel Morgan and Captain Briggs to get in before climbing in with Sergeant Pizzey, the other bodyguard. The policemen, Rehill and Plomer, got into a separate car. Two armoured cars with machine guns followed. They entered the city through Hall Gate, moved slowly past the gutted banks and the still-smouldering hulk of the Town Hall building. The pickets were dropped off at the stations assigned to them. Dyer, the officers, and the core detachment of troops headed through the narrow lanes to the heart of the city.

◦◦

Williams jumped out of the car as soon as it halted outside Jallianwala Bagh. Only a narrow alley led to the open space inside. There was no way the armoured cars could go in.

'Leave them here,' Dyer ordered. 'Guard them.'

The officers went through the narrow alley, followed by the troops on the double. They could see the gathering before them, an immense crowd listening peacefully to a man making a speech from a wooden platform about fifty yards away. Some men were less than ten yards away.

While Williams was still trying to look around, he heard Dyer bark out his commands:

'Gurkhas right, Frontier Force left!'

There was a small rise near where they had entered, and the troops took up positions on it as directed.

'How many do you think there are?' Dyer turned to ask Briggs.

'Perhaps five thousand, sir.'

Many more, sir, the sergeant was about to say. Perhaps four or five times more, sir. But he kept quiet; he had not been asked.

Many in the crowd stared at them in fear. Someone shouted: 'They won't fire. Only blanks.'

People began to run in all directions.

'Fire!' Dyer gave the command.

'Fire!' Crampton repeated after his CO.

There were whistles and then the volley of bullets.

Williams saw the crowd sink to the ground in a flutter of white garments as soon as the firing began, as if trying to vanish into the earth. Shrieks rose in the air. People ran towards the walls, towards the exits, towards a well. He didn't see any rushing towards the soldiers. The firing continued and those climbing the walls were picked off one by one.

Briggs grimaced as if in pain and plucked at Dyer's elbow, trying to say something. But the General was watching the crowd closely and directing the firing. There was no wild shooting. Each target was picked off carefully. The noise of the bullets ricocheting off the walls, the shrieks of the terrorized, and the cries of the wounded all mixed together in an unholy noise that would haunt Williams's nights for years to come.

Rehill, standing next to the General, could take it no longer. He turned and left. The firing stopped as the magazines emptied, and the soldiers began to reload. In the sudden silence Williams heard Plomer say to Dyer: 'Sir, you have taught them a lesson they will not forget.'

Dyer showed no sign that he had heard. He was completely calm and cold.

'Independent rapid fire,' he commanded. Crampton repeated his orders.

Finally, Dyer gave the signal to cease fire; they would need some ammunition to get back to camp safely.

Crampton shouted an order to his forty Gurkhas. They unsheathed their khukris and ran towards the drain to deal with those hiding in it. Then he immediately called them back; Dyer had ordered a withdrawal and was walking out through the narrow alleyway. Williams turned to look back before he followed his superior out of the Bagh and into the car. He would never forget what he saw in that rushed backward glance. The corpses were piled one on top of the other. The shrieks of the wounded were deafening. Men were running in all directions in panic and a dense crowd was concentrated around the far exit. Many were spread-eagled like white flies on the furthest wall, inching their way to safety. The sun was shot to smithereens and a terrible night was to follow.

Chapter 13

The Dead Were Everywhere

From where he sat, leaning against one of the few trees in Jallianwala Bagh, a blade of dry grass between his teeth, Kirpal saw the soldiers as soon as they entered. He didn't need a second glance to see that they were Gurkhas and Frontier Force Baluchis and Pathans. Once you have been close enough to a man in a muddy trench to see the whites of his eyes as shells burst overhead in the night sky, or spent hours lying with him behind a sand dune in a desert wadi to ambush an enemy convoy that may or may not ever come, you don't take long to recognize regiments. No question about it: Gurkhas and Frontier Force.

What were they doing there, lining up on the raised bank near the narrow entrance, and taking aim at the crowd? They were not too far away, maybe fifty, sixty yards. Just about as far away as the German dugouts had been in France, close enough for the Indian soldiers to make out that they were made of timber and iron beams, as if the Germans intended to stay there forever. He knew fifty yards was enough land for thousands to die for, eyes staring at the sky, their last words to beloved mothers and sweethearts frozen on their lips. And they could lie there a long time before someone won that piece of land and removed their bones and put their name and rank on a stone somewhere, far away from where they had fallen.

A glance can take in a lot, sometimes much more than the mind can process. Kirpal saw not only the Gurkhas and the Frontier men but also a young British captain. Behind him stood a senior officer, his face half hidden under his sola topi, a commander's cane in his hand. With him were a couple of police officers and two sergeants, who appeared to be bodyguards to the commanding officer. Even from that distance, one of the bodyguards seemed strangely familiar to Kirpal, there was something in the way he swung his right shoulder as he walked, jerking it towards his chin. He had seen him somewhere not too long ago.

The soldiers had their rifle butts against their shoulders. They looked ready to shoot.

'They won't fire! Don't run,' someone in the crowd shouted.

Kirpal heard the command from the senior officer: *Fire!* The young captain repeated the command. *Fire!* Someone blew a whistle. He saw the smoke rise from the barrels and a fraction of a second later he heard the volley of shots.

'Blanks! They are firing blanks!' a man in the crowd shouted, his voice fading.

But Kirpal knew that these were not blanks but real bullets, like the ones he had fired and faced for four years of the Great War. You did not line up and take such careful aim if you were firing blanks. You did that when you wanted to kill.

Instinctively, he flung himself flat on the ground and rolled over twice so that the tree trunk was between him and the soldiers, his mind black with anger. He had fought for the British king alongside soldiers like these and now they were shooting at him!

A screaming bullet glanced off the gnarled bark of the tree inches above his head; in a daze, Kirpal stared at the exposed chalk-white flesh underneath. What was happening was no mistake: the soldiers were firing to kill. The British officers were directing the fire. Impotent anger surged from deep within him and rushed through his veins. If only he had his rifle, he would get to them and stop them from firing; he had rushed fifty yards before.

In a flash he understood why the aeroplane had flown over the Bagh a couple of hours earlier. It had been a source of curiosity and much amusement to the crowd. They had all looked up, some lifting children onto their shoulders to show them the unique sight. But Kirpal had seen these planes before—in France.

It all came back because the strangest things come to mind unbidden at the oddest times: a half-forgotten dream, a face glimpsed in a passing train, a tune that will never play itself out, a hillside thick with green shadows seen in this or perhaps some previous life. And with death at the door, you recall things you thought you had forgotten. That was what happened to Kirpal as the sun descended to the horizon, and the soldiers took aim, and the bullets began to fly and people around him began to shriek and fall and die.

∾

The troop train was heading through France to the front. It was early morning and he, along with Hazur Singh and Bir Singh, sat on the footboard without their turbans, their long hair wound up in loose topknots, their beards still untied. Kirpal felt the rush of fresh air on his face and a sense of well-being, born of youth and vitality, overcame him. All he wanted at that moment was a cup of tea. This was a new thing for him, drinking tea in the morning like Englishmen. In the village it had been a glass of hot milk with a pinch of turmeric that gave it a mild orange colour—his grandmother said that turmeric kept away the flu and strengthened the bones. Tea was seen as something foreign, decadent, addictive. That morning he felt the pull of its addiction. But he would have to wait until the next halt where breakfast would be distributed to the troops. Then they would be able to stretch their legs and drink mugs of tea with the chapattis that the unit cooks would dish out.

The aeroplane came out of nowhere. They heard a steady drone and then it was over them, a huge metal bird flying over their train, keeping pace for a while and then curving away in a slow arc. 'Germans!' someone shouted. There was a burst of gunfire from up ahead on the train into the sky and soon the aeroplane became a speck and then vanished.

'He will go and report to his headquarters.' Havildar Natha Singh, who had come to the door to take a look, knew what he was talking about. He was an old-timer who had even seen service in China during the Boxer Rebellion. 'Trains are moving, many men are coming to the front he will report.... Then they will be waiting for us. But we don't have these birds on our side to go and see how many people are waiting for us.'

In those early days everything had an element of surprise, everything was new and alien. The endless deep blue of the Mediterranean on which the SS *Akbar* had sailed after a three-week break on the Suez. The impressive convoy of twenty-one ships, coughing thick grey smoke into the light sky, that carried the 3rd Lahore Division to France. The first sight of the French coast at dawn from the deck rail, its rounded low, green hills in the background, white cottages dotting the straggling slopes. It was difficult to believe that a war was going on there, so quiet and calm and peaceful did it look. The evanescent colour of the lavender fields, so gentle that it threatened to vanish any moment. The beauty and warmth and grace of the French people who welcomed the troops from India, standing three deep on the pavements, as the soldiers marched through the streets. Men wearing berets at stylish angles offered them cigarettes and women, amazing women with rosy cheeks and delectable curls and open laughter and white white skins, stepped up to the soldiers, handing them flowers, blowing kisses.... The sepoys had never seen such women.

'Fairies,' said Bir Singh, on the first day, just as they started walking wide-eyed through Marseilles, 'this is a land of fairies. I am fortunate I have been able to see all this.'

'Move Bir Singha,' Lance Naik Buta Singh butted him from behind, 'otherwise no fairy but the devil will come to you.'

The letters that the soldiers had sent home then were still untouched by the horror of war. They talked of the crossing of the dark waters to a land of beauty. And of how happy they were and why no one should worry about them and even if they were to die then they should be remembered in the nicest way, as ones who did their race, regiment, and religion proud, and how faithful they were in discharging their duty towards the king, the kind king who sat in vilayat. And of the food they got—chapattis rolled and made on flat metal tawas heated on wood fires burning in pits in the earth, and hot dal cooked in cauldrons by the langri, generously spiced with ginger, garlic, and chillies followed by sweet bits of gur. There was meat, too, and everybody could eat without breaking faith because the British officers of the Jullunder Brigade understood them so well. They had set up separate slaughtering stations where the goats were killed in different ways—halal for the Muslims and jhatka for those of the Sikhs and Hindus who ate meat.

෴

Another bullet ricocheted off the big tree and whined into the crowd not far from Kirpal. He turned to see a young man with a very dark face, made even darker by naked fear, howl and fall to the ground, twitching as his life ebbed into the dust.

These were bullets shot with deadly malevolence, intended to cause the maximum devastation. Like the bullets of the German snipers that had made life hell for the sepoys in those God-forsaken European battlefields. Those bullets came out of nowhere, from treetops, from behind mounds of earth, sometimes from behind a pile of dead bodies. The shells from the big guns could be heard before they burst, the bullet from the rifle gave no warning. Only gradually had he learnt that if he heard a bullet, it must have missed him.

But here in the Bagh, even if it missed him, the chances were that it would get some other man, or woman, or child. Here there was no place to run, no trench to hide in, no pit created by an earlier shell to jump into. The narrow exits were few and many were locked; meanwhile, death, hungry and demanding, was everywhere.

The soldiers continued to fire into the crowd, reloading their rifles. They would not stop, it seemed, until they had killed every single person in the Bagh. Flat on the ground, his face stuck into the grass stubble and dust, Kirpal waited for the firing to stop. When it stopped, he would have to do something, even if there were no havildar around to direct him. He began to plan, almost instinctively, as they had done in the platoon. The wounded would have to be carried off to shelter and bandaged. They could not be left to bleed into the dust. The dead, there must be so many dead, would need to be cremated else their bodies would rot. He knew the stench, the unbearable stench, of rotting bodies left in the battlefield. In the war, with the enemy only a hundred yards away, the troops could not reach them. But that could not be allowed to happen here. This was home, this was peacetime even if the Frontier Force men, whom he as part of the 47th Sikhs had relieved in the trenches, were firing at them.

On the other hand, this was just like war. It was about killing or getting killed. The memories flashed unbidden into his mind. At the front, the days had alternated between fierce fighting and quiet, tense waiting. The winter came, a kind of winter that the sepoys had never known in their lives. The wet cold cut like a butcher's knife right through to the bone and their heavy coats and blankets were no defence against it. When it rained, the trenches filled up ankle deep with chilly water and there was no place to sleep. On some days, the Germans seemed less dangerous than the bitter cold and monstrous trench rats. The mist hung low and heavy in which the faint silhouettes of abandoned village houses and leafless skeletal trees were just ghostly images which appeared and vanished at will. The snow when it fell, first in hard, pointed prickly drops and then in soft, floating flakes, seemed a benediction. The world would turn white and there would be no more killing but then that, too, was just an illusion. Blood continued to spill well past Christmas and young men continued to fall. The wounded tried to crawl back to the trenches, their blood trailing on the snow. The dead lay where they fell, and the fresh snowflakes fell gently on their bodies.

Somewhere, everyone hoped, there was a plan.

'This is not a war,' wrote Kirpal in a letter home when the guns fell silent for a while and the sepoys got time to sit and sleep. 'This is the end of the world.'

It did feel like the end of the world when the high velocity shells came from the German lines, screaming like banshees until they fell, and the earth shook like in an earthquake.

'Down they come, down they come these motherfuckers, like the rain in savan,' murmured Hazur Singh as they cowered in the trench, praying that there would be no direct hit.

A man couldn't take that sort of shelling for too long. It could make you stand up in the trench and shout at the gods with your fist raised or simply walk out into the open.

Like the ghost who, on a moonlit night, walked straight towards their trench across the devastated field. He was without a helmet and there was no gun in his hand or haversack on his back. His arms swung loosely and his head shook uncontrollably.

The sepoys watched fascinated. No one thought of shooting at him.

'Djinn or German?' Kirpal said loudly, as if to himself.

'Same thing. One more prisoner,' Lance Naik Buta Singh responded.

The man kept walking straight for their trench, oblivious of the screaming shells. The moonlight reflected off his half-crazed face.

Then Kirpal saw the grenade in his hand. Without another thought, he was out of the trench and even as the German raised his hand, he plunged his bayonet straight through the man's heart. A fountain of blood gushed forth as he pulled out the bayonet. For a moment he stared at the dead man lying at his feet, his unseeing eyes wide open, his thick-lipped mouth in an ugly twist. Kirpal had fired bullets before, in the dark, distantly aimed. He had never seen the face of a man whom he had killed. Until this djinn-German.

When there was a lull in the shelling. Kirpal lay on his wire bed, trying to get some sleep. The German soldier's face floated against his closed eyelids. Ultimately, he gave up trying to sleep and rose on his elbow.

Hazur Singh was leaning against the trench wall, his knees drawn to his chest and his arms clasped around them, his eyes staring into dark space. Kirpal knew that the boy was thinking of home.

'Oye Hazurea, not sleeping?'

'Not yet.'

'Don't think so much all the time.'

The boy looked away. The two of them sat in silence for a while.

'That German today—that one, the one who walked towards us,' Kirpal wanted to talk about what was on his mind.

'What about him? You killed him, thank God.'

'You know he looked like the sahibs, our angrez sahibs.'

'So what does that mean?'

'I mean they all look alike—the Germans, the angrez, the Francisi. Why are we fighting for one against the other? Why did I kill him?'

'That's simple, if you hadn't killed him, he would have killed all of us. Our sahib pays us, and we fight for him. Because there is nothing to eat at home if we don't send money from here. You know what a seer of grain costs this year? And if we fight well for the sahibs then we may even get rewarded when we get back.'

'If we get back,' Kirpal corrected him and put his turbaned head again on his folded elbow in an attempt to go back to sleep. The question did not leave him; it merely went away to come back at other times.

∾

It came back to him again in the Bagh. Why had he fought for the angrez? But there was no time for thought. The screaming and wailing were still all around him, but he could no longer hear the whistling bullets. The firing had stopped.

The soldiers had broken file. He saw a group of Gurkhas, khukris in hand, moving towards the crowd. They were moving towards the Hansli, the drain into which many of the crowd had jumped.

A bitter anger rose inside Kirpal. He didn't have a bayonet else he would have rushed the Gurkhas. He wouldn't let a single unarmed person be cut down by a khukri. Just then, there was a whistle from the captain and the Gurkhas turned back, sheathing their knives. Then the soldiers followed the officers out on the double, back through the narrow entrance through which they had come.

He looked around him. This was worse than any battlefield he had seen. The dead were everywhere: in the middle of the Bagh, at the foot of the walls they had tried to scale, piled up against the narrow exits. They were the fortunate ones who no longer felt any pain. Everybody else was suffering—those who were bleeding and dying, asking for water, trapped under dead bodies and unable to breathe, and those forlornly looking for their loved ones, hoping they would hear a call, a name, a sign— however desperate—of recognition....

This was a desperately unfair and unequal battle, he thought, as he began to help the wounded. And then he thought: this was no battle; the bullets had been fired by just one side; the other had been unarmed, defenceless, without even the uncertain shelter of a trench. There was no hope of any medicos coming out, or men carrying stretchers, or canteens of water. No hope of redemption, or rescue, or repair: the dying had been left to die on their own.

He tried as best as he could, tearing up turbans to make bandages. Shutting the eyes of the dead still staring at the darkening sky. Helping the lightly wounded to the exits. Dismantling the piles of dead bodies to pull out those who still had a chance to survive. If only Hazur or Bir or any of the others had been with him, he thought, he could have done much more. But they were with the unit or on leave. The thought still nagged: why had the boys of the 59th fired on him; he had fought everywhere with them, as part of the Jullunder Brigade.

And the British sergeant who had been standing there all the time: suddenly he knew who he was. There could not be two sergeants who walked like that, moving their right shoulder in that way. He had been in the receiving party at Jalandhar Cantonment railway station when they had come back from the war, watching them as they disembarked. For a moment Lance Naik Kirpal Singh had looked him straight in the eye and if Sergeant Nicholas Williams had returned his gaze attentively, he would have read many questions in his eyes. Why are you here? This is our country, and do you have to watch us on arrival in our own country? Have we not fought for the same king, the same flag? Then why can't you trust me? You are not superior— the white man's blood, when it spills, is the same crimson as mine. Perhaps you think I will revolt, or ask for instant freedom as reward for shedding blood, or want land or title or pension? Does it not occur to you that I may simply be tired, needing rest and sleep, and just wanting to be with my own? Then the look had disengaged, and both had gone their own ways, one back to his job as ADC to Brigadier General Dyer and the other to apply for long leave to first meet his father and Ralla mama at the gurudwara, and then go and lie in the sun at home in Dharamsinghwala.

The sun went down in an ocean of blood and the night that enveloped Jallianwala Bagh was death itself, visiting each shadow, teasing out and trapping each escaping life. The stray dogs, too, were soon out, sniffing blood and then warm, unresisting flesh. Kirpal felt his vision darken again and again. He needed water. But he carried on, willing himself on, encouraged by the presence of some others who had appeared. Two men were carrying a charpai on which they were moving the wounded two or three at a time. A young boy of thirteen or fourteen with a small saffron turban on his head was pouring water into outstretched hands from a huge leather mushki, almost as big as himself, on his back. He seemed to have appeared out of nowhere and the mouthful of water that he gave Kirpal revived him like amrit.

Someone tugged at Kirpal's sleeve.

It was a woman, her head uncovered, her hair in disarray. There was panic and untold grief in her wide-open eyes, and she was looking at him beseechingly, her mouth unable to form words at first.

'Help me, my brother, for the Guru's sake, help me...help me carry my husband. Maybe he is still alive.'

But her eyes told him that she knew he was already dead.

Chapter 14

When Angels Are Human

When two strong hands reached out to help her pull her husband's body from under a heap of other dead bodies, Maya Dei knew that Masi Karmo, her old aunt with the uncontrollable stammer, had spoken the truth, all those years ago. 'Farishtey,' she had said, 'angels…they come in the form of human beings. They don't have wings, but ordinary arms and legs, like all of us. It's just that they are sent by God.'

The man wore a soldier's turban, with neat even folds. She could make that out even in her grief; she had seen soldiers returning from the war. As she looked up at him in the falling darkness, his light beard and light eyes seemed otherworldly as if he was indeed no ordinary man, but one sent by God to help her.

'Hold his feet, mai,' the angel was speaking. His voice was soft, as if he knew what a difficult thing he was asking her to do. 'We'll pull him out.'

'Waheguru mehr kar, mercy God,' she managed to whisper under her breath before a dark wave rushed over her and she swooned to the ground. Her hands, as they touched the ground, were instantly covered with the dark stickiness of blood. To her, it was all her husband's blood and she recoiled as if stung, and stood up straight, shaking off the darkness with some deep inner strength.

God had given her this boon, this power to call on inner steel when she really needed to.

Like on that day so many years ago in Parhi, her village not far from the banks of the mighty Jhelum.

∾

She had rolled her long hair into a rough bun high up on her head. Hurriedly she slipped into the water of the mountain nullah and then jumped out again, as if some evil spirit had lunged for her. It was not yet November but the water was ice cold. She rubbed her palms vigorously over her young limbs to warm herself and then braved a second dip. This time it felt better. This nullah—called Khup by the villagers—was her favourite though there were three others that held the village in their embrace. She came to bathe in it every day in the last darkness before dawn. It had the friendliest sound; its water gurgled like deep laughter; it did not roar. Sometimes she found herself talking to it.

'Oh, my dearest Khupiya, take me with you one day, wherever you go. Show me the fields, the jungles, the big towns that you run through. Nobody else will take me, not even any of your three other nullah-friends. They are such angry nullahs!'

But that morning she was late. A rosy glow could be seen above the edge of the dark hills in the east. Hurrying out of the water, she pulled on her clothes. Any moment, the sun would rise clear of the hills with a surprising flourish and the entire village, all its thirty black stone houses painted over with limestone wash, would be bathed in a warm glow. The harsh silhouettes of the barren hills that stood in a semicircle around the village, unconnected to anything, would no longer look like a forbidding phalanx of prehistoric warriors, frozen in time. The first light would sweep up their straggling slopes, touching each rock and pebble that lay in endless sweeps and piles all around. Soon, there would be no place to hide.

She filled the two buckets that she had brought with her with water. Those wretched buckets. She wished under her breath that she could throw them forever into the nullah with the instruction—Khup, if you are my friend then take these wretches away and never bring them back.

But in her heart, she knew there was no escape. The two buckets of water were essential, day after day. With one, her aunt Karmo's husband, Makhan Singh, whom the entire village called Bhapaji, would bathe in the inner courtyard of the two-roomed house, and with the second she would run the kitchen and hope enough was left for her to clean the utensils at night.

But the full buckets were heavy, and her arms were still weak from the fever that had consumed her for a week. Her head had throbbed as if several dwarves were wielding hammers from the inside. She had tied her dupatta tightly around her forehead and repeatedly knocked it with her bunched-up fist, hoping to silence those hammer blows but to no avail. She had been scared to ask Bhapaji for medicine, though that was the first thing she should have done—after all, he was the only hakim in the village and that too one of some repute. People came from as far away as Sohawa to get the potions that he mixed from the two dozen bottles in his little shop, grinding the powders in a black stone bowl with a mortar whose silver knob had long lost its polish. She had not asked him because he would have been angry. If she were sick, who would get the bucket of water for his bath, who would make the roti and dal and saag for his meals or give him the glass of milk in the morning before he left for the shop? She should not fall sick, she could not fall sick, he would have said.

Instead, she had quietly gone to his shop. While he was busy trying to grind some medicine for the child of a sad, bony woman who had come from some other village, she had picked up two packets of medicine from a bottle on which was written in crimson ink—*Fever.* She dissolved one in water and as soon as she swallowed it, she had been drenched in sweat.

Soon her body had felt cold, so cold that she had pulled out her most valuable possession from the big trunk: the cream-coloured wool shawl on which the softest little flowers in peach and rosy-red with bright green stems had been embroidered by her mother. When she had thrown it over her shivering shoulders it became so much more than a shawl; it became an embrace, warm and unquestioning, all-forgiving.

The fever had hollowed out her bones. All she wanted to do was to lie down and sleep. But there was work to be done: the flour canister was almost empty. She would need to take the gram to the mill so that the next morning Bhapaji could get his two big rotis.

On such days she missed her masi, now dead three months, very badly. When she had been around, Maya did not have to do everything in the house. Masi would carry one bucket of water and would make one meal a day, almost to the day that she fell victim to the cholera that had swept the district that rainy season. The sweet turnip that she had pickled last winter was still in the clay jar. Thank God for it, Maya thought—as long as they did not finish that pickle, her masi would somehow still be around. She had never let Maya feel that she was an orphan. It was not the child's fault, she always said, that both her parents had died in the terrible plague in the villages around Jhelum.

Back home after her bath, she looked at the two heavy bags of gram that she needed to take to the mill. Her masi would have told her to go later, to first eat something and rest for a while. She might even have said, as she did every time anyone got fever:

'It's not good to move around in fever. If you get garam-sarad, then terrible things can happen. That boy Sai, Veero's younger son, went out with a fever into the cold rain and now he can't move half his body. Walks on one leg, dragging the other behind him, and his one hand is like the broken wing of a bird, and drool drips down his chin…. You rest, my child, otherwise my dead sister will curse me from heaven.'

But she had no advice to give herself when she fell sick two days after returning from the Teeyan fair in Sohawa.

'You must have eaten something filthy,' Makhan Singh admonished her, as she lay groaning, unable to hold back a drop of water or a morsel of food. He had unconsciously adopted the superior attitude and voice that he used when dealing with patients.

'I didn't eat anything. You know, I don't eat anything. Haven't eaten anything nice for twenty years.'

Makhan Singh disregarded her protestations. She said that all the time, even when she was eating. He went to his shop and, through the creeping cataract in his eyes, peered closely at the thick glass bottles on his shelf. Picking three, he measured and poured their contents into his black stone vessel and ground them fine.

That night, bent over the vessel that Maya held for her to vomit into for the sixth time in an hour, Masi Karmo decided to come clean, between painful breaths.

'I ate nothing all day. Then they forced me to eat that slice of watermelon…. But nobody gets sick with fruit. And a sadhu was giving cupfuls of Ganga jal. I gave him a damri for it and drank it…. It will wipe out my sins, all your sins too. It was from the Kumbh Mela, nothing could be wrong with that. This is just nazar, someone's evil eye…. I have always feared nazar.'

'Ganga jal from the Kumbh and a slice of tarbooz with the flies of the entire tehsil sitting on it and she says hasn't eaten anything for twenty years,' cursed Makhan Singh under his breath. 'How many have died of this haiza at that Kumbh only I know… these temptations of the tongue!'

She had lasted another day and a night, retching and groaning, unable to speak, unable to swallow even a sip of water. Makhan Singh sat at the foot of her charpai, bereft and helpless, his shoulders hunched in defeat, holding in his palm the uneaten packets of medicine he had ground in his magic vessel of black stone. Without his turban, his topknot was loose and unkempt. Maya stood rooted in the shadows, all strength drained into the ground.

Now she missed her—her warm, almost maternal presence, the shared hours spent cooking and cleaning, and the gossip sessions in the courtyard around the tandoor shared by four houses. While Masi Karmo was alive, Maya always felt that her mother was not too far away, was still present in a word, an accent, a twinkle in the eye, a way of unfolding and folding a dupatta again and again. But now, along with her masi, her mother, too, had gone away without leaving a trace. Makhan Singh was a stranger; he was distant and rough as if he resented her presence now that his wife, through whom they had been connected, was gone. Maya, too, felt uneasy around the house now. She was being given shelter and in return she was to cook and clean and fetch heavy buckets of water. And every month get sacks of gram ground into flour at Motilal's mill.

～

The grinding machine at Motilal's mill seemed to be more alive than parts of the village, particularly the houses which were permanently locked and whose inhabitants had gone away to Sohawa or Jhelum to find work. But even the machine's life was unsteady: it would stop and start at will and sound a death rattle every now and then. At any moment it seemed it would give one last gurgle and sink into eternal sleep.

At other times, the machine was like a whimsical bride dancing to Motilal's tune. Like a dandy groom, he would sit next to it on a comfortable bed with painted carved legs, constantly running a little ivory comb through his glistening hair. Or staring into an oval mirror set in a pearl-studded frame, scanning the two gold teeth that shone through his scanty beard. Or polishing the red stone in his ring with a corner of his silk handkerchief, delicately moistened with his own spit. Though his jowls now hung thick and loose, and the flesh on his neck gathered in ugly folds, and the squint in his left eye was more pronounced than ever before, and his two large hands seemed more grasping and greasy than ever, Motilal did not consider himself less attractive than any young man; his ugliness was visible only to others.

He was happy with the way things were. The mill run by his Kashmiri labourer, Hassan, was the only one of its kind in several villages and earned him enough to indulge himself. Every Tuesday, the mill would be shut down, Hassan would be told to take a day off and Motilal would set off on the narrow, steep path that led out of the village to Sohawa. He would return with enough liquor from the Sohawa theka in his saddlebag to last him a week. Once in a while he went off for a longer trip, all the way to Jhelum, where he knew more than one lady waiting for a gift.

Maya waited. The machine squeaked and then screeched to a halt. Hassan quickly picked up a tin of thick black grease and peered deep into the wheels and belts, a huge blob of grease ready on his index finger. Motilal turned his squint eye towards the machine, and it sputtered back to life, as if it had been throwing a tantrum only to get a glance from its dandy owner.

Relieved, Hassan turned to take the sacks from the girl's hands. His heart would always melt at the plight of this hard-working girl. The poor thing had been waiting so long, shrinking in a corner.

But Motilal would have none of it. He growled gruffly.

'Take it easy, girl. What's your hurry? Let's finish the big jobs first. And what are you doing just standing there? Don't you see all this wheat waiting to be sifted? Get to it!'

Motilal was second cousin to Makhan Singh and being, in a way, family could not take any money for grinding their flour. But there was nothing to stop him getting something in return, even if it was having a pile of grain sifted for free.

Fatigue had sapped the last of Maya's strength by then. The heavy sieve fell from her hands more than once and her vision began to blur at the edges as she tried to pick out little sticks and pebbles and the odd insect from the grain. Hassan watched her from the corner of his eye as he worked and there was sympathy and understanding, even affection, in the way he regarded her. Motilal too stared at her, almost without blinking, but in his eyes there was only naked lust. When Maya looked in his direction once or twice, his stare seared her being.

Finally, all the waiting bags had been turned into flour. Hassan looked up towards Motilal. He put his large hands on his knees and heaved himself up. Then he sauntered jauntily towards Maya and stood behind her. His wide smile revealed his gold teeth as he suddenly said: 'Meeow!'

Maya started, even though this meeow was not a new thing. It happened every time she came here.

'Scared, my cat? Come, enough of that sifting. Let's get your gram done now. Hassan oye Hassan! Oye, may thieves take your woman! Have you gone to sleep?'

'Ho Lala, I am here,' Hassan yelled back.

'Grind this girl's gram. Make it soft as cream otherwise I will....' Motilal swore.

'Will you eat some mice, my cat?' Motilal smiled slimily. 'Come, see how many mice I have saved for you.'

He caught hold of Maya by the arm and dragged her towards the grain store. Hassan frowned and looked away and began to cough loudly.

An army of mice was running helter-skelter among the haphazardly stacked sacks of grain. Motilal picked up a pair of tongs and set off after them. As he chased the mice, he cursed them loudly. Finally, he managed to get a mouse between his tongs. By then, he was breathing hard.

'Here, my cat, this is your cashew....' and he thrust the squealing mouse at the girl's face. Maya paled. Screaming, she tried to move back.

'You won't eat it? Even your mother will eat it! If you don't eat it, I will thrust it down your throat.'

Once again, Motilal brought the mouse close to the girl's face. Screaming loudly, Maya stepped even further back only to be brought up short by a wall. Outside, Hassan began to cough.

'Scared, eh?' Motilal giggled. 'Scared!'

He threw away the tongs, and the mouse scarcely believing its good fortune, scurried away.

'Scared? Foolish girl,' Motilal's voice had a simpering softness now, 'I was only teasing you.' He made as if to comfort Maya by rubbing her arm. The feel of the smooth young arm pleased him, and he began to rub it up and down, as if it eased some deep hunger within him.

Maya began to sob uncontrollably.

'Oh, oh, oh, what a foolish girl, a real child. I am your uncle, you know? Don't you? I am just being affectionate. Hush now.' He began to wipe the tears from her cheeks. Those cheeks felt as soft as freshly fluffed cotton and soon he forgot to wipe the tears away but began to squeeze the girl's cheeks between his thumb and forefinger. He looked very pathetic, every bit of him was pleading.

Maya felt those soft, spongy and slimy fingers on her face. She felt nausea rise in her throat, and she thought she would throw up any moment. Then, all of a sudden, she stopped sobbing. Edging sideways, she tried to make her escape. Motilal barred her way.

'Smile once, and I will let you go,' he pleaded. 'Smile, my dear one, smile.'

Then with a sudden heave he had her lying down on the sacks of grain and started tickling her.

'Hee hee…laugh, laugh, laugh.'

At the feel of the youthful limbs under his hands, Motilal's bony, middle-aged body came alive. His breath came in short, hot spurts. At that moment Maya felt that a blood-smeared, pus-infested insect from hell was crawling all over her. She reached deep within her for strength and stood up straight with a mighty heave. She stared firmly and coldly into Motilal's squint. He began to blink wildly and then seemed to shrink within himself, consumed by a sudden trembling. Fumbling in his vest pocket, he tried to hand her a coin. But she was already at the door. Outside, the machine had long come to a stop and Hassan was beside himself from coughing. That inner strength was her protection, perhaps a gift from God to make up for the early loss of her parents.

∿

The soldier held her husband's body by the shoulders, she lifted the feet, and they moved him out of the swamp of blood. She looked around. There was nowhere to go and the night was coming on. The narrow exit that led to the lane was choked with corpses. Men and boys and children lay piled up five, six, ten bodies high. Heads split by bullets, faces destroyed, legs shattered. She looked towards the exit by the well. There was a pile of bodies there, too, and another one at the corner near Mewa Singh Burj. The dark terraces and houses stood high above her on all sides. She felt her strength slipping away again. She knew she would swoon any moment. With great effort she opened her eyes wide to drive away the darkness. She could not fall down, she could not become one more body in the Bagh. Nobody else in the world knew that Joga Singh was dead, shot neatly through the forehead on Baisakhi day. Only she could do what needed to be done. She tried not to think of anything else.

They found a dry patch and put the body down. The soldier looked around quickly. Two small planks lay not far off, perhaps part of a makeshift stand for a basket of roasted gram that someone had brought to sell at the gathering. He put them end to end and they moved the body on to them.

'Chacha, water…' a young boy lying nearby pleaded with the soldier. 'Water…' The boy's shirt was drenched in blood.

There were other cries for water from all directions. Cries in the dark not directed at anybody. There were not too many people walking around. She could see a few dark shadows with lanterns wavering unsteadily in their hands, calling out familiar names, hoping for a response.

She looked up and her eyes met the soldier's. It was all right, she seemed to say. Her husband was already dead and nothing that they did would make much difference. There were others who needed help while they were still alive. The soldier put down Joga Singh's head gently and respectfully on the wooden plank and walked towards the well where a bucket hung on a rope near the ledge. He looked into the well to let down the bucket and stopped short. Cries echoed up from deep inside the well and he realized that a large number of people had jumped in to escape the bullets. Many must have drowned or suffocated to death. He would have to look elsewhere for water.

Maya watched him—a tall, broad-shouldered, nameless angel— as he rushed off with the bucket towards the Hansli drain. He whirled around as someone called out to him as if the voice were a familiar one. Then she saw him move quickly to a wounded man and, lifting him in his arms, walk quickly towards the drain for water.

She turned back to her husband, cradling his head in her hands. His turban had fallen off and his long hair had come undone. She gently wound it up in a loose topknot and taking off her dupatta tied it around his head. He did not like being seen without a turban with his hair exposed and somehow at that moment that seemed to be the most important thing for her to take care of. The blood from his wounds began to dry on her dupatta. His face was strangely calm. He had taught himself to stay calm all his life and had managed it even in death. Then she ran her fingers lovingly through his open grey beard and cupping his face in her hands bent over him and finally started to cry.

Chapter 15

A Matter of Pure Chance

A bullet had felled Ralla instantly. The pain seared through his leg and then the world around him, the dying day and the wavering sky, began to go dark. But the pain would not let him off that easily; it brought him back to his senses. His pyjama was drenched with his own blood. He tried to get up and then fell back again, unable to bear the excruciating agony radiating from his leg. All around him were bodies, lying on top of each other. It was difficult to say who was dead and who alive. All around him were cries for water, cries to mothers, cries to God. His own throat was parched, and the nausea kept rising to his mouth. Then an instinct for survival told him that he should do something about the wound in his leg. Taking off his turban, he tore off a long piece with his teeth and wrapped it tightly around the torn flesh on his thigh. Then he tore another long piece and tied it above the wound. The throbbing became almost intolerable. The only thought in his head was that he had to do something. Otherwise, the oncoming night would be his last. It was impossible to walk so he began to crawl towards the exit, dragging his wounded leg behind him.

It was then that he saw the young man with the soldier's bearing, walking hurriedly towards the Hansli, a bucket in his hands. He didn't need a second glance.

'Kirpu, oye Kirpu!' he called out, his voice faltering.

'Mama? Ralla mama?'

The next moment he was being lifted up in his nephew's strong arms.

'Have you seen your father anywhere?' was all he could ask before he lost consciousness.

Chapter 16

Ghallughara

Through his fever Gurnam had heard snatches of the conversation between Bhagwan and Sucha.

'...medicine, at six-hour intervals, even if the fever breaks... fevers come back.... I'm not a doctor. My first ishq is making bombs not grinding herbs.'

'What's happening on...Baisakhi.'

'...that jarnail who has come from Jalandhar and the DC... were making an announcement...nobody will come out after eight in the evening. And no processions or meetings allowed.... They didn't go towards the crowded areas of the city...help that man.'

'What man?'

'...never seen before...an educated man...bank clerk or an accountant. When...very polite....my son...soldier who has fought in the war...three, four years...a special permit...your soldier after all...your king...the jarnail gave some order and the soldiers dragged away that poor man...a jarnail or a jamdoot...God only knows.'

The firing woke him from the drugged stupor he had fallen into. A hundred guns seemed to be going off simultaneously just outside his window. Not a round or two, but a relentless long burst that wouldn't end. He tried to stand up but, weak from three days of fever, he felt faint and fell back. Fighting back the darkness, he called for Bhagwan. But Bhagwan was already at the front door, opening it and then shutting it again, not knowing what to do. He was without his turban, as he had been lying down in the shade waiting for the afternoon to pass; his topknot of grey hair hung loose on his forehead.

There was a pause in the firing.

'Goliyan,' said Bhagwan, 'must be in Jallianwala Bagh. That boy Sucha said there was going to be a meeting there....'

The barrage of bullets started again, as if they intended to bring down the sky. Once or twice, a shriek managed to rise above the staccato firing, like a thin scrawny hand reaching up to any God who was listening. Then, as suddenly as it had started, the firing stopped. A collective groan seemed to rise up from behind the window, then it became a whimper and then that too died out.

Bhagwan rushed in like a man possessed. Hurriedly he put on his turban and, pushing the straggling hair under it with his index finger, rushed out of the house.

'I'll be back,' was all that he said.

When he returned three hours later, Bhagwan could barely speak. His chest heaved and his mouth formed words which Gurnam did not hear.

At long last he managed one word: 'ghallughara'. Gurnam knew what that meant. A holocaust, mass murder, like the one that the Afghans had wreaked on the Sikhs in the eighteenth century. Sitting on his haunches, his face looking a decade older than when he had walked out of the house, Bhagwan began to speak, hesitatingly at first and then in an angry, bleeding flood.

'Corpses, heaps of corpses. Blocking all the entrances to the Bagh. With their eyes blown out, skulls split, arms and legs smashed. Cries coming from all directions, asking for help, asking for water. And children. Already the dogs are feeding on them. I tried to go in from Navi Gali but bodies blocked the way. I saw Khairuddin of Teli Mandi lying dead in a ditch with his son in his arms, also dead, and not more than six months old.

'I managed to get in through a small entrance near the

timber stall. Again, the dead and the dying, so many clustered near the well, so many near Mewa Singh Burj. Nobody to help the wounded. A few people were walking around with charpais, looking for their own, turning over bodies. One or two had a lantern but it was getting dark. I saw a tall man, a Sikh—he looked like a soldier. He was trying to get water from the Hansli but how much could one man do? I helped him for a while and then I left—you were lying here alone and someone said nobody should be out after eight. As I hurried back, I heard a woman asking a group of people in the gali to help her carry her husband's body out of the Bagh. They said, "Bibi, it's already past eight o'clock, we cannot be out." By Waheguru's grace I reached home without being stopped.'

Then, his fists clenched into his eyes, the sixty-year-old man sank to his haunches and began to sob. Body convulsing, heaving sobs of helpless desolation. He would not be able to forget what he had seen as long as he lived.

Gurnam knew that he had to throw off the fever. With a determined effort, he pushed himself upright and drank a full glass of water. Then he pulled up Bhagwan by the shoulders and hugged him tightly. With an effort, he climbed the high steps to the terrace and sat down on a charpai. From here he could look into the lanes around the house and towards the flat patch of dark emptiness further away, which he knew was Jallianwala Bagh. What Bhagwan had told him was tearing his chest apart.

Chapter 17

In the Garden of Desolation

The darkness thickened around Maya Dei. She could see two or three lonely lanterns swaying some distance away. Once in a while a lantern would stop, stoop low, and then, already dimming with disappointment, move on. What were the lanterns seeking, she wondered: everybody was the same in death, one body the same as another, equally bereft of breath and life. Then she corrected herself as she looked down at her husband. Even in death one needed to belong. Each person was looking for the one they had been born to or given birth to or shared a bed with or perhaps just a meal....

She heard a familiar voice and looked around. It was the younger son of Lala Sunder Das. The boy—in that numb moment she could not recall his name—had come looking for her. She had rushed out of the house without telling anyone when she had heard the firing in the Bagh.

'Bibiji,' the boy said, and then stopped, his eyes fixed on Joga Singh's face, calm in death. His mouth fell open and he could not say anything to her.

She spoke finally: 'Help me, Kaka, call your brother. Let us take him away from here.'

'Yes, Bibiji,' the boy said, and rushed away, glad to be given something to do that would get him away from there.

For an hour Maya Dei waited, her eyes fixed at the point at which the boy had vanished into the darkness. A man carrying the dead body of a young boy over his shoulder was walking away, not too far from her. He seemed taken aback to see a woman sitting in this garden of desolation, among the dead and the dying. Then he seemed to understand that she was waiting for help.

'Bibi, it is difficult for people to come. It's past eight o'clock and there is curfew. They are afraid of being shot.... Everybody, even this, my only boy, has been shot....' And the man trudged away under his heavy burden, each step taking him further into unending grief.

The clock from the tower began to strike. She was not sure what hour it struck, perhaps nine or ten, but she knew it was late. If no one was going to come to help her then she must go herself and find help. She would go to Lala Sunder Das's house and get the boys herself. But they must be afraid of the curfew otherwise they would have returned by now. But surely there must be people who would listen to her pleas. Perhaps some of the students she had seen in the evenings, who studied and slept at the dharamsala attached to the temple complex in Ablowa Katra. She picked her way through the piles of bodies, careful not to step on anyone or hurt anyone who might be wounded or step into someone's blood. But without a lantern it was impossible to be too careful. She found herself asking forgiveness from everybody and everything and only one word kept quivering on her lips.... Waheguru, Waheguru.... He alone would guide her through the darkness, through that night.

The temple compound was dark, its heavy door chained from the inside. She tried to push open the door, then knocked on it with the flat of her right hand. A window opened in the upper storey of the house across the lane. A bald, middle-aged man, wearing a vest was framed behind the rounded iron bars.

'What is it, mai? There is nobody in that dharamsala. The boys who were there have gone home for Baisakhi.'

'Bhai sahib, can you help me, then...my husband....' she could not bring herself to say the words. Her jaw quivered and tears began to flow down her cheeks.

The man understood.

'I have two wounded men lying in my house and I am the only one to take care of them. It is also curfew time. I wish I could help you...but look a bit further on...see if you can find someone.'

She walked on. There was nothing else to do. A man sat on a low charpai, smoking a hookah. Folding her hands, she told him what had happened and begged him for help.

He turned to the two men who were sleeping in the entrance to his house.

'Get up you two! Go with bibiji to the Bagh.'

The men stirred but they were not willing to go with her.

'What are you saying, Choudhry? It's almost ten o'clock. Isn't it enough that so many are dead today? Why do you want us to die too?'

Slowly Maya Dei walked back to the Bagh. She knew she had to be with Joga Singh and she would stay there until someone came to help her, even if she had to wait all night. As she was about to enter the Bagh, her foot stepped on a lathi, the kind that peasants often carried when walking long distances. Its owner, lying face down in the drain, would not need it any more and she picked it up instinctively. She had seen dogs prowling among the bodies. Holding it in both hands she returned to her vigil by Joga Singh's body.

The boy to whom the soldier had given water was still alive.

'Mai, please stay here, don't go anywhere,' he entreated as he saw her return and sit down.

'I am not going anywhere, child, my world is here,' was all she could say as he shut his eyes. His breath came in low, wheezing gasps. She wished she had some way to give him water and something to wrap him in. But her dupatta was already soaked in the blood that had oozed from Joga Singh's forehead.

A wounded bull was dying slowly nearby and every few minutes Maya Dei closed her eyes in pain as the animal bellowed hoarsely, kicking its legs in the night air. There was nothing she could do to ease its pain except pray: 'Have mercy on the poor animal, Waheguru, and grant it release.'

Slowly the night began to pass, marked by the striking of the clock on the hour. There was hardly any movement any more and only one or two lanterns could still be seen in the Bagh. There was no wind, as if it were staying away out of respect for the dead. With a last quivering croak, the bull, too, had fallen silent. Only the dogs barked, their noses covered with blood.

Just after the clock struck two, a peasant who lay not far away called out to her.

'Mai, give a hand and lift up my leg.'

She held and raised his leg with both hands for a few moments to give him relief and then gently put it down again. Her hands were covered with fresh blood from the gaping wound in the man's leg that had soaked through his pyjama and plastered it to his skin.

Finally, she was able to count five chimes of the clock. It seemed that for an hour or so she had fallen asleep where she sat, her husband's head in her lap.

She looked around, bitter, burning bile rising in her throat. A weak dawn was hesitating across the sky. In the wan morning light, swarms of kites could be seen circling and swooping, ever lower. Joga Singh's body was stiff, and his leg stuck out at an unnatural angle. She tried to straighten it out and managed with some difficulty. Hundreds of bodies still lay around her as far as she could see, some with their faces to the sky, eyes open, mouths screaming silently. She had not realized that so many of them were children. The boy who had been begging her not to leave was quiet now, his painful gasps stilled forever. What she had not seen in the dark, she saw now: he had one arm around a dead child, no more than three years old.

Many people were now in the Bagh, searching for loved ones, helping those who were still alive. In a daze, she saw Lala Sunder Das and both his sons hurrying towards her. The boys were carrying a charpai between them. She touched the Lala's feet and then he held her close as her body was racked with uncontrollable sobs. The boys put Joga Singh on the charpai and the small group began to walk towards the narrow exit at the far end, just like all the other little groups on that killing field carrying away their dead.

PART IV

Chapter 18

A Sanction for Mass Murder

It was very late in the evening, much after he had woken up from his nap and had his tea, when the first report from Amritsar reached Porter in Lahore. Troops had fired at a huge crowd was all it said. He didn't know quite what to make of it. He needed to wait for a proper briefing.

He asked for another cup of tea and moved out to the armchair on the veranda. Just before his nap he had again read Milly's wire, a month old but still lying neatly folded on his bedside table, one end tucked under the brass table lamp. And that had put him in a pensive mood.

'Coming early as soon as passage available.'

There had been silence after that wire and now he himself was feeling the separation. She had been away almost a year, determined to spend as much time as she could with Tim and Willy before they went away to university or the army or whatever awaited them. If she did not come, he should apply for leave. But if the disturbances continued, then leave in July would be impossible. If there were to be the slightest opening, he told himself, he would go. At this stage in his life, it was not his career but the happiness of his family that must come first. Milly had suffered on his account earlier and he must not make the same mistakes again. He should not repeat what he had done in his younger days in Montgomery district.

He could see it clearly now, from the distance of all these years. He had allowed himself to be ensnared in the rat race for appointments and postings very early on, even as he had criticized others for doing just that. His justification had been nothing new: 'Well, now that I am in it, I better have a good go at it. No point ending up second best. Otherwise, I may as well have joined the church as I once wanted.'

Montgomery had been an important step; it had the promise of setting him up for greater things. But the district was known for its annual wave of deadly influenza. Milly had fretted about his health and hurried to join him and selfishly he had encouraged her to do so.

Those early days of their marriage—a rosy-hued cocoon of love and tenderness—would live for him forever. Milly was the kindest, loveliest wife that he could have imagined and the comfort that she gave him in Montgomery had exceeded all his dreams and expectations. The joys of physical love, the warmth of a cosy home, and the social acceptance that had eluded him as a bachelor, overwhelmed him and he often wondered if he could really ask for more.

But, in the summer of 1902, Milly had come down with a fever that wouldn't go away. Hour after hour she lay quiet and uncomplaining, and he watched her with rising panic as she became pale and weak. The station's doctor came in daily and, one day, after the fever had subsided, and Milly had fallen into a deep sleep, he ventured to say to Porter.

'It might be best to send her away to Dalhousie for a while. She needs the cool air and mountain sunshine. That will bring her back to normal like nothing else.'

He had agreed reluctantly, but the day she left, the house seemed awfully empty.

Milly had indeed recovered at Dalhousie and when they discovered that she was pregnant they decided that she should go and stay with the Campbells in Simla. Lucy Campbell was a second cousin of Milly's but in India that made her close family. He planned to take leave for the last two weeks of her confinement and spend it with her in Simla.

But Milly was already writhing in pain by the time he reached, covering the last few hours from Kalka on muleback. A runner was sent from the Campbell cottage, which stood high up on Summer Hill, to get the doctor from the Town Hall. But the runner had to go even further, chasing the doctor to the village of Mahasu where he had gone on an urgent house call to the Chief Conservator's residence.

By late afternoon, Milly had delivered a lifeless baby. Porter read the news on Lucy Campbell's dismayed face. Something seemed to die within him when he saw the child, its tiny body still to be cleaned of the blood. He steadied himself before he went into Milly's room to hold her hand as she lay there, her face steadfastly turned to the wall.

The next morning, he saw the body of their little baby girl, bathed and dressed and lying in her small decorated coffin that had hurriedly been arranged by the Campbells. He touched her forehead with his lips and put the lid down on the coffin. A very small group from the station accompanied him to the cemetery of the local church under the deodars. A short ceremony took place in a light drizzle, even as the sun shone on the far mountains that stretched in hazy ranges to the snow peaks.

They never talked about their little child again except in their silences. Every year in October, he would visit the cemetery in Simla and calculate for himself how old his daughter would have been that year. And every year he blamed himself for urging Milly to join him in Montgomery.

Those memories saddened him, and he began to walk slowly from one end of the long veranda to the other, his hands in his pockets, his shoulders in an unusual hunch. Beyond the veranda, the buzzing of the insects had become louder, and he watched a bearer light the gas lamps on the two pillars of the gate. Yes, he thought, life had not been easy. The victories had come at great cost.

The telephone rang when he had just switched off the lights after dinner and got into bed. A garbled message had been received from Deputy Commissioner Irving. All that could be understood was that several arrests had been made and a prohibited meeting had been dispersed. There were rumours of heavy casualties. The report was still too sketchy to disturb the Lieutenant Governor with. Porter turned on his right side—he had come to believe that sleeping on the left side would burden his already weak heart—and went to sleep.

◌

His staff officer woke him up. O'Dwyer wanted him at Government House straight away. Porter glanced at the bedside clock. It was just past four in the morning. He got out of bed, then sat down again immediately to slow down his breathing. Then he pulled on his dressing gown over his pyjamas and rushed to Government House.

O'Dwyer was already in office, clearly unhappy at being woken up at that hour, along with his staff officers. Commissioner Kitchin, also in his dressing gown, was entering just as Porter was arriving. Two men, Porter recognized one of them as Gerard Wathen, the principal of Khalsa College in Amritsar, had brought a message from Irving. O'Dwyer read it and then handed it over to Porter. Putting on his glasses, Porter quickly noted the main points: despite announcements in the city prohibiting such meetings, a meeting of six thousand had taken place. Brigadier General Dyer had gone in with his troops and opened fire without warning. The Deputy Commissioner had not been with him. About two hundred were believed to be dead. The city was quiet that night… but more disturbances could be expected.…

Wathen was in a state of high agitation.

'British soldiers shot down men like rabbits. Majha will be up in revolt. Your Honour, the only thing that can save the situation is for you to disown the action taken.'

Sir Michael stared at Wathen in annoyance.

'Please don't tell me what I should or should not do,' he said icily.

'I tell you, Sir Michael, if you want to avoid deep trouble and bitter political feelings which will last years, please go to Amritsar immediately and replace Dyer and say that a mistake has been committed, not in the firing itself, but in its extent.'

At that point Wathen was thanked for his efforts and asked to leave.

O'Dwyer then dictated his own message conveying the essence of the DC's message to the Government of India in Simla. It worried him that no civilian officer had been with Dyer. He was also worried at Wathen's remark that British troops, and not Indian soldiers, had been used in the shooting. He looked around the room, his narrow face pinched in arrogant anger. His eye settled on Kitchin.

'Leave immediately for Amritsar. Meet Dyer and let me know exactly what happened.'

The military report written by Dyer was received by Major General William Beynon, the GOC, in Lahore the next day and he brought it to O'Dwyer's office. It was almost noon, and everybody had managed to sleep for a couple of hours.

O'Dwyer read the report in silence and passed it to Porter across the desk. Porter went through it quickly. He read the crucial paragraph twice, almost consigning it to memory. He had a feeling that he would need to know this sequence of events well enough to answer questions on it.

Dyer had written:

At 16 hours I received a report from the police that a gathering was beginning in the place mentioned above. I immediately sent pickets to hold various gates of the city (to prevent a renewal of the attack of the 10th on the British quarter) and marched with 25 Rifles 9th Gurkhas, and 25 Rifles from detachments of 54th/59th Rifles Frontier Force, making a total of 50 Rifles, and also 40 Gurkhas armed with khukris. I entered the Jallianwala Bagh by a very narrow lane which necessitated leaving my armoured cars behind. On entering I saw a dense crowd, estimated at about 5,000 (those present put it at 15,000 to 20,000); a man on a raised platform addressing the audience and making gesticulations with his hands. I realized that my force was small and to hesitate might induce attack. I immediately opened fire and dispersed the mob. I estimate that between 200 and 300 of the crowd were killed. My party fired 1,650 rounds.

Porter could read between the lines. Dyer had decided in advance to open fire if he saw a crowd gathered. There had been no warning to disperse. The estimate of 200–300 dead was based on the experience of firing 1,650 rounds in an open battlefield and not into a densely packed gathering in an enclosed space. And, mercifully, only Indian troops had been used.

Benyon was addressing the Lieutenant Governor.

'Sir Michael, I believe Dyer's action has crushed the rebellion at its heart in Amritsar and soon we won't need to fire a shot. I am conveying my approval of Dyer's action to him. May I take it that I can add yours?'

Sir Michael was quiet for a moment and asked: 'Is there any need for that?'

'I think General Dyer would be glad to have it,' Benyon replied.

'You can then add my approval,' said O'Dwyer, adding, 'not only has he killed the rebellion in Amritsar but also prevented it from spreading elsewhere. If he had delayed action or given warning, then his force would have been swept away like chaff in the wind, and Punjab would have been in flames.'

As the lines were still not functional, the short but very important message was sent to Dyer in Amritsar by aeroplane: 'Your action correct and Lieutenant Governor approves.'

Sitting at his desk that night and hoping for a few hours of undisturbed sleep, Porter made the day's entry in his Collins diary. He wrote a short summary of Dyer's report, concluding that 'it seems to have been a bloody business—200-300 killed in a garden. Probably it will be justified by the results achieved. I ventured to ask the Lt. Gov. the reason for his hesitation before according approval. He had hesitated only, he assured me, since this was a military matter and not a civilian one.'

The next morning not too much time could be devoted to Amritsar alone—in fact, Amritsar was shrouded in deathly silence—as news of mayhem poured in from other parts of Punjab: the railway station at Wagah burnt down, telegraph lines cut, and railway tracks pulled out; hartal and disturbances at Gujranwala, the station, telegraph office, post office, and church set on fire; serious rioting in Chuharkhana, Wazirabad…all the way to Lyallpur along the railway line. Even his beloved Gurdaspur was not free from problems: the railway and canals were under attack and the small British community and American mission were in danger.

Sir Michael's orders had been clear and precise and had to be carried out. He had planned long and in great detail for what he was convinced was a well-scripted uprising. Armoured trains were dispatched in every direction. Aeroplanes were fitted with machine guns and prepared to drop bombs on civilians.

Porter worked late. into the night. It was good that Milly was not there, he thought; she would never have let him keep these hours and keeping both her and Sir Michael happy was not an easy task.

Chapter 19

An Evanescent Flower in
Sandal Bar

The sound of the guns had not come as a surprise to Mehtab in Ram Bagh. He had seen the Gurkha and Frontier Force soldiers march from the camp shouldering their lethal Lee–Enfield rifles. He had seen the crazed anger in the General's eyes, the determination in his step, the arrogance in his voice. He had feared the worst, even as he had prayed to Waheguru that it should not happen.

If something happened to Kirpal he would never forgive himself. In his frustration, he struggled to free his wrists; the rough rope only cut further into the flesh. The red welts were beginning to bleed. If something happened to Kirpal how would he face Jindi when he met her in the heavens? And explain that he had been unable to protect their dearest possession, their only son…. That he had failed to keep the promise of their beautiful marriage.

❧

When Mehtab was about twenty, word spread quickly that Dhanna Raja had arrived in Dharamsinghwala. He was well known in Tibba and the surrounding villages because everybody needed him at some time or the other: he was both a nai, a barber, as well as a matchmaker, just as his father had been. It is said that what the jackal is among animals and the crow among birds, the barber is amongst men. Clever and cunning. Not to be annoyed, not to be slighted. That's why the title of Raja was added to his name, as it had been to his father's. Being called a Raja removed the stain of the menial caste that he had been born into. His eyes, narrow slits under bushy grey eyebrows, did not miss anything and his sharp mind filed away for later use all he saw or heard as he went from family to family. The secret of his success was his timing: he always knew the right moment when to whisper and convey a message or entreaty. More often than not, it would be when he had his target sitting before him, eyes shut, waiting for the razor to shave his beard, or the scissors to begin its digging for the ingrown toenail. And, more often than not, he got his way.

Everybody knew that he had not come all the way across the Ravi to Dharamsinghwala to shave and trim beards, and that too in a predominantly Sikh village. He was there as a matchmaker. Everything about him—his self-important manner, the silk scarf knotted around his neck, his eyes heavily lined with thick black kohl—showed clearly that he was carrying a marriage proposal.

Dharam Singh was open and welcoming.

'Dhanna Raja, you have come all this way to see us! Some good news, I hope?'

But the barber would take his time.

'All in good time, Dharam Singhji. It's been a long journey. Some rest and food and sleep first? Then we can take care of the world's problems.'

Dhanna Raja sat in the courtyard and ate well, his narrow eyes fixed on the blob of white butter that Dharam Singh's wife, Pritam Kaur, put on each large roti as she took it off the fire. Then he retired to the small room in the far corner of the courtyard, the room with the big trunks stuffed with quilts and mattresses, and slept soundly.

It was evening when he emerged from the room and sat on his haunches before Dharam Singh, cupping a tall glass of steaming hot tea in his hands. He then revealed the purpose of his visit.

'Dharam Singhji, you may have left Tibba but Tibba hasn't forgotten you. Everybody remembers your calm, saint-like personality. And when I come here, I see for myself that you are blessed. With your hard work and prayers, you have turned this wilderness into paradise. And your sahibzada, this wonderful young man, Mehtab, who was but a child when you left Tibba, he is your true son. In his eyes I see the same wisdom, the same saintliness.... He needs a life partner now, a nice girl who will take care of him, a healthy young Punjaban who will bear him sons. He is getting to be twenty, and that is already late.'

'And you have just such a girl in mind?'

'More than one in Tarn Taran tehsil. At least a dozen families would be honoured to tie a bond with your family. A boy like Mehtab, as they say, you cannot find even if you go out looking with a lamp in your hand. But I don't want to take this relationship too far from Tibba. The biradari of Tibba is so closely knit and I want that bond to grow stronger. I bring the proposal of Jindi, the beautiful daughter of Bhaiya. She will fit into your family like she was born here. She has seen only fourteen winters yet but youth has favoured her with its freshness and energy. Fair as milk, her face like the moon, her cheeks are like gardens of wild roses. But, most important,' and at this the barber turned towards Pritam Kaur, Mehtab's mother, 'is her seerat. Her temperament is that of a dove, a sweet tongue, not a harsh word for anyone. And, as you know in women, it's not the surat that matters so much but the seerat, because the comeliness of the flesh fades. God has been very kind to this girl, he has given her both.'

That night, when Mehtab returned home from work, Dharam Singh mentioned the proposal brought by Dhanna Raja.

Mehtab was upset; this sounded too much like the old corrupt ways of the villages. 'These barbers and purohits are cunning men, cultural parasites. We can't be encouraging them.'

'What you say is correct,' Dharam Singh responded, 'but these things will not vanish in a day. This is an old tradition of our villages. It also helps the barber caste earn a decent living. Let us appreciate what he has done—he has brought us a good proposal for you, my son.'

Mehtab had never argued with his father before, and that realization made him refrain from taking the argument further.

Five months later, Mehtab Singh and his parents made the journey to Tibba for the wedding, accompanied by a group of landowners from Dharamsinghwala, most of them members of the new village Singh Sabha. They made up a serious looking barat, not at all interested in the feasting and dancing and drinking that would normally be associated with a wedding.

In Bhaiya's courtyard, the vedi, a small pavilion raised on four stakes with a red cloth roof stretched across bamboo cross beams, was already set up for the religious ceremony that would sanctify the wedding in the eyes of God. Rough foliage and a few flowers hid the base of the stakes. The fire would be lit in the small hollow of stones at the centre of the pavilion and the couple would go around it seven times, four times led by the groom and then three times by the bride, while the pandit chanted mantras from the sacred texts.

That night a troubled Mehtab decided to take matters into his own hands.

'This is not the way I'm going to get married,' he told his father. 'This is against everything that I have learnt, against all that I believe in.'

Dharam Singh knew what his son meant: with the encouragement of the Singh Sabha many marriages among the Sikhs were being formalized through the Anand Karaj, by going four times around the holy Granth, not the fire, and to the accompaniment of verses from the Granth.

'We will talk to Bhaiya...in the morning. Now go to sleep,' he told his son.

But it was not an easy conversation. Nobody in Tibba had ever seen a marriage that was not performed around a vedi fire: that was the only way to give it sanctity.

'But even Sikhs have been performing marriages like this,' Bhaiya said. 'Dharam Singh, even you were married like this.'

'True, Bhaiyaji, but things are changing, customs are changing. Our families have never thought too much about differences between Hindu and Sikh traditions. In fact, we have been doing other things too that are now frowned upon by reformers— keeping fasts, visiting shrines of pirs and maulas...that has been the way of life in our villages. But this is a new awakening, and I must admit I see nothing wrong with it.'

After several hours, hours that would remain a confusing childhood memory for Ralla, the bride's younger brother, the elders struck a deal. There would be a marriage according to the established rites under the vedi, and the next morning, there would be a wedding in the presence of the Granth Sahib. Mehtab Singh acquiesced. Jindi went through it all in a daze, wearing a red velvet salwar-kameez that had once been her mother's and which the village seamstress had altered for her. The only thing she knew for certain was that she would soon go away, from the only place on earth that she had ever known, from her childhood games and distractions. Her head covered with a red dupatta with a gold border, she looked down at her feet as she went around first the fire and then the Holy Book, aware only of the little bells on her toes that tinkled naughtily at each step. Her heart fluttered anxiously every time she thought of the man who walked ahead of her, whom she had never seen before, to whom she was now bound forever, no matter how long that forever would be.

There was to be no muklawa, no mandatory waiting before

the bride was taken away: Mehtab had had enough of meaningless ritual. The same day, the small barat left for the canal colony beyond the Ravi, taking with them Jindi, trembling and sobbing in her loneliness, wondering when she would see Tibba again and worrying about how her young brother, who stood forlornly in the group bidding farewell to the caravan as it left for Patti railway station, would spend his days.

Jindi's arrival ignited Dharamsinghwala. People would talk of nothing else but her beauty and warmth. Her open face, sparkling eyes, and inviting voice won over every heart in the village.

'Dharam Singh and Pritam Kaur are lucky,' the women said, as they gathered in the winter sun of the afternoons for their gossip sessions. 'They have found an angel to look after them in their old age. They must have done some very good deeds in their previous lives. All this, the good and the bad, is written. You see everything here itself.'

Mehtab Singh fell headlong in love with his young wife. None of his restraint or control seemed to be able to hold the flood of emotions that spilled over from his heart each time she smiled at him. He talked to her of things he had never mentioned to anyone else, each desire in his heart, each wild dream in his head. He wanted their souls to merge into each other, and so it seemed did she. There was not a moment's discord between them, no issue or conflict. Just a continuous joy, the like of which he was certain could not have been felt by any other man in the whole world.

'Jindi, you are life itself, that's what your name means, and it is true. You are all my life, all I ever wanted from life,' he found himself whispering to her night after night, as he cupped her tender, soft face in his hands. She felt like a flower that might get crushed if handled roughly. More than once she would wake up in the night and find him looking at her, his raised head resting on his palm. Even in the darkness, she could make out the lightness of his gentle eyes, even more gentle when filled with love.

∾

The nausea left her feeling faint and helpless. The smells from the kitchen, even the sweet smell of the halwa being cooked for the gurudwara, made her feel so sick that she would want to run away into the fields or to the high bank of the canal. She began to miss the mother she had lost too early. Pritam Kaur understood.

'Come, child, I am your mother, too. A beautiful thing is happening to you for which we have been waiting four years now. A little child is coming to you, a gift of Waheguru. I am sure it will be a nice healthy boy; I can see it in your walk already. Every evening you must go to the gurudwara and pray and all will go well. In my time we used to go to Gugga pir but my son will not let you do that.'

Jindi went to the gurudwara morning and evening. She prayed hard for a little boy, a boy like Ralla, playful and carefree. It was during those days that she went back to Tibba, the first time after her marriage and Ralla found her grown up and different. The women of Tibba could make out from her walk that this was not only a bride returning home after four years, but a mother-to-be.

'May you have a son like four moons,' was the blessing that she received in every house she visited.

There was only one midwife in Dharamsinghwala. She had lived in that area since before the arrival of the Sikhs from Tarn Taran tehsil. Nobody knew her full name; the whole village called her Rani the dai and everybody knew she was Muslim. However, her faith was of no consequence to any of them; every child born in the new settlement had been born into her practised hands.

She came in a week or so before Jindi was due and issued instructions to Pritam Kaur about the preparations that would need to be made when the time came. As she was leaving, Mehtab was entering the house.

'A son is to be born in your house, barkhurdar. Make sure you tell your wife good stories, tales of the valour and courage of your Gurus and make sure your wife wakes up and looks at only good things early in the morning. Keep her away from beggars, the lame, and the blind.'

When the time came, a boy ran three miles to call Mehtab from the canal lock that he was inspecting. He sought the supervisor's permission to leave early and walked home. Rani was bustling around the house and he could see that his mother was quietly submitting to her instructions. Wanting to stay out of the way, Mehtab went to the gurudwara and sat down quietly. It was not yet time for the evening prayers and the hall was empty. Worn out by the tension, he leaned against the wall and nodded off.

A gentle hand on his shoulder woke him up. It was Dharam Singh, outwardly calm but Mehtab noticed a lurking shadow of concern in his eyes.

'Give thanks to Waheguru. He has given us a son to carry forward our name and His message.'

'Is everything all right?' Mehtab asked.

'In Waheguru's hands,' his father replied as they hurried home.

A flood of emotions churned through Mehtab as they approached the house, a mix of responsibility, exhilaration, confusion. But there would never be any doubt about what he felt when he entered, forgetting even to take off his shoes, caked with the mud of the canal bank. An icy fear took instant hold of his heart. Instead of the chaos of joy that he had expected, he was met by a worried silence. Rani was rushing out of the room in which Jindi lay and he saw her carry away a large brass bowl; the sight of the blood in it terrified him. The look on his mother's face needed no explanation. He knew Jindi was in danger, his entire world was in danger.

'Maybe I need help,' Rani told him. 'There is too much

bleeding. I will try to do what I can, but there is an injury
inside, I think.'

It was a long bicycle ride to the outskirts of Lyallpur, though
he took every shortcut that he knew, riding hard through the
dark fields. His legs were numb and trembling by the time he
reached Dr Chadha's home. The doctor was about to retire for
the night but one look at Mehtab's face told him that he was
needed, no matter how late the hour. The ride back, with the
doctor riding pillion, clutching his bag, was harder and slower.

Dr Chadha took one look at Jindi, felt for her pulse, lifted
her eyelids, and then looked down. With his hands he indicated
to Dharam Singh that Jindi should now be put on the ground,
her head towards the north. But Dharam Singh shook his head
in disagreement. She would lie where she was. Then he began
to recite hymns from the Granth Sahib, his voice steady, his eyes
lightly closed.

The night of a death can be a long night, every moment weighed
down with questions that have no answers. Mehtab wondered if
he should have made that long journey at all and wasted those
precious hours while Jindi was still breathing. Perhaps if he had
sat next to her and held her hand, she may have lived. Perhaps
if he had gone to the gurudwara and prayed very hard, giving
his entreaties the full weight of his mind and spirit, the bleeding
might have stopped. Perhaps she had looked for him as her vision
began to cloud and fail, perhaps she had wanted to say something,
perhaps.... He wrestled with those questions until fatigue began
to gnaw at his bones. As the first licks of light began to light up
the sky, he heard a little cry and saw for the first time the gift that
his Jindi had left him.

Four days later, he took the train from Lyallpur with the
little bundle of her ashes held close to his body. It had taken
all his courage to pick the bone fragments out of the cooled

pyre and bathe them in milk. On this last journey, he wanted to be alone with her. At Kartarpur, at the holy place where Guru Nanak had spent the last years of his life, he watched Jindi mingle with the eternal in the fast-flowing waters of the Ravi and drift away. For a moment, he felt peace on her account as she raced towards the setting sun but it was only for a moment—a large, looming loneliness swallowed him in an embrace that would not ease for years.

They say that in Sandal Bar some flowers bloom only for a day or two.

Even now, more than twenty years later, there wasn't a day that Mehtab didn't think of Jindi. Often in times of trouble, and always in times of joy, he conversed with her, gently, softly, as if holding her face tenderly in his hands. He felt certain that her spirit was always at his side and it was she who must have shielded Kirpal from every danger in foreign battlefields. And he, fool that he was, had let the boy walk into trouble, here at home.

Chapter 20

Sucha Lends a Helping Hand

When he heard the long spell of firing, anger flamed in Sucha's head even as he watched Dr Hardit Singh shut his eyes as if he were in sudden physical pain. So many bullets could only mean one thing: hundreds dead and hundreds more wounded. The shooting of three days ago on the railway line would seem like nothing in comparison to what was happening now, he thought despairingly. It should never have come to this; it should never have been allowed to come to this. The brothers of the Ghadar had the right idea. This government was not one that you could appeal to or reason with. Men like O'Dwyer could not be expected to recognize sacrifices in the war and reward them. They would never accept Indians as equals or let them have a say in their own destiny. But O'Dwyer's government would have understood bombs and assassinations and rebellion in the ranks of the army. Ten men like Rash Behari Bose or Sohan Singh Bhakna or Kartar Singh Sarabha would have brought them to their knees. For the hundredth time, Sucha cursed the traitors who had betrayed the Ghadar conspiracy of 1915. It was only because of them that a passion that had seemed so invincible had been ruthlessly snuffed out.

Umrao had simply vanished. Sucha had heard once that he had been seen in Kashmir but there had been no way to confirm that. But Sucha was glad for even that rumour; the British had hanged to death so many of the conspirators. Others had been tortured, beaten, broken, imprisoned, exiled. Yet, the ghadar that they had dreamt of remained in their hearts, no matter where they were...in the Cellular Jail in the Andamans, or wandering in Europe or America, or hiding in Punjab's villages, waiting for the moment they could fight again....

The wounded came all evening, some dragging their way to the clinic and others being carried. Each man brought a story of shock and sorrow. A storm of bullets had been unleashed. No warning. No way to get out. Blood everywhere. No water. Sucha and the doctor had no time to find out details. They did what they could; most of the victims needed a hospital if they were to have any chance of surviving.

At eight the curfew came into effect and nobody could step out to help the wounded and the dying. Sucha cleaned up the clinic as best as he could and tried to persuade the doctor to eat something before going to bed. But Hardit Singh just shook his head in silence and turned away. He looked very frail and tired.

Just as he was about to put out the last lamp, Sucha heard an urgent knock on the door. Then it was repeated, even more urgently. It must be someone bringing a wounded person, Sucha thought, but how could they have come through the tight curfew.

He opened the door a few inches. A tall, broad-shouldered young man stood there, carrying an almost unconscious older man in his arms. Sucha opened the door fully and helped to put the wounded man on the old examining table with its chipped white enamel paint.

'Bullet?' he asked the tall man.

'Yes, but I think it has gone through him. I know, I've seen these wounds in the war,' Kirpal told him. At once, the soldierly bearing, the neat turban, the beard tied in a net made sense to Sucha.

'Yes, we've seen many injuries like this one today. But how did you...there's a curfew...?'

Kirpal's look told Sucha that he would not have let anything stand in the way of his trying to save Ralla.

'I had to. Somehow. Otherwise he would have bled to death.'

'You were together?' Sucha asked, even as he tore away Ralla's pyjama and started cleaning the wound. Ralla winced at the touch of the spirit.

'It's okay, Ralla mama,' Kirpal held the older man's hand. 'It'll be okay. We are with a doctor.'

'Your mama?' Sucha asked.

'Yes, he's the only one I have on my mother's side. Her younger brother. It's a miracle he spotted me in that hell where hundreds are dead or are dying. It's a miracle that I could bring him here…someone told me about this Doctor sahib. There was nowhere else to go.'

Dr Hardit Singh had come into the room, pulling on a shirt. As Sucha put water to boil, he tried to remember where he had heard the name Ralla before. Finally, he turned to Kirpal and asked: 'Are you from Tibba?'

'He is,' Kirpal pointed to Ralla. 'I have been there once, it was my mother's village. Can't remember much, except the wrestler.'

'Bhimaji,' said Sucha, 'I stayed at his akhara for a while when I was much younger.'

A dim memory of a boy helping the wrestler with the weights stirred in Kirpal's mind.

'He will be all right,' the doctor was saying. 'The bullet went through the flesh; the bone is okay. But he has lost a lot of blood. I will bandage him up and let him rest here tonight. Sucheya, make tea for all of us and then you both can talk of your Tibba village.'

Sucha would not let Ralla leave the next morning or the next. For him, this was not just another wounded man from Jallianwala Bagh. This was his childhood, an extension of Bhima and the akhara, a part of the only home he had known. Ralla and Kirpal stayed at the doctor's home for the next two weeks and then moved to the Golden Temple to await news of Mehtab.

Chapter 21

The Humiliation of
Gurnam Singh Gambhir

Gurnam's fever had faded only to be replaced by a deep torment. And anger. Anger at the helpless misery of his countrymen. At the injustices meted out to them by an unheeding God. He could not understand why a people who prayed day and night, who genuflected towards any possible manifestation of divinity, had to suffer so much. Wasn't it enough that they were writhing under the onslaught of epidemics and famine, that they were burdened by debt and poverty? God had also placed over them an unfeeling, unrelenting arbiter of their daily destiny, a foreign ruler who believed that he was born to rule because of the colour of his skin, who believed that one European life was worth ten Indians, who had no intention of ever leaving this land that had furnished and financed his palaces and treasures and industries, who dragged out the whole political game gambit by gambit, dangling a distant hope in one hand while taking it away with the other. He cared little that thousands of Indians had spilt their blood in distant battlefields for his glory, fighting an enemy that was not their enemy for no reason except loyalty, a reason of no value in his eyes. Indians were nothing but just some low form of life—to be tortured, exploited, deceived, robbed. And then when the whim took the killer, to be shot in cold blood.

Like they had been shot on the railway line four days earlier and the previous evening in Jallianwala Bagh. Not in some distant town, secluded valley, or desert waste but right here in his city.

His city! The city that ran in his blood. He knew how its earth smelt after the first shower of rain after the long summer or how light, airy, and vast its skies could be in the summer dawn. He knew the warm glow of its winter sun and the teeth-chattering cold of its winter nights. This cold-blooded murder was being carried out in broad daylight in the kuchas and galis where he had spent his carefree childhood, whose every turn and twist was inscribed on his heart. The boys with whom he had played gulli-danda in these squares, or jumped from terrace to terrace in the desperate chases of chor-police or hung around with in Hall Bazaar as an awkward gangly teenager, were all still here.... The elders of this beloved city had all been his fathers no matter which sort of cap or turban they wore, which God they worshipped, whether they turned towards the rising or the setting sun. To see death and bloodshed in these streets, to hear wailing on Baisakhi, broke his heart. He felt the cuts on his own body, the whiplash across his soul. And he knew, even when his anguish was raw and fresh and his body still weak from the fever, that he must do everything he could to help those who were being brutalized. He was one of the few of his generation who knew the ways of the oppressor, who had managed to walk at the edges of the world of the tyrants.

∾

The next day, at four in the afternoon, the Public Library was already filled with barristers and pleaders, municipal commissioners, magistrates, and prominent merchants. Commissioner Kitchin spoke briefly in Hindustani. He said that the city was in the hands of the General who would give further orders.

A bit later, General Dyer accompanied by DC Irving, and escorted by military and police officers rushed in. He began to speak fast in Hindustani, not even bothering to sit down. The audience, too, had to stand up.

'You want war or peace....? If you wish for war, the government is prepared for war...if you want peace, then obey my orders, and open all your shops.... For me the battlefield, whether in France or Amritsar, is the same.... Obey orders. I do not wish to hear anything else. I have served in the military for over thirty years. I understand the Indian sepoy and the Sikh people very well. You will have to observe peace, otherwise the shops will be opened with rifles.... Speak now, if you want war....'

Then the DC spoke: 'You've heard the General. The whole city is in his charge.... Open the shops....You have committed a bad act in killing the English. They will be avenged.... You and your children will pay the price....You people must open shops at once. The government is very angry with you....'

Then Dyer and his party left the hall, just as they had come, in a flurry of red-faced anger and arrogance.

Gurnam wanted to bar their way. To ask them what God-given right had permitted them to commit these atrocities on his people. He felt the blood throbbing at his temples but restrained himself: his seniors were sitting in stunned silence.

As the gathering broke up, there was talk.

'Englishmen killed? How many? Five, six? And what did these maderchod sons of bitches do in Jallianwala last evening? The murder of hundreds by these bastards? They have killed so many that there is no wood left for cremation!'

'The bodies are still rotting in the lanes, dogs are feasting on them. And the DC talks of revenge! *We* need revenge.'

'And martial law has not even been announced! No formal orders—they will issue them tomorrow and then backdate them. That's what they do.'

∾

Second Lieutenant Newman was bursting with self-importance. Members of the Bar had been lined up before him in Ram

Bagh, their hands behind their backs. Among them were vakils, barristers, municipal commissioners, title holders. Men like Lala Dharam Das, Badrul Islam Ali Khan, Maqbool Mahmood, Mohammad Amin, Gurnam Singh Gambhir....

'You have all been appointed special constables. The General's orders are that you will patrol the city throughout the day and help keep peace and order. And if you do not follow orders, you will be punished, depending on your behaviour. Flogging, imprisonment, or death. You will report here three times a day—at nine in the morning, then at one, and then at five in the evening and answer your roll call. A number is being given to each of you.'

One of the younger pleaders made to step out of line and speak. The lieutenant immediately kicked him hard on the shin. The pleader doubled over in pain and then fell to the ground, clutching his leg.

'This is what will happen to anyone who does not agree with our orders. Or worse.'

∾

A filthy smell pervaded the lane that ran between small houses and shops for a hundred and fifty yards. Blind alleys led out of it. It was like any other lane in the old city—narrow, overpopulated, with drains running on both sides. Most of the houses were old and rose to two storeys; the walls were made of brick into which were embedded narrow windows with small sunshades of corrugated iron and the occasional balcony with a wooden carved balustrade. If the missionary lady, Miss Sherwood, had not been passing through this lane on her cycle when an angry crowd had attacked her, provoked by the firing on their compatriots on the railway bridges earlier, this lane would have remained indistinguishable from a hundred others in the city.

But now this lane was destined to become a symbol of the worst kind of humiliation and punishment. A special wooden structure, called a tiktiki, had been set up near its centre. Gurnam was made to stand next to the tiktiki, alongside three British soldiers of the 25th London Cyclists, and witness the flogging of anyone whom the authorities felt had flouted the orders that were now in force in the city. His insides burnt with resentment. It was not enough for Dyer that hundreds of unarmed citizens had been shot dead. There also had to be random torture and then humiliation heaped upon the tortured so that the proud spirit of Punjab was crushed once and for all. And he, Gurnam, had to witness it all. He was a vakil, not a special constable. It was not his job to witness floggings or to teach people how to properly salaam every passing Englishman.

Dyer had also ordered that anybody using the lane would have to crawl. The soldiers stood by and laughed as the people living in the lane crawled in and out on their bellies, pulling themselves along by their hands in the grit and grime. If they fell ill in their houses, they remained ill. No doctor was going to crawl his way in. If the latrines filled up and overflowed then so be it, no jemadar was going to crawl in to clean the latrines. And if they did not crawl properly, and lifted themselves up on their knees, they got the hard butt of a rifle or a heavy army boot on their backs. The soldiers relieved themselves against the walls of the houses. They shot and roasted the sacred pigeons that frequented the Jain temple. When they flogged six young boys at the tiktiki, on the charge that they were among those who had attacked Miss Sherwood, the entire lane watched from their houses in shock and revulsion. Each of the naked boys passed out after a few lashes. They were given water and when they revived, they were whipped again. Their cries and appeals for mercy became fainter and fainter even as Gurnam witnessed it all helplessly, almost unable to hold his rising anger in check, an armed soldier on either side of him.

∿

Towards the end of May, while Gurnam was tying his turban
in front of the small oval mirror on the mantelpiece, Bhagwan
came in, flustered. The police were at the door. Gurnam had been
expecting this to happen any day. Some lawyers had already been
taken away, after being relieved from the humiliation of serving as
special constables. Calmly he finished tying his turban, straightened
the angle and neatened the folds with the help of a knitting needle
he kept for this purpose and then turned to Bhagwan.

'Let's go.'

A sub-inspector and six armed sepoys stood at the door. The
SI spoke aggressively.

'DSP sahib wants to see you at the kotwali.'

'Why?'

'Orders, let's go.'

'Am I under arrest?'

'No, these soldiers are here to protect you.'

They walked through the lane to the police kotwali. Plomer
was waiting, along with an Indian inspector, Buta Singh, and
started questioning Gurnam immediately.

'You were present on 10 April when the disturbances took
place. You must know what the conspiracy was?'

'I know of no conspiracy. I was only trying to help you
send the crowd back.'

'Yes, yes, but you're one of them. You know who killed the
Europeans that day?'

'I know nothing.'

'We know you were inciting the hartals too. You were present
at the meetings on 5 April and 6 April.'

'Only on 6 April.'

At a signal from Plomer, the inspector took Gurnam to a
cell and slammed the door on him. Even in the day the cell was
dark and damp. When his eyes adjusted to the darkness, Gurnam
saw that it was bare but for a small earthen pot with water and

a metal cup. There was a small heap of roasted gram next to it on the floor. In the corner was a small tin canister with its top cut off for him to relieve himself. He could not eat the food that was slipped in through the hatch in the door, dark chapattis and an oily mess of a dal. Gurnam swallowed a handful of the gram with half a cup of water and lay down. He knew this was going to be a long haul.

In the evening he asked to see the kotwal. But it was Buta Singh who came.

'I want my food from my house and my bedding to sleep,' he told him.

'We'll see about that. I thought you were ready to talk.'

'Talk about what?'

'Some things you may have remembered after a few hours here? It happens to many people. You should know—your father was a police inspector, famous for making people talk. Maybe you can now recall the names of the people who called the hartal, the conspirators behind the disturbances, those who burnt the bank and killed those angrez on the tenth...perhaps those goondas who attacked Sherwood memsahib?'

Gurnam ignored the reference to his father, though he knew what Buta Singh meant. His father had trained his dog, a German shepherd called Ruby, to gently hold the testicles of suspects in her mouth to make them talk while he sat calmly in an armchair, whistling a tune.

'I don't know about any of that, or of any conspiracy,' he said.

'Pity...if you did remember, then food and bedding, perhaps even a government award, would be possible. Maybe even a jagir.'

❧

The mornings were all the same: a forced walk for fifteen minutes at seven in the courtyard with the other prisoners, a hurried

visit to the filthy and smelly latrines, a quick wash with a rubber
hose in public, and back to the cell for the day. There would be
one more brief outing at five in the evening. His bedding from
home was finally given to him but the food did not change. He
continued to live on handfuls of gram.

Four days later, there was early morning activity in the jail.
Handcuffed, he was taken to the outer room to join three other
prominent prisoners. He recognized Girdhari Lal, the managing
director of the Amritsar Flour and General Mills Company,
Dr Bashir, and Pandit Kotu Mal. The four of them were bundled
into a horse carriage and driven to the railway station. Several
other prisoners followed on foot and there was armed mounted
police in front and behind. At the station they were all put in
a third-class carriage meant for prisoners being taken to Lahore.
One of Bashir's relatives called out to him from the crowd that
had gathered at the station.

'Don't worry, bhai. We'll get you out soon even if we have
to spend all we have.'

The man who shouted was pulled out of the crowd by two
policemen. His hands were tied behind his back, and he was
marched off to the kotwali.

From Lahore railway station, they were made to walk in the
midday sun to the sessions court. Halfway there, Gurnam asked
the police escort for water. The constables looked at each other,
then directed the group to a nearby well. Just as they were about
to drink, an inspector rode up.

'Are you out of your mind?' he shouted at the constables,
and they were pulled back to the road without being given any
water. At the court there was no place to sit, so they sat on the
ground in the courtyard. It was not till seven in the evening that
they were taken to the Central Jail.

Each of the four men was put in a separate cell, about seven
feet long and two feet wide and two feet high. It was impossible

to stand and one had to crouch or lie down all the time. Gurnam refused to eat the food that was put into the cell; it was as bad as that he had been given in Amritsar. He also refused to take a bath when he saw that he had to use drain water. It would be two weeks more before he was put in a proper cell with three others and allowed better food at a payment of thirty rupees a month.

Chapter 22

Dyer Changes His Tune

Punjab's crimson spring gave way to a summer of arbitrary arrests, quick trials by special tribunals, and mass imprisonments. Martial law was brutally implemented. Civilians were bombed by aeroplanes. Peasants and their families trudging home after a day in the fields were machine-gunned from the air. Villages were strafed indiscriminately as if this were a war. Gallows were set up in public places to instil the fear of instant death. School children, even infants, were made to parade for hours in the heat, saluting the Union Jack. Tight censorship had thrown a veil around the province while the government brutalized a helpless population for an imaginary conspiracy and non-existent uprising. Despite the repression and news blackouts, reports of the massacre in Amritsar and its aftermath began to gradually filter through to the rest of the country and the world. The clamour of questions grew louder: what had actually happened on the thirteenth of April, how many people had been killed, was the shooting by Dyer justified, what further atrocities were being perpetrated by the authorities?

Even as the agony of Amritsar and Punjab continued, its top official, Sir Michael O'Dwyer, who had contributed so much to the ongoing tragedy by his repressive orders, his support for Dyer's actions, and his lack of sympathy for the Indians he ruled over, made a perfunctory assessment of the situation on the ground. He drove down in an armoured car to Amritsar on 20 April with Commissioner Kitchin. He met General Dyer, toured the city, talked to some of the families in the Fort, but did not visit Jallianwala Bagh.

Then O'Dwyer, whose long tenure of six years as ruler of the province was coming to an end, got busy with a farewell round of leave-taking and partying. Running a crucial part of the country during the war, and especially during the recent disturbances, had been hard work, but not hard enough for Sir Michael to skip his morning ride or afternoon game of golf or tennis and, in the cold days in Lahore, two mornings a week with the hounds! There had been time, too, for the duck shoots in Bahawalpur and pig-sticking in Patiala and stag hunting in Kashmir. One of the days with the hounds was always a Sunday and often the Lieutenant Governor would head straight from the hunt to the cathedral for the morning service. Nobody dared to nudge him awake as he inevitably fell asleep during the sermon.

One evening, returning from a farewell event, O'Dwyer confided in Porter: 'I have absolutely no ambition for further employment, even if it were to be offered to me. In any case to become the Viceroy one needs to be a hereditary peer with private means.' That night, Porter could not help noting, in the confidence of his diary, that in those last days the Lieutenant Governor was at his most boorish.

At the end of May, Michael O' Dwyer left Punjab for Bombay, not in a blaze of glory but very quietly, secretly. A decorated decoy train went in front and his followed. He was convinced that he had crushed the problem in Punjab at the right time and Dyer's action had served to deliver the right lesson. On the last day of the month, he and his wife boarded the ship to England. He was not to know it then, but India would follow him relentlessly.

ᖇ

The good news came after O'Dwyer had left. Hugh Porter had been made a Companion of the Order of the Star of India, or CSI, as it was more modestly known. When he received the news in his office in Lahore, Porter had to sit down, and take deep

breaths to calm his pounding heart and still his racing mind. The
news was one that would make anyone happy, certainly a civil
servant reaching the end of his India tenure. What a long journey
it had been, from the time he had walked the Lakeland Fells
reading Rider Haggard and trying, as young men are wont to do,
to find himself. Sitting by streams, catching fish, and indulging in
long, meandering, self-conscious conversations with other young
men about what was important in life—achievement or happiness,
culture or money....

He wired Milly immediately and then lunched with a sense
of quiet satisfaction. He was still in a generous mood when his
attendant brought in a request that Kesho Ram, the pleader,
wanted to call on him.

'Five o'clock this evening,' he said; that would give him enough
time for his afternoon nap.

~

Kesho Ram was affable, spoke reasonably good English, and was
straightforward about his loyalty. He was not 'double-facey' as
Porter described most Indians, including the notables who were
actually beneficiaries of the British Raj; it wasn't quite duplicity
they were guilty of, but certainly insincerity. Or a lack of moral
courage to say it as it was, to speak their mind fearlessly. But
Kesho Ram was different: he believed in stating the facts. Porter
liked that.

Kesho Ram sat very straight in his chair, taking out the
watch he wore on a gold chain from his waistcoat pocket as soon
as Porter walked into the drawing room as if to note the time
when the meeting started, so as not to overshoot. He kept his
hands on his knees firmly all the time he talked. Porter thought
to himself, half amused, perhaps that posture helped Kesho Ram
form his English sentences better, like a child who holds his
hands clasped during elocution.

After the courtesies, the talk turned to Amritsar, from where the pleader had returned only the day before.

'The behaviour of the police has been very bad, Porter sahib, very bad. They do not treat us like human beings.'

Porter kept quiet, knowing this statement was a preface for some hard information.

'And Deputy Superintendent Plomer is making money. Arresting people without reason, using the martial law as an excuse, and then releasing them after taking money. It is known that he has made more than a lakh of rupees.'

'If there is evidence then perhaps prosecuting Plomer will help to settle the situation?'

'He should be prosecuted though I think it would take more than that for the people to feel that justice has been done after what General Dyer did. The figures you have been given are all wrong. More than a thousand people died. I am not sure if there were many women there but certainly there were children.'

Porter thought of something that he had been told by an officer who had visited Amritsar with O'Dwyer. The officer had said: 'It is probable that not 200 but nearer 800 were killed at Amritsar. I have heard some mention the figure of 1,800. The fact is that the dead were not counted so no one really knows.' Porter had written the figures down in his private diary, but it would not do for Kesho Ram to know this, so he said: 'Let us not forget that people had been warned by Dyer not to hold a meeting.'

'That too, Porter sahib, needs checking. Dyer's proclamation was only made at some points in the city. Most of the people in the Bagh hadn't heard any announcement. Many were visitors from villages, simply resting there after the Baisakhi cattle fair or after visiting the Golden Temple. And, most important,' Kesho Ram paused for dramatic effect in pure pleader fashion, 'if he didn't want the meeting why didn't he have the entrances guarded once he had come to know it was going to be held. It seems he was waiting for people to trap themselves.'

'Kesho Ram,' Porter felt his blood rising, 'that is not how our officers think or behave.'

'I will believe you, Porter sahib, if you say so, for we in Punjab know of your long service. Then why did he continue to fire when the people were trying to run away? Why did General Dyer make people crawl on their bellies in the lane where Miss Sherwood was assaulted? These were people who lived in that lane, they had nowhere to go to but their homes. In fact, some of them were the very people who had protected Miss Sherwood.'

'That order has been rescinded now.'

'Yes, that's true, but it will be a stain on the good name of the British Raj for a very long time.'

Porter knew that the pleader was right. An inquiry into the Punjab disturbances seemed inevitable now. The signs were clear: a confrontation was building up. Most of British India supported the government's measures in Punjab, including Dyer's action in Jallianwala Bagh, convinced it had prevented a repeat of the mutiny of 1857. For them, Dyer was a hero. The Indians clearly thought otherwise. Gandhi was peppering Delhi and London with messages calling for an inquiry, and in a major blow to British prestige, Rabindranath Tagore had sent a telegram to the Viceroy relinquishing his knighthood.

The news from home was also worrisome; there was criticism in some quarters in London of the manner in which unarmed Indians had been shot down with machine guns and bombed from aeroplanes. Michael O'Dwyer's version of firm government, Edwin Montagu, the secretary of state, had noted, had produced its 'invariable and inevitable harvest'. Keen to prevent the derailing of his planned political reforms by the bad press that the government was getting, Montagu told the House of Commons about his intention to hold an inquiry and by end of May, he directed the Viceroy, Lord Chelmsford to start the process of setting up one.

Porter knew that he would have to go to Amritsar and prepare himself.

༽

Dyer came to call in early August, a day before Porter was to take the train from Lahore to Amritsar. They had not met for a couple of months during which Dyer had achieved much military success up north against the Afghans, particularly in relieving Thal.

But Porter's honed political instincts told him that Thal was not going to wipe out Amritsar. Despite his recent success, Dyer's face was haggard and drawn and Porter noted dark shadows around his eyes.

Later the Chief Secretary recorded in his diary the essence of his conversation with Dyer:

> Dyer seemed aware of what we were up against. He told me that he had been in Delhi on 30 March when the disturbances began. He was spat on in Delhi and his car was stoned as he passed through Ludhiana. He had reached Amritsar on the night of the 11th and went around from street to street on that night and again on April 12th and 13th. He had announced that no meetings should be held. But behind him were men beating a ghee-tin and announcing that a meeting was to be held. This all should be seen as one transaction, he said. This was important. When he entered the Bagh with his troops it took him three seconds to decide that the insurrection should be ended there and then. This was no local disturbance but a full rebellion and before him was the epicentre of that rebellion. The gathering was nothing short of a declaration of war. Dyer said he opened fire and the crowd collected in knots and he thought they were going to attack. He kept on firing till the ammunition of the troops was nearly exhausted. He regarded it as his mission, his religious duty to

kill the rebellion. He did not arrange for the wounded to be treated because he thought it was not his responsibility. The mutineers were so numerous that they could well take care of their own wounded. That is more or less what he has told Simla. He added before going that the people needed to be taught a lesson that would end the rebellion in Punjab. For that reason, he continued to fire even when they were trying to escape and personally directed the fire where the crowd was the thickest; if he had more ammunition, he would have fired longer. He did not regard this just as a rebellion but open mutiny. Dandas were being brought into Amritsar in large quantities and a Danda Fauj was being readied. What faced him then was the Danda Fauj in the making.

A warning bell went off in Porter's mind after that conversation: Dyer was clearly changing his tune. There was now only a casual mention of the fear of attack from the crowd, on the basis of which his action had been approved by O'Dwyer. Instead, there was now a clear belief in a bounden mission, a religious duty, the teaching of a lesson to the natives that would resonate across Punjab…all this was very different from the earlier story of firing in self-defence in the face of an advancing crowd! Dyer had obviously decided to don the mantle of the hero that he was being painted out to be.

Porter left for Amritsar the same night, reaching the town at a quarter to seven in the morning. After a quick breakfast, he toured the places connected with the riots, accompanied by Captain Massey. He saw the burnt-out hulks of the National Bank building, the Town Hall, the Alliance Bank, and the gutted church. Then he reached Jallianwala Bagh.

He went in through the same entrance that had been taken by Dyer and his troops. The Bagh was smaller than he had thought: just about two hundred yards in length and not quite so wide.

He estimated the area to be around six to seven acres. Much of it was under early green corn, unlike the time of the shooting in April when it had been dry and brown. A line of an Urdu poem flashed through his mind:

Talwar ka khet kab sabz hua....
Never grows green the field sown with swords

Captain Massey pointed out the location of the platform, the troops, the well, the exits. The number of people who had been present on Baisakhi day was now being placed at twenty-five to thirty thousand, much more than the six thousand or so Dyer had said. Carefully and methodically, Porter went around the other points of interest in the city. They ended up at the Gobindgarh Fort; on 10 April, Massey had moved all the women and children from the Civil Lines—about a hundred and thirty-five of them—to safety behind its imposing walls even as an unarmed crowd had collected on the railway bridges.

Porter was in a pensive mood on his return journey to Lahore. The visit to Jallianwala Bagh had only confirmed what he had felt earlier, but never admitted fully even to himself. Dyer had been shooting fish in a barrel; the people could not have escaped even if they had been given a warning. The exits were too few and narrow and mostly barred; to a man who could feel it, the Bagh, four months after the massacre, still smelt of death. Dyer had created a convenient duty for himself, a duty to kill ruthlessly, and O'Dwyer had egged him on and then patted him on the back. Dyer and O'Dwyer were one of a kind—narrow, cruel, unfeeling. Hugh Porter knew all that but he also knew that he would say no such thing even by implication when questioned by an inquiry committee. He was steeped too deep in the imperialist hue; he would stay true to the civil service code, true to his oath of loyalty to the King and government.

Chapter 23

Maya Looks Back in Sorrow

Maya Dei could not bring Joga Singh's ashes to the home of Lala Sunder Das. That would be against all tradition; ashes once collected from the pyre had to be immersed in flowing water. Even though there was no knowing when she would be able to do that, she did not want to trouble Lala Sunder Das any more; he had already done more than enough for her. The family had kept Joga Singh's body with all respect in their baithak from the time they brought him home from the Bagh on a charpai till they took him for cremation beyond the Sultanwind Gate.

She had insisted on going to the cremation ground. They all knew it was not normal for women to do so, but on that day, nothing was normal: people were scrounging around for wood to burn the bodies of Hindu and Sikh victims even as the shrouded bodies of Muslims were being rushed to hastily dug graves. She had lit her husband's pyre and nobody had objected to that. When the heat from the flames reached her, her legs gave way. Lala Sunder Das put a protective arm around her shoulder.

'Come, my daughter, keep faith in Waheguru. You have done what you could. Let's go home now. The boys will watch over the pyre and we will come to collect the phul in two days.'

There were others collecting the splinters of bone and ash from the cooled pyres two days later. Among them were the volunteers of the Sewa Samiti, the local charity that had performed many cremations of unclaimed bodies and had started a count of the dead. Bisheshwar knew one of the volunteers and so it was worked out that the Sewa Samiti would keep the urn containing

Joga Singh's ashes in their office until Maya Dei could make some arrangement for their immersion. The volunteers added some marigold petals to the ashes, covered the urn with a red cloth, added a name tag, and took it away while Maya Dei watched in helpless silence. She stayed on in the Lala's home, a sad, quiet presence who spent several hours every day staring at the desolate Jallianwala Bagh from the window with the rounded iron bars. On the tenth day, the family accompanied her to Harmandir Sahib and they all prayed for the peace of the departed soul. That was all. She knew Waheguru would forgive her for not organizing an Akhand Path, a full reading of the Granth Sahib or for not keeping her vow of going barefoot to the Harmandir to pray every morning for forty days.

∿

Two months after Baisakhi, Lala Sunder Das saw her off on a train to Lahore. From there she took a train to Jhelum, all the while hugging the precious urn with the ashes to her breast. Three hours after reaching Jhelum, she got a seat on a lorry headed to Parhi. She broke down when the familiar landscape of rounded hills appeared around her with the realization that Joga Singh would never come back here, to the beloved village of his childhood. Once home, she set the urn among Joga Singh's precious books. She knew that there was no other place he would rather be.

Very early the next morning, without a word to anyone in the village, she took the urn to the Khup nullah, and after performing a short ardas, sprinkled the ashes in the churning white water. The Khup would know where to carry them. The Khup belonged to the two of them. The Khup could be trusted. It was the only witness to their first meeting. As she turned, she looked up at the steep path above the nullah to where he had stood, looking down at the village in unbelieving wonder in the first light of dawn.

That was when she had first seen him, when she had been sixteen.

It had been four years since Masi Karmo's death. Her sharp features had softened with dimpled curves and an early wisdom had touched her youthful beauty. Shadows now darkened her eyelids and a sadness seemed to hover forever above her lips, a sadness that only heightened her attraction to anybody who looked at her face carefully. Her lithe, youthful limbs gave the impression of some flowering creeper as she swayed through the village with soft light steps.

That morning, no sooner had she picked up the buckets than she let them drop back to the ground. She froze, her upper lip curled attractively in surprise. A man stood silhouetted against the dimly lit sky on top of the hill. She knew that a path came that way from Sohawa, but it wasn't a path that many travellers took. Most preferred the safer detour around the jowar fields. This one was precipitous and slippery and one wrong step could plunge you into the swirling Khup. It was said that a village beauty hurrying down that path in darkness, after a tryst with her lover, had fallen into the Khup and been carried away in an instant; her spirit was still seen on that path on some dark nights.

The man stood absolutely still, transfixed by the sight that greeted him. A heavenly mix of saffron and rose seeped gently from the silver line of the horizon into the dome above. He was drinking in the scene as if he had been waiting to see it for a long time. Then reluctantly he turned to the village below him and saw the girl with the buckets, wary and still. He began to walk down the path swiftly. She watched with trepidation as he descended the precipitous slope, but he seemed to know the path well and was soon on safe ground. As he came close, he greeted her.

'Sat sri akal, bibi.'

'Sat sri akal. You should not have come this way,' she found herself saying.

'Yes,' he said, looking back up at the steep path. 'It's a difficult slope, though in my childhood it never seemed so steep.'

Facing her again, he responded to the questions in her eyes.

'I was born here. This is Khup, no? And there are three other nullahs and I can tell you their names too—Bayi, Khurniyan, Parate...' he said, as if giving proof of his belonging.

She couldn't restrain her smile.

Kneeling down, he cupped his hands and washed his face with the cold water. Then, he broke a layer of ice from the surface and wiping it with his handkerchief tried to see his reflection in it.

'Very misty...when we were young, we could see our faces clearly in these mirrors. We took them home and put them on the shelf hoping they would stay. But in a couple of hours only a cupful of water would be left.'

He raised the thin layer of ice towards the sun's slanting rays.

'See these colours...they are still the same,' he said as the rays broke into a spectrum. She caught a glimpse. It seemed to her that he would go on like this all day, lost in his memories. But it was getting late for her.

'Are you going to the village?'

'Let us,' he responded quickly. 'Let me carry those buckets for you.'

'No, no, please don't take the trouble.'

'What trouble? We used to get water like this every day.'

He began to walk beside her with the lightness of a boy, not that of a man whose beard was already showing the first signs of grey. It appeared that the surroundings had invigorated his body and spirit, awakened memories of a treasured childhood.

'Please give me the buckets now,' she pleaded as they entered the village lane.

He emerged from his reverie and gently handed her the

buckets. Then, without a word, he walked towards the village gurudwara, bent under the low door of its outer courtyard, and vanished inside. Maya realized she was alone again, but strangely she did not feel alone.

Joga Singh's arrival became the immediate subject of curiosity and gossip among Parhi's residents.

Even Motilal squinted curiously at the man in neat, clean clothes who walked through the lane with boyish energy and stopped to talk to Makhan Singh outside the hakim's shop. Putting on his soft white turban, Motilal gave his ring a quick shine on his waistcoat and landed up at Makhan Singh's shop after the stranger had walked away.

'I say, old man, who is this Sardar?'

Makhan Singh continued to grind his medicine, his head shaking in rhythm to the circular motion of his hand. He didn't say anything but couldn't hide a smile.

This made Motilal even more angry and more curious. He repeated his question and this time there was an edge to his voice.

At last Makhan Singh stopped grinding and looked up.

'Our Joga Singh, that's him. Son of Choudhry Mukand Singh. He owned the house across mine in our lane. A kind, gentle man, a true friend. His wife, too, was a true Potohari lady, not a harsh word in her mouth. You don't know them. Your mother was still wrapping you in diapers when they passed away.'

'How?'

'How? They both passed away, as people pass away. No plague, no influenza, no cholera, just passed away. Joga Singh went away to Rawalpindi to some distant relatives to study. And study he well did, even at the college of the angrez priests. He speaks English like Englishmen. He teaches in the Rawalpindi college.'

Makhan Singh's face had flushed, and his chest had expanded

in the telling, as if he was relating not some stranger's but his own achievements.

'Then why's he back here?' Motilal asked pointedly.

'He wants to live here, wants to bring down the old crumbling house of his parents, and build a new one and spend his life here.'

For a long while Motilal was silent, wondering at the wisdom of the man who would leave a vibrant town like Rawalpindi and willingly bury himself in this hellhole of a village.

By evening, the entire village knew why Joga Singh had come to Parhi. Maya, too, knew and more than once she glanced towards the abandoned house across the lane with its weather-beaten door, its faded blue paint and flat low roof. A new house would come up there and this stranger, who had come down the steep path that morning—was it only that morning?—would live there. A ripple of excitement went down her neck and the sides of her arms.

Soon strings of mules loaded with bricks began to arrive from Sohawa. Along with them came six Kashmiri labourers and a young man in khaki shorts and khaki bush-shirt, sent by Joga Singh, who had returned to Rawalpindi. Using their pickaxes and spades efficiently the labourers brought down the old house in two days, sending countless snakes and scorpions to an untimely death under the falling debris.

The labourers were keen to finish their job quickly and return to Kashmir before the sultry heat set in. If they did slacken, Makhan Singh, who had virtually stopped going to his shop since the construction had started, would berate them:

'Get to work, you good-for-nothings. You haven't come here on your mother's wedding. And take off those bloody shawls first.'

The new house became a mission for Makhan Singh, as if it was the fulfilment of his own dream. He followed each day's progress closely, watched the rising walls, marvelled at the coloured glass panes, and fondled the blue tiles that would make diamond designs on the floor. When the young foreman showed curiosity about the old man's interest, Makhan Singh told him in gentle but firm tones: 'Joga Singh requested me to take charge. He said that my experience was invaluable and he knows I will treat this as my own project.'

He had repeated this thought to himself so many times that he had begun to believe it.

One morning Makhan Singh was walking around on the top floor of the new house. His step was unsteady because he had rather indulged himself when taking his morning dose of opium. When he went close to the edge of the building his foot faltered, and his heavy body fell two floors. His head split open like a melon as it hit the iron girders piled up below. The labourers stared at the body open-mouthed, unable to believe that this important man who had cured so many sick people, and taken so much interest in this house, would never move again.

The dark night rushed in. The stars wore mourning veils and the moon hid away behind a dusty haze. An unseasonal cold wind swept purposefully through the village as if searching for someone and the open doors of the outer courtyards banged and banged again. The wildly flickering flame of the lantern brought alive ghostly forms in the dark corners of the room.

Maya leaned against the pillar listlessly, her long hair open. Fresh tears had left grimy marks on her pale cheeks. Her eyes were fixed on the dark form of the newly constructed house across the lane. She could see the labourers huddled around a chula set on bricks, quietly cooking their food.

The cold wind pierced through her clothes but she did not move into the house. There was nothing there, just a vast emptiness. The place had never seemed so bereft, its nooks and corners never so full of spirits.

She started at the sound of a heavy step from the direction

of the lane. Then a shadow thickened the darkness at the door. A sweet smell of oil drifted towards her. Motilal. She shrank into herself.

He brought his face close to her. She could see the kohl in his eyes, the dark red of his turban.

'You have been crying, little girl? For that old man? Thank God that he has died. Now you are free of him and his demands.'

She stared back into his lecherous eyes. The deep hatred in her look was like a slap. He withdrew back a bit and spoke in a different tone.

'I will not let you want anything. I will do what you say. You will have anything you want before you name it.'

Tucking up his crackling starched white salwar, he sat down on his haunches at her feet, his hands involuntarily clasped as if he were beseeching her.

She stood upright, her determination strengthened by the desperation in his eyes.

'You will live with me, won't you?' he simpered.

'No.'

'You will live with me?'

'No, I will live here.'

'You are sad tonight. I will come again tomorrow morning. Or should I sleep here itself?'

'No, no, no!' she screamed, holding the lantern high up as if showing him the way out. Taken aback, he turned and began to walk away, telling himself that he had chosen the wrong moment.

She lay awake a long time, with the lantern undimmed, waiting for the dawn. Finally, she fell into an uneasy sleep.

There was a knock and she looked towards the door. Sunlight came through the cracks. Motilal was back. She should not open that door. A couple of minutes later, there was the knock again. Now fully awake, she noted the gentleness of the knock, as if someone was knocking with just one finger.

It was Joga Singh.

'Sat sri akal, Maya bibi. I came this morning by the early lorry from Jhelum.'

Her lips quivered in response and she covered her head with her dupatta.

'Is Bhapaji not awake? I thought he was an early riser.'

She stood silent, unable to say anything. Her eyes welled over with tears.

He stepped inside and looked around. The silence of death was everywhere.

'Was he unwell?' he asked in a subdued soft tone.

She shook her head.

'No…he was getting the last bit of the roof done, of the new house. His foot slipped and….'

'New house? What new house?'

'Your house. He's been busy with building your house for three months now. He had even stopped going to his shop. I think he felt it was his duty to help with the house, a duty towards your father.'

Joga Singh stood there, shoulders slumped. Several times he wiped his eyes with his folded handkerchief. Then his attention turned to the despondent girl who was now sitting on the charpai in the veranda, unable to stand any more, scratching the green paint from one of the pegs of the cot with her nail. He wondered what she would do with her life.

He looked around. He could hardly stand around here much longer and he could not leave her alone or take her to his house where only one room had been made ready for him. Then he knew what to do.

'Maya bibi, get up and wash your face. Let's go to the gurudwara. It will be time for Japji very soon.'

She lit up the red, blue, and yellow glass windows with her youth. The flowers she planted in the four pots on the terrace bloomed instantly. Birds that had never been seen in that valley before came flying every morning to the carved iron railing of the top veranda just to talk to her. As she walked on the diamond shaped blue tiles of the floors, they seemed to dance with her. Fascinated and entranced, Joga Singh watched her quietly, not wanting to say anything lest the spell break. It was not just that he had built himself a new house in his ancestral village: an entire new life, it seemed, had presented itself to him.

Very soon after they were married, he had resigned his job at the Mission College in Rawalpindi. All he brought back, loaded on the back of a mule, was a metal trunk full of books. She arranged the English books on one shelf, the Punjabi books on another and marvelled at their beauty, their shining leather, their gold lettering and all the knowledge locked up inside. Poetry and plays, novels and essays. Every morning she meticulously wiped the dust off those books, knowing that Joga Singh liked nothing better than that hour or two in the evening with his books when he returned from the orchard that he was planting on his family patch. They would have their tea on the balcony, watching the sun sink towards the flat thin horizon and then he would settle into his armchair while she sat on the bed, embroidering or cutting vegetables or just watching him quietly. And thinking how much good she must have done in her last life to have got a husband like Joga Singh. Once in a while, he would want to tell her what he was reading. It opened new worlds to her. Names of cities beyond Jhelum and Rawalpindi, lives of Englishmen and their memsahibs, and sometimes when he tired of the formality of the English language, he would pick up the poets and start reciting—Bulleh Shah, Shah Hussain, Bhai Vir Singh…these all made more sense to her and she flowed easily with the rising falling inflections of his voice, the lilt and the swing, the colour that came into his cheeks and the half-smiling half-wistful look that came into his eyes.

Those had been beautiful days, and had left their gentle memories
of love and caring. But now he was gone, just like her parents and
her masi and her masi's husband. She was again alone in Parhi,
weighed down by the thought of a lifetime of lonely tomorrows.
The once new house to which she had brought life and joy now
seemed a death trap, its walls forever closing in on her.

Chapter 24

The Truth Will Out

Finally, in the beginning of July, Gurnam Singh Gambhir was taken to court in a carriage with three other citizens. That day they were not in handcuffs but were closely guarded by armed constables. The first charge against him was that he had attended several meetings at Dr Kitchlew's house between 30 March and 10 April in which plans had been hatched to burn European bungalows and kill Europeans, boycott courts and British trade, and deliberately spread false rumours. The second charge was that he had been part of the conspiracy to show Hindu–Muslim unity on Ram Navami and the third, which to Gurnam sounded the most ridiculous, was that he had been involved in the conspiracy to incite the crowd on 10 April at the railway line and had later gone around town on horseback, delivering inflammatory speeches.

'This is a falsehood,' Gurnam responded. 'I have never attended any meeting at Dr Kitchlew's house during the period mentioned and have not attended any meeting anywhere for that matter where the issues mentioned were discussed. As to the second charge, while I have advocated fraternization between Hindus and Muslims, I do not believe there was any secret meeting held anywhere for the purpose of creating a show of unity on Ram Navami. And the third charge is a mockery of justice since it is well known that I did my best to disperse the crowd on the bridges and that too at the instance of the Deputy Commissioner. I deny having gone on horseback into town to deliver speeches. I returned Mr Plomer's horse there and then and walked home.'

He was finally acquitted but only on 6 July, after being kept in custody on the flimsiest of grounds for nine weeks and even beyond the martial law. Another prisoner was being released on the same day from Lahore prison. A man of a very gentle demeanour with the organized manner of a government functionary or bank clerk. As they were both waiting to collect their personal belongings from the prison officials, Gurnam looked at the man's face and was surprised to see that it still glowed as if with some inner spiritual light, which months in prison had not been able to take away.

On an impulse Gurnam introduced himself.

'Sat sri akal, ji. I am Gurnam Singh Gambhir, pleader.'

'Sat sri akal. Mehtab Singh, irrigation department,' the man responded. Then he carried on, as if unable to stop himself from sharing what was uppermost in his mind. 'I am happy, not just at leaving prison but because my son will be waiting outside. He has been a soldier in the war and I am going to see him after four years.'

Outside the gate, when Gurnam glanced back after hugging Bhagwan, he saw Mehtab Singh walk up to a tall young man with a soldier's bearing, hold him by both shoulders as if appraising him from head to toe and then hug him tightly while another man resting on a crutch, twirling a cane with a silver lion head handle with his other hand, looked on smilingly. Then he watched them mount a tonga and ride away in the direction of the railway station to catch a train to Amritsar.

૰

The courts were functioning by the time Gurnam came out of prison but he felt a deep abhorrence at the thought of going there again to work. He was aware that several lawyers were still in jail pending their trials; others had started taking cases to defend those being tried by martial law tribunals. But, for Gurnam, something fundamental had changed in those three months. Many things had contributed to the way he felt now. It was not just the flaming anger he had felt at the murder of his countrymen and the humiliation and tribulations that he had suffered himself. Nor even what he had seen as a special constable—the floggings, the whippings, the enforced salaams, the torture of innocent students. Nor the stories coming in about the martial law from Lahore, Kasur, Gujranwala where other incarnations of General Dyer—Lieutenant Colonel Frank Johnson, Colonel O'Brien, Major Carberry, Captain Doveton, and Mr Bosworth-Smith— were teaching their own lessons to the people of Punjab. It was a realization, an immense clarity that had overcome him when he had gone to the Golden Temple after his release: God had given him one life and that too a very finite one; it was up to him to make it count by doing what would allow him to sleep peacefully at night. To go to a British court, even to defend his own countrymen, to address the judge as milord knowing the hollowness of the justice being rendered, was something he would no longer do. If Rabindranath Tagore could renounce his knighthood, Gurnam felt that he could give up pleading in British courts.

His first thought was to write down everything that he had seen or heard in the last three months. He needed to get down on paper as much detail of the events, of individual stories as possible. He didn't know then to what purpose he was doing this but he knew that the government would try to suppress information and then to whitewash it. To counter that, things would need to be on paper and in so much detail that the narrative could not be denied. Indians may be happy to go by word of mouth but if the truth of all that had happened in his city had to be told someday to the world outside, then it needed to be specific—with names, dates, ages, addresses, and it needed to be written down. That was the way the British worked. This was the way their civil service, their judiciary, their newspapermen, their parliament ultimately understood things. And sooner or later more and more people would start asking for the truth. Even when the province had been under a blackout the impression had gathered that things in Punjab had been much worse than the government admitted. Now, with the martial law lifted, political leaders and journalists were beginning to visit Amritsar. Motilal Nehru and Madan Mohan Malaviya had already visited Jallianwala Bagh while Gurnam was still in prison. Gandhi had formally written to the Viceroy demanding an inquiry. Once an inquiry started, Gurnam knew, the detailed columns of information—names, dates, descriptions, eyewitness accounts he had heard, all written down in his neat, slanting writing in long registers would be useful.

∿

Bhagwan could not help a slight start as Gurnam came out of his room wearing a new white khadi kurta pyjama set with his white turban.

'It makes your complexion look a bit dark,' was his only comment. 'That black coat, a lawyer's coat, lifts it.'

'Yes, perhaps,' Gurnam replied. 'But if I go as a Sewa Samiti volunteer from house to house wearing a lawyer's black coat, the doors will not open for me.'

Gurnam had learnt that there were others working at recording the truth. The local charity organization, the Sewa Samiti, which had carried out cremations of more than forty unknown bodies on the day after the massacre, was now collecting information to assess the true number of the dead and wounded. Gurnam joined their efforts. Small teams of volunteers would go from door to door, starting from the lanes around Jallianwala Bagh and fanning out even to the surrounding districts to gather names, ages, photographs. Being a known local person helped: initially people were reluctant to come out and speak; they feared that revealing connections with the victims may get them into more trouble.

When he and fellow volunteers were collecting these details, Jawaharlal Nehru and the Englishman, C. F. Andrews, came to Amritsar. Gurnam and other members of the Sewa Samiti guided them on their visits to the Bagh. Nehru wanted to take as many photographs as possible; he meticulously tried to count the bullet holes on the walls which someone had already circled in white chalk. On one section of wall alone he counted sixty-seven. During those days it fell to Gurnam and the Sewa Samiti members to make sure that the right people, those who had been directly affected or had seen the action with their own eyes, came up to be interviewed by the leaders. One of the people that Gurnam brought was Lala Sunder Das. He told the leaders about Maya Dei, who had sat all night amidst the carnage and of what he had personally seen when he went to get Joga Singh's dead body the next morning. Maya Dei had since left Amritsar with her husband's ashes for their village but if required could always be brought back to record her statement. Lala Sunder Das promised to send his own son to fetch her from across the Jhelum.

Gradually the figures began to emerge. Malaviya said that a thousand people had been killed in Jallianwala Bagh; Gandhi, starting a plea for funds to assist the families of the victims, put the figure at fifteen hundred. Gurnam and his fellow volunteers sat in his old office at home, while Bhagwan brought them round after round of tea and atta biscuits, and tallied the names from their various lists. The figure that they got even at that early stage was of five hundred and thirty dead and the majority could be identified by name. The estimate of the wounded would end up at three times that figure.

'This is going to be crucial evidence,' Gurnam said, holding the lists in his hand. 'These are not just numbers, each number represents a life cut short, a family bereaved. This will be the strongest argument that our leaders will have.'

The government was forced to come up with a figure of its own. At first this was put at less than three hundred but faced with the Sewa Samiti's detailed lists, was later increased to three hundred and seventy-nine; in the weeks to follow even this would widely be seen as an underestimate. Meanwhile, the initial trickle of news of the barbarity of the Baisakhi shooting, the horrible excesses of the martial law, and the callous indifference of Michael O'Dwyer began to spread with even greater speed across the country and to liberal sections of the British media.

The news of Gandhi's impending arrival in Amritsar—his visit having been approved by the Viceroy in October—reached the city a day ahead and caused huge excitement. Gurnam headed out to the railway station much ahead of the arrival time. As he walked across the iron footbridge over the railway line he stopped for a moment and looked around him. Here was where it had all started for him in real earnest just over six months ago when he had tried to stop the shooting by riding on the white police horse between the police and the crowd. So much had happened in those six months, so many people had died, so many lives disrupted. And some things had changed forever: he no longer believed that it was possible to work with the British or expect understanding and accommodation. Probably there were thousands more who had come to the same conclusion, including the slight, bald man with the reedy voice dressed in a white homespun dhoti who was about to reach Amritsar by train.

The railway station was choked with people; it seemed the entire city had turned out to greet the man whose name was on every tongue, but who had not been allowed to come here during all these difficult months. His arrival itself was a victory, a vindication. Gurnam joined the joyous procession that escorted the

Mahatma to the bungalow of Lala Girdharilal Malik in Panjmahal.

Gandhi's arrival galvanized political activity in the city. The Hunter Committee had been set up by the Viceroy in the middle of October. But its refusal to interview imprisoned nationalist leaders like Kitchlew and Satyapal resulted in the Committee being boycotted by Gandhi and the Congress. Gurnam joined a few other workers in pleading with Pandit Malaviya:

'This is so much evidence we have collected that will go waste if we don't get it to the Committee. There are statements, eyewitness accounts....'

Malaviya agreed but he also knew that beyond a point it was futile trying to change Gandhi's mind.

'Nothing will be wasted,' he assured the workers.

And so it was to be. A non-official inquiry committee was set up by the Congress and all the collected information would be studied by it in the coming months. Gurnam's work was cut out for him. He helped the Congress Committee—the bulk of the work of which was being done by Gandhi himself along with C. R. Das—to record and verify the statements of hundreds of people. The statements had to be checked, translated from the vernacular, and checked again. Once the hearings of the Hunter Committee started, the evidence being presented there was also used to corroborate the conclusions that the Congress Committee was reaching on its own. A lawyer's eye and drafting skills were crucial assets. Gurnam did not have a moment to think about anything else: he knew instinctively that he was being far more useful than he had ever been in his life this far. His work, he didn't need to tell himself, would continue not just until the Congress Committee published its report, not just until the December session of the Congress was held in Amritsar, but until the day the firanghi rolled up his Raj and left Indian shores forever.

Chapter 25

Udham Singh Finds His Cause

They called it the Lunatic Line, the railway that ran for 600 treacherous miles from the coastal town of Mombasa to the shores of Lake Victoria. You had to be mad to come to work here, and if you weren't then you would become mad by the time the line was done with you. The coolies from India were bonded labour; they were working to pay off loans they had already taken, and often already consumed. They were powerless to protest the brutal conditions of work imposed by slave-driving railway managers, the filth of the labour camps, the lack of medical provisions to stave off the ravages of malaria. The trains had to be kept running on the line that had been built a few years earlier; British troops and guns were to be deposited into interior Africa and valuable materials brought back to the coast to be shipped home. Day and night they worked to keep the line open, to maintain the dozens of wooden trestle bridges, to lay the branch lines and even reassemble old steamers for Africa's rivers and lakes. Through all this, the workers died or survived depending on how tough they were.

Udham Singh was tougher than most. He could handle the hours, the mosquitoes, the plank beds, even the wild animals: he had scared off a leopard as a child near the rail crossing of Upali. The conditions and the work didn't get to him; he let it all slip off his broad shoulders. The managers hated the swagger in his walk but when their abuse had no impact, some of them began to treat him differently, as if he were a cut above the others. His ready smile, glib talk, and easy charm could win over the unlikeliest of men.

But what he found difficult to handle was the news from Punjab that had started trickling through in letters and from fresh arrivals on ships. News of how Dyer had killed hundreds in Jallianwala Bagh, how he had made people crawl, how he had young boys whipped till they fainted. A wild rage seemed to take hold of him every time any fresh news came. The blood would rise to his head and his whole body would be afire. He seethed for revenge and the fact that he was not there among the dead and wounded gave him the conviction that he had been saved to be their avenger.

However, the realization soon settled in that impotent rage alone would lead nowhere. The men that he wanted to get his hands on were citizens of a distant world of privilege and position and he needed to find a way of equipping himself to crash into that world. And he would get there, he told himself over and over again; while both O'Dwyer and Dyer seemed out of reach at present they could be followed to the ends of the earth: all that was needed was to find a way to bring them within his grasp. The Uganda Railway Company though was not the place to be and even though two years still remained of the contract he had signed with Mr Andrews in Lahore, Udham Singh gave the managers the slip and disappeared into Africa.

～

The four Indians in the dimly lit room were trying to assess him. Impassive faces watched his every gesture, weighed every word. Udham had to make this meeting count: this would be the closest he would ever get to the inner team of Sitaram Acharya, the leading Ghadar revolutionary in east Africa.

The questions continued into the night but gradually he began to feel an acceptance.

'And you are willing to go back to Amritsar?'

'If necessary.'

'You can be arrested on arrival. You have broken your contract.'

'I need a fresh passport.'

'How can you get that?'

'I have another name. Many people only know me as Sher Singh.'

Then Udham tried to push his luck.

'I will do what I have to in Hindustan; I have worked for Ghadar before. But I can do more than just distribute newspapers and carry messages. I need to get to America, to England. I can be very useful.'

The men exchanged glances; yes, they seemed to say, they might find something useful that needed doing.

But first there were jobs to be done in India. He travelled back on a new passport issued in his birth name, Sher Singh. On one page of that passport, thanks to his revolutionary friends, there was a valuable endorsement for travel to America. His arrival in Sunam, his home town in Punjab, caused a minor sensation—here was not just a man who had been overseas but one with a new motorcycle and cash to spare. Every few days he would vanish on the motorcycle for brief periods. But he never said a word about where he went.

In the evenings, the town's young men would gather around him, drawn by his adventurous ways but also by the fact that once in a while he would reveal the existence of some secret purpose. On those occasions, in the midst of his bragging, his face would become steely still, his eyes would narrow, and his voice would take on the tone of a holy promise.

'Haan, this motorcycle is mine, bought with my own money. Who else can it belong to? Has anybody else in Sunam been across the sea? Only I. And only I have close friends in other countries—in America—who love me. Sab jigri dost hain mere, bosom friends. They will help me and together we will throw out these firanghis. They have ruled enough. Someone has to do it. One of us has to do it.'

Nobody knew whether all this was just empty talk. But one thing seemed certain: a restlessness in his manner made it clear that he wouldn't be staying in Sunam for long. And so, nobody was surprised when one day Udham Singh sold his motorcycle and simply vanished, not to return for a very long time. He is meant for bigger things, his admirers said, we will hear news of his exploits one day.

Chapter 26

Hugh Porter Goes Home

In December 1919, four months after his visit to Amritsar, Chief Secretary Porter started his appearances before the Hunter Committee. By then he was well prepared to answer the questions posed to him even by the more aggressive three Indian members. He reiterated that General Dyer was correct in opening fire when he did in order to quell the uprising. He dodged the question as to whether the Punjab government had approved of the killing of three hundred and seventy-nine unarmed people—the final number officially given out. There was no way of saying how much bloodshed was the right amount under these circumstances: the amount of bloodshed that produced the right result was justified. All very clever answers, the sort that are given by lawyers and debaters and diplomats. But he had to admit: the number of deaths was probably more than that needed to produce the desired effect.

The real test came when one of the Indian members of the committee, Sardar Sahibzada Sultan Ahmed Khan, asked him point blank:

'Do I understand that if you were placed in the same position as General Dyer you would have acted in the same fashion?'

'Probably not—I should not have had the pluck.'

'We will presume you had the pluck.'

'Possibly I should not have gone on firing as long as General Dyer.'

A few weeks after that, Porter finally started on his voyage home for his long-awaited vacation with his family, having answered the questions posed by the members of the Hunter Committee as best as he could have. Nobody in the system, he was certain, could fault him for showing any doubts or misgivings. The Committee would take some months to come up with its report and Porter knew that Gandhi would come up with his own report by then. Porter had no doubt that the Indian members of the Hunter Committee and Gandhi's report would come down very hard on Dyer. He wondered what they would say about Sir Michael O'Dwyer, whom many people in India believed to be the real villain of the piece: they even conflated the two similar names to make them into a common symbol of hate. One point still troubled Porter on occasion—and this had also been the subject of some questioning by the Hunter Committee: the Punjab government had given their approval but had they done so believing that Dyer's action had been right, or to show solidarity within the government and reveal no cracks between the civil and military authorities? O'Dwyer had identified totally with Dyer but Porter was not too sure about himself. In the quiet of the voyage, far away from Amritsar, he could acknowledge to himself that he had defended the approval because no amount of disapproval could have brought the dead again to life; on the other hand, any sign of disapproval would have shown the government's vulnerability and that was not the way of the Punjab school of administration. How innocent had he been, he thought, when he had reached Gurdaspur on his first posting; he had no idea then of what all one has to do in the line of duty.

As the journey progressed, his thoughts moved on from the difficult events of the past few months and ranged across the twenty years he had spent in India. By and large it had been a rewarding time, perhaps it had even spooled out a little too quickly for his liking.

He recalled that faraway November day, at the turn of the century, when he had boarded the P&O SS *Malabar*, and an India career seemed to stretch forever into the future. Full of exciting possibilities, adventure, and glory. All that he had ever read about men like Hastings, Wellesley, Dalhousie, Bentick had been very much with him and the thought that he had joined their ranks always brought a smile to his face and a slight sense of disbelief that such things could happen.

That first journey, although it would be followed by many more in the years to come, was etched in his mind. That handing over the last letter, written to his father, to the lanky, square-jawed pilot wearing velvet gloves who turned back from the Isle of Wight. The last view of the English coast and the Dover cliffs in the early morning haze. That warm feeling that he left without any regret in the world, all loose ends of his youth neatly tied.

The *Malabar* was a luxurious ship with at least fifty in first class and thirty in second. It could move fast, covering two hundred and eighty miles every day. There were leisurely dinners on board of soup, fish, steaks, and several kinds of dessert to follow. Coffee and whisky were served by Anglo-Indian and Goan waiters who would stylishly lean towards the guests and whisper 'say when' as they topped up the drinks.

In the Mediterranean, a flannel suit was enough to keep one comfortable on deck, staring at the sparkling blue sea in all its moods, with playful porpoises performing for the passengers all day. Or smoking on deck on starlit nights with eyes half shut, and deciphering the strange language that the lascar shiphands shouted out across the deck over the noise of the wind and the sea.

There was even a game of cricket when they disembarked to stretch their legs in Malta; Porter had felt good, limbering up for a patch of half decent spin bowling. There were no dances, largely on account of the shortage of women on board. There were two or three, all slightly faded wives of officers stationed in India who seemed content to talk to each other, or smoke quietly at one end of the deck, experimenting tentatively with a new-found freedom.

In his mind that journey was linked forever to the taste of Arabic coffee, first sipped in Alexandria. He had never been able to get the cooks in India to reproduce that thick texture, sweetened with sugar granules, rich with warm cardamom. And the magical sights that he saw from the deck as the ship went through the Suez and the Red Sea: the hills melting into a mauve haziness at dusk, the water turning the colour of molten lead, the sand of the Arab lands changing colour—from gold to brown to pitch black—as the sun reached for the horizon, and the stars that hung bright and low above the sea, some of them bright enough to leave their own separate paths of light on the water.

Then, one morning, the chief engineer, a huge, gregarious Irishman with a barrel chest and a sailor's white beard, came by to the dining hall where most of the passengers were sitting with their second coffees after finishing breakfast.

'Excuse the break, gentlemen. One of the lascars died last night. We will soon conduct a funeral.'

They stepped out on deck as the ship's engines died out and watched in sombre silence as, after a brief prayer, the body, wrapped in a sheet, and weighed down with pieces of lead, was lowered into a restless sea. Then the waves closed over the body, and it vanished into the deep. Porter thought for a moment that if he had indeed been a parson, and travelling on this ship, it would have fallen to him to perform the service. But then he dismissed the thought. He was not a parson but a fresh recruit in the Indian Civil Service and he could guiltlessly turn back to *Wuthering Heights* for the rest of the day.

But all that was long ago. Now he was going home, where Milly and the boys were waiting for him. It would be a good time to listen to them; he must take care not to talk too much

himself. It was also a good time to rest; his heart needed it. And
to catch up on his reading—Sophocles, Turgenev, and Conrad.
He intended to play some tennis on deck too. His latest medical
examination had shown that his kidneys were free of albumen.
It would also be useful to catch up on writing his still fresh
recollections of the last few weeks in his Collins diary, in which
he devoted one page to each day, keeping the back pages for
a monthly cash summary. A full page would be devoted to the
special visit he had paid to his daughter's grave in Simla, after
handing over charge.

He did not know it then but he would visit the grave once
more, in 1948, a year after India's Independence, and a year before
his own death. He would note then that if she had lived, she
would have been forty-six, exactly the age he had been at the
time of the massacre in Jallianwala Bagh.

PART V

Chapter 27

Many Streams Make a River

Before heading home to Dharamsinghwala, Mehtab insisted that Ralla and Kirpal accompany him to the Golden Temple. The three of them were alive and together and that was a miracle in itself, given all that had happened in Amritsar over the last few months. At the gurudwara, they bowed before the Granth Sahib in thanksgiving, took the prasad, and ate a quick meal at the langar before their journey. As they were leaving the complex, Mehtab Singh stopped for a moment and turned back to look. He shook his head in a gesture of helpless disappointment and then the three of them headed off to the railway station.

The train journey to Lahore and then to Lyallpur was long and Mehtab found himself ruminating on much that had happened and so much that needed to be done. When he had looked back at the Golden Temple, it had been with pain: the holiest of sites was being misused by the wrong people. It was known by then that three weeks after he had opened fire on the unarmed crowd at Jallianwala Bagh, General Dyer and his brigade major, Captain Briggs, had been honoured at the Golden Temple by its manager, Arur Singh. They were invested with the five symbols of the Khalsa: Dyer had boasted that he had been made an honorary Sikh and even been exempted from keeping long hair. Everyone knew that Arur Singh was a sycophant and puppet of the DC and that Dyer was using him, and he was willing to be used.

But the problem was bigger than one Arur Singh, bigger than even the issue of who had control of the Golden Temple. When the Sikhs were being persecuted by the Mughals and Afghans, and

were forced to hide in forests or live in the saddle, the control
of their shrines was in the hands of the priests of the Udasi sect,
the mahants, who could escape persecution since they wore no
outwards signs of being Sikhs. But in the days of Maharaja Ranjit
Singh and the Sikh chieftains, the austerity and religious purity
of the mahants had deteriorated quickly under the temptations
of rich offerings to the gurudwaras; the coming of the canals
had increased manifold the value of the lands granted to the
gurudwaras and the mahants had turned the shrines into personal
fiefdoms. In exchange, they were happy to be the cat's paws of
the rulers. Not just satisfied with being corrupt and venal, the
mahants had also shown a flagrant disregard for Sikh scriptures
and practices. Polite demands by the community presented through
weak resolutions passed by Sikh organizations had little impact on
the situation. The vested interests of the mahants, the loyalists, and
the British authorities had come together in an unholy alliance.

The train rolled over the bridge on the Ravi and into the
dark night. Mehtab watched his son, sleeping with his head resting
on an army kitbag in which he was carrying all his belongings.
His son was now a grown-up young man, one who had already
travelled more than he could ever dream of doing, one who had
seen war and death, victories and setbacks, blood and pain. And
he himself was going to be forty-seven. He didn't know how
much time he had left. Life, as had been so obvious in the last
few months, could throw up unpleasant surprises. Soon, he must
bequeath the world to his son. A world that consisted not just
of his house and fields but a world of values, beliefs, traditions,
convictions. Whatever he did now, Mehtab was clear, would not
just be a job and certainly not a job for this brutal regime.
A mission was tugging at his mind: Arur Singh's treachery in
honouring Dyer had again awakened his passion to work towards
recovering the purity of the gurudwaras that had been so badly
besmirched these past decades; the sanctity of these holy places

had always been deeply ingrained in his soul, it had been part of his heritage. If only he could leave a heritage for his son of the kind that his grandfather and father had left him!

◈

Mehtab had heard the story many times from his grandfather. Of the time when Rattan Singh had been a young man, riding furiously through the driving rain on his black horse to Tibba.

'It was a very dark night,' Rattan Singh would say almost in a whisper to his grandson, rocking him gently on his knee. 'Very dark. Not a star, no moon, and thick jungle. The jungle of Harike. You've seen the Sutlej, that big river? There is another big river, called the Beas and the two meet at Harike. There is so much water at the confluence; it's like an ocean out there. When you grow up, you should go and see for yourself.'

The scene would come alive before the young boy's eyes. The black horse, the tall grass, the flashes of lightning that lit up the clumps of trees with their vast trunks, spreading canopies, and laughing, shrieking demons swinging from the branches.

'But Dara, my horse, was very strong. He could run a hundred miles without stopping. I patted him on the neck and we carried on, keen to reach our home in Tibba. We were not going to be scared by a simple storm.'

Mehtab would wait for the moment in the story when the lightning crackled all over the sky and the night suddenly turned into day and a man could be seen standing in the swampy grass under a tree, one arm outstretched towards the rider. The first time he heard the story, that moment had scared him but after that first telling as he knew what would come next, he no longer felt afraid; rather a feeling of warmth and reassurance would come over him.

When he came to this point in the story, Rattan Singh would gently put down Mehtab from his knee and stand up himself. He liked to act this bit out, as if it were all happening right then and not thirty years ago. That image would stay with Mehtab all his life: his grandfather, with his short white turban and his thinning white beard, walking to and fro on the flat roof of their village house, silhouetted against a moonlit sky, playing both himself and the man he had met.

'"Who's there?" I shouted. At first, I heard nothing, only the rain, and I thought I must have imagined something. Then I saw the man again and went closer. Again, the lightning flashed and it was clear as afternoon. It was not a demon, just an old Muslim man with a long white beard.'

And Rattan Singh would make a gesture as if elongating his own beard.

'He was wrapped up in a thick blanket and his face was wrinkled. But his voice was strong.

'"You have a beautiful horse, Sardara. I have been walking for many days. There were troubles up north. I left in a hurry. That was the only way to save my life. I don't know what happened to the others."

'"Where are you going? Do you want to ride with me?"

'"I have to go very far; I don't even know where. You cannot take me there. Give me your horse."

'"Give you my horse? This horse has fought with Maharaja Sher Singh at Chillianwala! Are you out of your mind, old man?"

'"No, I'm not. And I am not robbing you of your horse. I have something which should be of great value to you."

'Then he opened up his blanket and revealed a bundle wrapped up in a thick shawl. I looked at it closely.

'"Don't ask me questions now, Sardar. This is your Guru Granth, your holy book. Take it and go, and may your God bless your coming generations."

'I don't know what happened to me. I began to shiver uncontrollably. I got off the horse and took the Granth Sahib in my hands and bowed my head over it. Then I wrapped it up again in the shawl. I looked up—the man was already in Dara's saddle and was wheeling him around.

"'Khuda hafiz, Sardar. You will never regret this deal."

'Then he was gone as if he had never been there. If Dara had not vanished with him or the Granth Sahib hadn't actually been in my hands, I would have thought the whole thing had been a vision, that someone had made me swallow a ball of opium without my knowing. But it was God's will, his way of giving me a mission in life.'

All his life, every time that Mehtab prayed for strength, he prayed for the steadfast resolve that his grandfather had shown. For the next thirty years, Rattan Singh had devoted his life to the care and service of the Holy Book. He first built a small wooden shack in Tibba in which barely six or seven people could sit and listen to the recitations. Soon, the shack made way for a room of burnt mud bricks. A small triangular yellow flag fluttered at the door. An oil lantern threw shadows on the walls as Rattan Singh read the hymns, more from memory than by sight.

Even in the freezing months of Poh and Magh—and even on his last day—he would be up at half past four, with the stars still bright in the brittle sky. He would bathe in the open patch behind the gurudwara with a bucket of water that had been drawn from the well the previous evening and kept indoors under a blanket, lest it become ice during the night. Reciting the Japji under his breath he would change into his long white shirt with the silver buttons, which were his one luxury in life, and pull on a fresh pair of stitched breeches. He did not need a mirror to tie, with three left-handed swivels, his white turban and to run his fingers through his sparse beard. Then he would enter the gurudwara, open the Granth Sahib and start reciting the Asa di Var. If there was no one else present, he would recite it under his breath but the moment he saw anyone, usually one of the older men or women, framed in the doorway against the inky dawn sky, he would raise his voice.

Soon, his wife Satwant Kaur would take the halwa off the chula and put it into the wide brass bowl and, wrapping it in clean muslin, would carry it across the small patch of grass that separated the house from the gurudwara. The smell of the sweet halwa—that heavenly mix of flour, sugar, and home-made ghee—cooked over the wood fire was one of the earliest smells that Mehtab Singh could recall. Whenever he got a whiff of that smell anywhere, in any gurudwara or at a wedding ceremony, he would recall his grandmother's face, the fair, dimpled face with its golden nose ring and deep-set, honey-coloured eyes. This was forever her smell; not only did it fill the house in the mornings, it remained in her clothes and her dupatta and hair all day and when she hugged him close to her, it rubbed off on him, too. This halwa, consecrated in the presence of the Holy Book, would become prasad, something sacred, which each of the members present would eat as if it were touched by God himself; sometimes they would not eat it all, because it was not the eating that mattered, even a speck was enough for salvation. They would take it back home in a shiny brass katori, covered with a white embroidered handkerchief, to their sleeping sons and daughters, who upon awakening would look for it, on the only stool in the house, or on the mantelpiece. And those who had no sons and daughters to give it to would give it to the birds that sat on the gurudwara wall, the sparrows and common black crows, or to the three dogs lazing in the village square, to enable them to transmigrate to a human existence, if not complete liberation from these eighty-four hundred thousand relentless cycles of life and death.

Mehtab would always turn to that vision of the gurudwara and of his grandparents whenever his mind was troubled, or the conflicts and contradictions of the moment seemed insurmountable. Then he would withdraw inwards, searching for strength, perhaps in his soul, perhaps in the subconscious understanding of the scriptures that he knew so well by heart. But always first, that vision of dedicated service from the ethereal ambrosial hour of dawn to dusky twilight, would sustain him, telling him who he was, where he came from, and what he should do.

By the time they reached Dharamsinghwala, travelling the last bit from Lyallpur in a lorry, Mehtab's mission was fully formed in his mind. He would join the Akali movement and work to oust the mahants from the gurudwaras. In his mind, the colonial oppressors and the corrupt controllers of the Sikh shrines had become one; his duty now lay at the Harmandir Sahib, as an active Akali. A few weeks later he left Dharamsinghwala and headed to Gujranwala to hand in his resignation to the irrigation department and then went back to Amritsar. His conscience wouldn't let him take another day's salary from a government that had been responsible for Jallianwala Bagh.

૨

Ralla was happy to stay those few days in Dharamsinghwala. This was the only family he had and even now, so many years after her death, he could feel the warm presence of his sister Jindi. Nobody mentioned her name but it was she who tied him to Mehtab and Kirpal in a circle of affection and caring. Mehtab's mother, almost seventy now, had been so excited by the return of all three of them that she had shed the aches and infirmities of her advancing years and given herself over to feeding and looking after them. The tandoor would be fired up in the forenoon, and she would herself put in the rotis, then take them out with the long iron seekh and lather them with white home-made butter. The saag and the dal would already be on the chula in earthen pots, creamy and fragrant. And she had made a full jar of Kirpal's favourite sweet pickle—cauliflower, carrots, and thinly sliced turnips cooked in mustard oil and jaggery.

As he rested in the village, Ralla began to recover the strength
in his wounded leg. Every day he tried to walk a little more,
and see if he could walk a few steps without his crutch. Kirpal
would walk with him, on the same paths that they had walked
when Ralla had visited them once before, up to the canal and
back. And when Ralla tired, he would hold on to his nephew's
strong shoulder.

On those walks, Kirpal often talked to his uncle about the
war and of things that he hadn't even had the time to tell his
father. He told him of the loneliness of his first voyage in 1914
from Karachi when he had first understood the meaning of kala
pani, the dark waters, and why sending somebody across the kala
pani was the ultimate exile, the final banishment, the breaking of
caste, the loss of faith. And he talked of his fellow recruits—or
rangroots—as the veterans of the battalion referred to them, sepoys
Bir Singh and Hazur Singh, all of whom were taken under his
wing by Lance Naik Buta Singh. And of how, months later, a
German bullet got Buta Singh through his left temple, and he
fell like a stone and Kirpal had got his body back to the trench
pushing it inch by inch on the icy ground, pretending to be dead
whenever he sensed that the enemy could be watching. And of
the German he had killed with his bayonet and how the blood
had spurted from his dying heart.

Ralla listened, patiently, quietly, knowing that the boy needed
to talk of all these things, to unburden himself. At times, Kirpal
would be overcome by emotion. At other times, he would lapse
into long silences. But soon, once Mehtab got ready to leave for
Gujranwala, these walks ended. Ralla too felt the need to return
to his duties with the Sant of Alibegh.

As he prepared to say his farewell, Ralla said: 'We will try
to meet at least once every year. And I will make sure that I
reply to all your letters.' What he left unsaid was that the awful
night in Jallianwala Bagh had shown him the fragility of life, the

suddenness of death, and how important it was to be with one's loved ones as often as one could be.

∾

After his father had gone away to Gujranwala with a new determination in his step, and Ralla had returned to Akhnoor, Kirpal was overcome with a fatigue that showed no signs of going away. He knew that this was not fatigue of the body, not of bone and muscle, but of the spirit, deep inside. Not yet twenty-three, he was already tiring of the world; in four years of war and in the last few months at Amritsar he had already seen too much for one lifetime.

Life and politics, all talk of rulers and ruled, of protests and agitations, of freedom and Empire only brought up the bile in his throat. He no longer felt the strength in him to protect or to overcome, to kill or be victorious. All that he had been doing with pride now seemed so useless, futile. The uniform, the rank, the glory of battle was a sham, a huge deception. He had been blind; his friends had died for the wrong reasons. Now that he could see things clearly, he should never have allowed himself to be recruited, to be beguiled by that obsequious tehsildar, to be tempted by the gun and boots, the uniform, the eleven rupees a month, and the promise of adventure in foreign lands. Tehsildars, he now knew, had been given quotas to fulfil; their own future depended on being able to recruit more and more young men to please their colonial masters. He and his fellow soldiers had just been fodder, cheap fodder—black pepper, as they were known—for a king who was not his king, for a king who didn't care for them and was still punishing them. The vision of his company trudging back from the front lines in Europe in 1915 came back to him: tired men pushing one foot after another, sleepwalking. Blood-stained bandages, mud-caked stiff boots, torn and bedraggled puttees on their legs. Weeks of crouching in trenches had given them bent knees and bent backs. The stench of the heavily fermented straw of the trenches would stay long in their nostrils. And what had he come back to? The senseless murder of his people at Jallianwala Bagh by men with whom he had gone to battle shoulder to shoulder.... To martial law, humiliation, floggings, arrests, torture.... To wheat at five-and-a-half rupees a maund and barley at three-rupees-and-a-half and even straw at two rupees a bundle.

For days he lay from morning to dusk in a charpai at the edge of the fields. The sun was no longer that of high summer, and the green was comforting to eyes tired by months of staring at snow and desert. His grandmother would bring him his food and take care of anything else he might need but she understood, with the wisdom of age, why he preferred his solitude. The only way he could calm his mind was by being alone with his thoughts.

∾

About a year after the shooting in Jallianwala Bagh, the protests against the corrupt controllers of the Sikh gurudwaras, in particular the Golden Temple, became louder. Akali reformers began to gather day after day on the parikrama, the marble walkway around the sarovar. Speakers demanded the resignation of Arur Singh, the sarbrah who had honoured Dyer. The DC tried to protect his man and sent him away on two months leave. But that only infuriated the protestors even more. In a large gathering held at Jallianwala Bagh at the end of August 1920, the leaders of the reform movement threatened to burn an effigy of the sarbrah. Suddenly, Arur Singh came out of hiding and, apologizing before the congregation with folded hands, resigned his position. A committee was formed to take care of the affairs of the Golden Temple and Mehtab Singh was nominated as one of its members. But the battle was only half won; the government would continue, through one device or another, to keep a hand in the running of shrine.

The call for reform spread to other shrines. The Akali jathas, realizing the power of non-violent protest, used it to wrest back control from the mahants of various gurudwaras. The mahants of the smaller shrines read the mood of the people and gave up without much resistance but others, such as those controlling the major gurudwaras at Panja Sahib and Tarn Taran, had to be pushed out through determined campaigns.

The fight for the freedom of Nankana Sahib, the birthplace of Sikhism's founder Guru Nanak, from the hands of the licentious Mahant Narain Das would exact an even higher price. The mahant had invested deeply in cultivating the local British authorities and had fortified himself with an army of mercenaries with sufficient quantities of arms and ammunition as well as swords, axes, sickles, and lathis. The commissioner of Lahore, C. M. King, assured him of protection in case of an Akali attempt to take over the shrine. When, in February 1921, an unarmed Akali jatha landed up with the intention of praying peacefully at the shrine and departing, they were trapped and massacred by the mahant's men. Their bodies, some badly mutilated, were then unceremoniously burnt by pouring kerosene on them.

This was no longer a matter that concerned only the Sikhs. National leaders such as Mahatma Gandhi, Maulana Shaukat Ali, Dr Kitchlew, and Lala Lajpat Rai visited Nankana and condemned the murder of innocents. Nor was it just the corrupt mahants who would be held culpable; the foreign government was equally to blame: the police, the administration, and the judiciary had all turned a blind eye to the killings. Mahatma Gandhi called the tragedy at Nankana a 'second edition of Dyerism'; Jallianwala Bagh had given a new idiom to the struggle from colonial rule. When the names of those who were killed at Nankana were compiled, among them was Ralla Singh of Tibba village, a follower of

the Sant of Alibegh who had joined the call for the reform of
gurudwaras issued by his brother-in-law, Mehtab.

The tragedy at Nankana had made one thing clear: it would not
be possible to fully oust the mahants as long as they enjoyed the
support of the government. The Akali movement was broadened.
It became a part of the mainstream non-cooperation movement
and received full support from the Indian National Congress and
other nationalist forces. When in January 1922 the government
buckled under the Akali agitation and handed over complete
control of the Golden Temple, symbolized by the keys to the
toshakhana, the treasure house of the shrine, Mahatma Gandhi
congratulated the Akalis for winning the 'first battle for India's
freedom'.

◇

It would soon be three years to the massacre but the echoes of
those gunshots were still reverberating throughout the country.
Something had changed fundamentally on that day. All talk
of gradual political reforms, all pretence of benign rule by the
colonialists had been shown up for what it was—a cynical and
wretched charade.

   Dyer, the Indians knew, had been virtually allowed to go
scot-free. Only removed from his military appointment in India,
only prevented from getting further promotions, and allowed to
go quietly into retirement. Huge sums of money were being
collected for him. That was no punishment. A sizeable section of
the British political establishment, the public at large, and the media
lauded him for saving India for the Empire. And even those who
criticized him sought to limit any damage to the larger reputation
of the Empire by treating him as an aberration, a man who went
rogue for his own reasons. Nobody was held responsible for the
imposition of martial law and its excesses. Sir Michael O'Dwyer,

who was responsible for enforcing conscription, throttling political aspirations, abandoning judicial process, and abusing every aspect of his power in his attempt to crush the spirit of Punjab, was a grandee in England, vigorously defending Dyer. It was only to be expected of a man whose own record in Punjab was reviled by those he had been expected to rule with a just and fair hand.

The news, a few months apart, of the death of Ralla and the repeated arrests of his father during the reform agitation brought Kirpal back to Amritsar. His time in Dharamsinghwala had settled his thoughts and clarified his mind, and he was ready to join battle again. He no longer had any doubts which side he was on and what he was fighting for. He would fight, by the side of his father, against the forces of colonial brutality, first at the Guru ka Bagh agitation, and then at Jaito. Without raising a hand, for these were battles of the spirit, he would suffer the lathi blows of the mounted police on his shoulders and his chest, each blow fuelling his determination to resist the oppressor.

Kirpal was one of many millions of ordinary Indians sickened by depredations and injustices such as Jallianwala Bagh, who now rose up against the foreign rulers. There was to be no compromise; the battle for freedom was now on for real and could only end in one way. All the streams of the struggle—Gandhi's non-cooperation, the Khilafat Movement, the revolutionaries, and the Akali agitation for the reform of the gurudwaras—would mingle into a river of national awakening flowing inexorably to its ultimate destination: swaraj.

Chapter 28

A Butcher Gets Full Honours

'Bloody rain. It had to today,' thought Nicholas Williams, as the retired sergeant pulled the waterproof cape over his shoulders and brushed the raindrops off his peaked cap. He thought of opening his umbrella and then decided against it. It would be difficult to manage the cape and the umbrella and shake hands at the same time with the other old soldiers of the 25th Cyclist Battalion of the London Regiment waiting outside the Wellington Barracks this rainy July morning. Besides, there was no dignity in marching behind the cortege holding an umbrella. A soldier must always look like a soldier, so let the damn cap get wet. A small gesture for a former boss, especially one who had been a good soldier and of whom it was said that he didn't know the meaning of fear, whether in the jungles of Burma or on the wild Afghan frontier.

Brigadier General Dyer's body would soon be brought out of the Guards' Chapel and put on the waiting gun carriage. It was right, Williams thought, to think of one so recently departed only in good terms. This was not the time to dwell on the General's tarnished reputation, besmirched by the relentless rat-a-tat of bullets in Amritsar over eight years ago now. There were enough bad nights when he would wake up to silent screams and a memory of hundreds of men in white, running in every direction in an enclosed space, towards unrelenting walls and narrow crowded exits and falling, always falling. Today, he didn't want to tempt that nightmare. He would rather keep his mind on Dyer's good qualities and his eyes on his former mates.

And on the women. The number of women waiting for Dyer's body to come out was surprisingly large, carrying wreaths, dressed in mourning black, wiping tears. Women saw Dyer as their saviour, the man who had prevented another mutiny. He had shielded them from the worst nightmare of every British family in India: the rape of Englishwomen at the hands of the barbarian natives. More than six hundred women had written to the *Morning Post* seeking to get the government's judgement against Dyer revoked. Many even believed that Dyer had been right in making Indians crawl in the lane where Miss Sherwood had been assaulted.

Lost in his reverie, Williams found himself staring at the inscription on a wreath held by an old lady: '*To the great, gallant, noble soldier, General Dyer, from a Major's daughter.*'

Yes, the sergeant nodded to himself, in some lives it was all about rank. Even now, five years since the 25th Cyclist Battalion had simply petered out—some men taken into Signals and the others allowed to go home—he perked up when people called him sergeant—in the neighbourhood, or at the school where he worked, or even among the costermongers. He found himself straightening up, holding his head higher, walking smarter. He missed those years with the battalion in India; he missed being a sergeant on active duty, the uniform, the salutes, the responsibility, the pride: it had all ended too soon. He understood how important it was to that old lady to say that she was a major's daughter. For the same reason, the man being buried was being called a general. That's how he was known—among the India hands and among the Indians too—to all those who supported him or hated him. Few would bother with the detail that he had held only a temporary rank of brigadier general, which was taken away from him when he was relieved of the command of 5 Brigade after the controversy. He didn't get to keep that rank after retirement too, though he did try; an almighty fight had erupted between the high-ups in the War Office and the India Office and the issue of his rank got lost somewhere in all that. The man now lying in his coffin was Colonel Dyer. But he would always be called General.

Williams was drawn to the soldiers gathered in the courtyard. They were all like him, a little older now, a little less cared for, a bit worn out. He could identify with their bereft looks and uncertain demeanour, somewhat lost out of their crisp uniforms with lapels and patch pockets and shiny buttons. All that had vanished with the battalion; they were just a bunch of ordinary men past their prime, struggling to make a living.

A few men recognized the sergeant and saluted him. Some others who could not place him immediately, saluted too because the others had. They began to speak, saying the usual things that are heard on such occasions.

'You were close to him, Sarge. Hear he was sick lately.'

'Stroke, they said. Hard arteries, that's what took him.'

'Brave man, though, bravest in India.'

'Didn't get a fair deal, they did in him, all of them.'

'The Lords saved him, else they would have hanged him.'

'No way, the people were for him too.'

'Who knows what would have happened in Punjab if he hadn't opened fire that day. Another mutiny. Sure did away with that one.'

Williams's heart warmed to the men. This is where he belonged, where he was respected, where he was known. And it had been a long journey getting there. A journey that had begun in the slum tenements of Admiral Mews in London and carried on to the railyard where he had joined a gang of boys to clean the coal dust from the seats and floors of rail carriages for a few shillings.

Everything had changed the day he had seen the beautiful poster glued on a rail carriage, a poster that showed three men in uniform: army tunics, peaked caps with chin straps, polished long leather boots. Two of them were carrying rifles while one leaned on a bicycle and looked on. Two bicycles lay on the ground, all kitted up with leather pouches and rolled sleeping bags. The bold text on the poster said *A Few Smart Men Wanted for The London Cyclists* and in smaller letters below: *25th (C. Of L.) Cyclist Bn of the London Regiment.* When war broke out with Germany, the Cyclists, fast-moving and light, were the first line of defence against any large-scale invasion from Europe: their job was to deter and harry the invader on the coast. That's where Williams had stayed for the first fifteen months after recruitment, almost in sight of France but not destined to go there. One November night the orders came to proceed to Chiseldon, without their bicycles, and prepare for service in East Africa as infantrymen. Topis, drill uniforms, and stores were issued to the battalion marked '4th East African Brigade' and then suddenly taken back. Revised orders were on the way for the new infantry brigade: they were to sail not for Africa but for India. Somewhere in all this reorganization of the Cyclists into infantry, Nicholas Williams had been promoted to a sergeant.

It was all destiny, thought Williams now, in the sombre, pensive mood that had descended on the gathering outside Wellington Barracks, even as there was some movement at the chapel entrance. He again brushed the rain off his cap and finally opened his umbrella. Just destiny: if the brigade, including the 25th Cyclists, had gone to Kenya as intended, he would not have been standing in the drizzle, waiting for the body of General Dyer to be brought out. It was Dyer's destiny, too, that he was getting a full military funeral in London—the Guards' Chapel, the gun carriage, the streets closed; in one stroke, all the infamy and disgrace of his departure from India was being wiped away. A short family memorial service had already been held at the All Saints Church in the village of Long Ashton where he had lived out the last two years of his life, cloistered in a tucked-away cottage.

Williams had visited him there once after writing to Annie Dyer, the General's wife, asking for permission. She had written back that he did not see anyone except his sons, daughters-in-law, and grandchildren when they visited, but since Williams had been his ADC, he would make an exception. Williams recalled walking along a narrow path between a hedge and stone wall to St Martin's Cottage. People in Long Ashton barely seemed to know that Dyer lived there so Williams had to ask at the post office. The afternoon had been a disappointment. Dyer could hardly speak and had just nodded to Williams's courtesies from his wheelchair in which his wife had rolled him out in the small garden that overlooked the surrounding countryside rolling away towards Bristol. She had said that the General spent most of his time reading or sitting in the garden watching the birds, unable to move after his stroke.

'He suffered a lot,' one of the men said, reading Williams's mind.

Williams knew what the man meant. For weeks after the shooting, Dyer had been unable to sleep, walking up and down in his rooms, telling himself that he had done his duty. Even years later he had relived the nightmare of Amritsar every day, each time concluding that he had done the right thing by giving the order to fire. The twenty-six thousand pounds collected for him by the *Morning Post* had provided some comfort. More than the money it was the thought that so many people saw him as having saved India for the Empire that cheered him up. It even lessened somewhat the bitterness of being booted out of India by the higher ups, denied any further appointment in India or without, and put on half pay. But he was never the same man after Amritsar. His spirit, his love for science and mathematics had all soured, his life-long dream of inventing a rangefinder abandoned, and gradually he had collapsed under the weight of his own doubts. One stroke and then another one in the final hours had turned him into his own caricature.

The coffin was brought out by eight Irish Guardsmen, their scarlet tunics and bearskins brightening up the grey day. Slowly, they carried it down the steps and placed it on the gun carriage. Dyer's Union Jack, the one that had flown over his headquarters in Jalandhar, was draped over the coffin and on it were placed his sword, medal, and sola topi with its white feathers. Williams, as Dyer's bodyguard at the most crucial time in his career and an NCO, stepped up with the wreath of red carnations from the 25th London Cyclists and placed it on the coffin towards the head. The inscription read: *With the deepest respect and admiration of all Other Ranks of the Battalion.*

The procession moved slowly out of the gate and turned towards the Horse Guard Parade, led by a lone policeman. Three pairs of horses, each with a trooper riding the horse on the left pulled the gun carriage. Behind the carriage were some officers and then the civilian mourners in black. Williams's gaze sought out Annie Dyer, the woman who had guarded Dyer every minute, protected him from all criticism, read to him in his loneliness when his own eyes tired, protested against every slur on his name. She was there with one of her sons and his wife, her own old mother, and other family members that Williams could not identify. Three more cars with family and friends followed slowly, and as the last of these moved out of the courtyard and turned right, the men of the 25th began to march, falling into formation instinctively. It was quite a procession, usually accorded only to public heroes and certainly not to colonels, or even generals for that matter, and all because of destiny, thought Williams.

The cortege turned slowly at Horse Guards Parade and went past the Memorial and past the small groups huddled under umbrellas. Williams looked for any familiar face and then looked away. It was difficult for him to keep his mind on any one thing; thoughts rushed around in his head with a will of their own. This always happened whenever he thought of India or Dyer or

Amritsar and the disjointed memories would leave him with a splitting headache.

On such days he would wish that the 25th had just been demobilized after the Armistice in 1918 like so many other battalions and put on one of those military trains that steamed every eight hours out of Jalandhar station. They would have returned to England and become clerks and teachers and instructors and musicians right then and things would have been so different. But instead, they had been kept back in India and put on a rigorous drill. Some were put on bombing training, others on the Lewis gun and yet others simply spent their days cleaning windows. Patiently, they had lived out each day, one after another, waiting for the time when they could head home. But soon it was Christmas once again and again they had started to decorate the cottages. And the clouds of political discontent had begun to gather.

On such days, a face would come back to him, the face of a Sikh soldier. The man had come off the train at Jalandhar Cantonment while Williams had been on duty with his picket on the platform, looking out for any untoward incident, or sign of restiveness in the returning units. Spared from bodyguard duty since Dyer was spending most of those days in Flagstaff House, Williams had been glad to be away and curious to see these men who had survived the European battlefields to which the Cyclists never made it. All these Indian soldiers were now suspect, they might indulge in looting or join the protests against the Rowlatt Bills or mutiny with the surviving Ghadar revolutionaries.

That Sikh soldier, tall and straight with a light beard and light eyes, had walked by close to the picket, supporting a wounded colleague whose eyes were covered with a bandage. As he passed Williams, the soldier looked him in the eye. Williams was transfixed for a moment by the directness of that look. It showed no hint of any subservience or inferiority. It was a level, fearless, fully honest look that seemed to convey to Williams: yes, I know you are suspicious of me and my colleagues. But we have fought bravely and been wounded and killed. We have nothing left to fear. For you too are mortal even if you are white.

The Admiralty Arch rose before the funeral procession; behind, far away, stood the commanding statue of Queen Victoria, half hidden in the grey of drizzle and cloud. Whenever he passed through the arch, Williams had always looked for the pointed projection that stuck out from one of the pillars. It was said to be the architect's nose immortalized in his creation forever. But that day he forgot to look for it; his mind was very far away.

'That's a crowd,' the soldier marching next to him turned and said, the awe evident in his voice. The comment brought him back to the reality of the present. The man who had wanted to bring not just Amritsar, but all Punjab, to heel with his action, was now lying in the coffin up ahead.

A sea of black umbrellas was parting to allow the coffin bearers to go up to the portico of St Martin-in-the-Fields. After the family members had entered the church, the umbrellas closed up again. The rest of the mourners would find their way into the church on their own and look for whatever place they could find. Williams found a seat in the balcony and looked around as the hymn 'Lead, Kindly Light' was struck up. He had a good view of where the coffin lay and of all those who were present, all the big shots from the army and the imperial establishments, many representing even bigger shots, and he could see well what was happening. It was just like that April day in 1919, he realized, when he had stood behind Dyer and had been able to see clearly everything that happened.

After the speeches and the service came the Last Post from the buglers. The coffin was being taken out of the church and the people had started filing out. Williams hurried down and stepped again into the grey afternoon but in his head the blazing Indian April sun had still not faded. He could see the wreaths being piled into two cars. They would be taken and put at the base of the cenotaph in Whitehall.

A man with a small notebook in his hand was blocking his way. As Williams tried to push past him, the man spoke.

'You a soldier, sir?'

'Yes, a sergeant.'

'You served with him in India, sir? Amritsar?'

'Yes.'

The man had taken out his pencil. He clearly had been shooting his questions in the dark and was not a little surprised that he had struck it so lucky.

'Can you tell me? What sort of a man was he? Did he do the right thing at Amritsar.'

Nicholas Williams paused before he spoke. A part of him wanted to say: 'He was a good man but he did not do the right thing. He may even have been alive today if he had and we all may have slept better all these nights. He should have fired in the air first; he should have given them a chance to run away, to disperse. They were not rushing us, they were dying like flies. There was no danger to us or the Raj. There was no real rebellion that we had to crush. And even if had fired, he should have stopped much earlier, much....'

But instead, what he said was: 'He was a fine officer, one of the finest. We would have followed him anywhere and proudly. He did the right thing. He saved India for the Empire.'

'Thank you, Sergeant,' the reporter gratefully scribbled down the quote and putting up his collar against the drizzle took the steps of St Martin's two at a time and hurried off towards the Strand.

The coffin had been loaded on a vehicle. Annie Dyer and the close family were getting into the car. They would accompany the body to Golders Green for the cremation. Williams gave the car a long look of farewell and pulling down his cap, hurried off across Trafalgar Square. He knew that where Dyer was going, he would have no need of a bodyguard.

Chapter 29

The Dancing Dervish

In early August 1927, the SS *Jalapa* dropped anchor in Calcutta for a ten-day break before it continued its eastward voyage. One of the crew members, Frank Brazil, dressed in western clothes, stepped off the ship, carrying his toolbox and suitcase. But this was no Puerto Rican ship carpenter coming ashore to find his land legs. This was Udham Singh coming home, using the identity under which he had already performed several jobs in America and Europe for the Ghadars. His toolbox contained, besides screwdrivers and hammers, three revolvers and over a hundred bullets. He did not know it then but one of the men for whom these bullets were meant, General Dyer, had slipped away into the safety of death a fortnight earlier. The suitcase was full of incriminating, seditious Ghadar literature. Somehow the customs official who had checked the ship at Karachi had overlooked all that; his eye had been distracted by a stack of picture postcards of naked women. Udham Singh found these incredibly useful to bribe his way through problems but this time he had been careless in hiding them. Somewhere, he knew, a red flag would have gone up against his name and he realized there was no way he could board the SS *Jalapa* on its return voyage to New York without getting into trouble and possibly even finding himself in jail.

For a while, he dissolved into Amritsar's familiar lanes. These lanes were his, these smells and colours and sights were those of home. Nothing that he had seen, none of the places he had managed to get to—Africa, Mexico, California, New York, Detroit, Europe...nowhere had he ever found more comfort than in this city. He rented a small room attached to the brothel run by the popular Madam Nur Jahan, above a bustling jungle of shops, not far from Jallianwala Bagh. Here, the restless traveller could be himself and shake off the dust of many foreign shores.

But soon the desire to show off got the better of him and he made a second mistake. He started sauntering around in the bazaars in his fancy foreign clothes. He liked the look that he saw on the faces of friends and acquaintances—ah, that orphan boy, he made good. Just look at him. All decked up like a sahib. He always had something in him. This city was not big enough to hold him.

Somebody who didn't know him, or perhaps didn't like him, told the police that a foreigner was staying in the brothel and that made them suspicious. When they jumped him in Hall Bazaar one evening, he was carrying a loaded gun, and that was it. They beat him and questioned him for fifteen days, keeping him hungry and thirsty, splashing his face with cold water so he could not sleep, until the stories, bordering on the incredible, came pouring out. The shifting identities of Sher Singh, Ude Singh, Udham, Frank Brazil...the links to the Ghadar revolutionaries...a Mexican wife named Lupe...the life of a daily wager, of a railway worker, of a car factory mechanic, ship carpenter...the life of a well-dressed world traveller, mysteriously funded. He told them what he had to; he saved what he could. But it was more than the stories that came spilling out. The suitcase and toolbox with their damning contents—the revolvers, bullets, and seditious literature—hidden away with a friend, were ferreted out: the additional district magistrate didn't take much time in passing a sentence of five years. Rigorous imprisonment. Udham Singh's plans to exact vengeance for the shooting at Jallianwala Bagh would have to wait.

~

Over the next four years, Udham earned the stripes on his back.

Flogged again and again for insubordination, for sowing rebellion among fellow prisoners, for spreading the message of revolution, he was transferred from jail to jail. Then, by a strange coincidence, for a while he was in the same Mianwali jail as the man whom he would come to regard as his guru—Bhagat Singh, the young revolutionary. Bhagat Singh was not just a young man with a gun who had murdered a British police officer. He was also a thinker, a philosopher, a writer. A true revolutionary who had the courage to walk into the Central Legislative Assembly in Delhi and throw bombs, not to kill but to attract attention to the cause of India's freedom, and then make no attempt to escape. Everything about Bhagat Singh was a lesson for Udham—his calm courage, his extreme disinterest in any reward for his struggle, his ultimate and utter lack of belief in any god. Bhagat Singh was moved to Lahore but the news of his hanging two years later, in 1931, spread fast through the country and reached Udham who was still in jail. He heard of the farce of a trial, the terrible prison conditions, the refusal to eat in protest by the prisoners. Then the cowardly hanging of his twenty-three-year-old guru and his companions, Sukhdev and Rajguru at twilight, ahead of the time that had been fixed, with not even a last meeting with the families. He heard too of the disposal of the bodies in the dark, the hasty cremations on the banks of the Sutlej, the shovelling of the ashes into the river. For a while, Udham Singh was crushed…and grew docile, at least outwardly. Perhaps because of that his sentence was reduced by a year. He came out of prison and vanished. He needed time to recover, both his wasted body and subdued spirit.

Disguised as a sadhu, wearing the thick saffron robe of a holy man, a hooked walking stick in his hand, he reached Kashmir. This was the haven he was looking for. Nobody knew him there; nobody would suspect a sadhu. On the contrary, often when he was sitting by the lake in the fading light of the day, someone would leave him some chapattis, or a little basket of fruit. In response, Udham Singh would raise a hand in blessing and say: 'Jai Bhole Ram!'

One of those evenings, Udham was surprised to see a sharp-featured young man with a short curly beard and a flat blue turban sitting a few yards away from him in silence. The man didn't say anything but occasionally Udham could feel his eyes on him. Then the young man got up and went away. This happened again the next evening, and the next. Udham Singh began to suspect that the young man was a CID agent tailing him. He decided that he would confront the man if he saw him again; they couldn't put him in prison for disguising himself as a sadhu.

The next evening, the young man in the blue turban was already sitting by the lake by the time Udham reached his usual spot. Going behind him, Udham Singh shouted: 'Jai Bhole Ram!' The man turned around and, in that instant, Udham Singh recognized him. This was the boy who had lived with the doctor in Amritsar, the one who had made copies of the Ghadar literature for Udham and others to distribute. He decided to play the game a bit more.

'I can see your past in your face. You have left Amritsar but I still see it in your face.'

Sucha froze and was immediately on the alert. Was this sadhu a CID man? Years had passed but it seemed they were still looking out for anybody who had any connection with the Ghadar movement.

Then the sadhu let out a loud bellow of laughter and slapped Sucha's back.

'Don't worry. I am with you. I recognize you because I never forget a face. How is the old Doctor sahib?'

Things fell into place in Sucha's mind, too. The square shoulders, the eyes shrouded in deception. The boy from the Putlighar orphanage.

The next few days were full of talk.

'Doctor sahib passed away two years ago, in his sleep,' Sucha related. 'I was alone once again. I had nowhere to go, and yet I could go in any direction. Then I heard again that the Ghadari bhai who first brought me from Tibba, Umrao Singh, had been seen here, in Kashmir. So, I came here hoping to run into him. I have been here six months now but there has been no sign or word of him. When I saw you, I don't know why, I thought it was a kind of sign, which is why I kept coming back here. But then when you startled me I thought you were CID, and I was done for....'

Udham too was glad to have found a companion whom he could trust. For a while he did not need to hide things or tell half-truths. He told Sucha about his days in America and Europe, about the men and women he had met, about the woman who loved him and had no idea where he was. One evening he lifted his shirt and showed Sucha the scars on his back where jailer after jailer had vented his anger and frustration with whip and cane over the last four years. The welts had healed on the surface but were still painful to the touch.

Sucha confessed to him that he had no desire to go back to Amritsar. There was no fight left in the city any more. He wanted to find the surviving Ghadar revolutionaries, no matter where they were hiding. That would give him back his purpose in life and with time, the fight would begin again.

Udham Singh looked at his companion with sympathy; he understood Sucha's passion instinctively.

'Carry on the battle, Sucha bhai, movement is the essence of life. If you have a mission then don't wait for a permanent home. I will show you the way out of here, all the way to Europe. I too am your Ghadari bhai. And I can do this with my left hand. I have moved many men from Mexico to California and other places. I too am leaving soon on a journey, and I will travel wherever I have to—Europe, America, England, and as long as I have to until I get within reach of my objective and do what I have sworn to do.'

And then he recited:

Ek jagah rahte nahin aashik aur badnaam kahin
Din kahan raat kahin, subah kahin sham kahin

They do not tarry at a place, the lover and the damned,
Here day, the night away; morning home, evening away.

In all the time he spent with him in Kashmir, only once did Sucha see anger rise in Udham's eyes. They had been sitting by the lake and Sucha was reminiscing. He was telling Udham Singh about how he had learnt to mix medicines and help the doctor to treat and stitch wounds.

'That was the worst time, the time of Jallianwala Bagh, when we had to treat so many of the wounded. What a terrible evening that was; I can still hear the barrage of bullets if I shut my eyes and think of that Baisakhi.'

Udham Singh froze into stone. His entire body became taut as a coiled steel spring. His fists clenched and unclenched in restrained fury. The blood rose to his eyes even as Sucha watched. When he finally spoke, it was through clenched teeth.

'Dyer is dead and gone and there is not even a grave I can find. His clever wife decided to burn him rather than bury him. Otherwise, I would claw him out of the ground with my bare hands and shoot six bullets into his dead body. But O'Dwyer is alive, still alive. He is mentioned in newspapers. He is still telling lies about us, about what happened, about Punjab. He has even written a book, a collection of lies, about it. It is not easy to get to him, but nothing that is worth it is easy. Look at this man, my guru, my deity, was his life easy?'

He took out a photo of Bhagat Singh from his wallet. A

photo cut out from a newspaper, showing the revolutionary in a hat. Holding that photo above his head with both hands, Udham began to whirl, in slow swirls at first, his saffron robe spread out like a dervish's gown, his eyes shut. As he whirled, he began to recite the well-known verse of the revolutionaries:

> Sarfroshi ki tamanna ab hamare dil mein hai
> Dekhna hai zor kitna bazue qatil mein hai

> Our hearts yearn now to sacrifice ourselves
> We yearn to know how strong is the killer's arm

Then he was whirling faster and faster and descending deeper and deeper into a trance...until he was lost to Sucha and the world and became his own obsession.

Chapter 30

The Maverick Martyr

12 MARCH 1940

Finally, the day I've been waiting for is here. My tapasya has been rewarded, my prayers answered. The long journey of this orphan gypsy is almost done. The blood races in my veins like the Chenab in flood, but my heart is calm. And cold. That maderchod Michael O'Dwyer, whose very name makes me mad, will not escape me now. Through his death I will pay my homage to Bhagat Singh, who raised the flag of inquilab ten years ago. Udham Singh too will go smiling to the gallows like him. I too will be immortal.

This old revolver is good. Bloody good Smith and Wesson .455. Did some shooting—target practice only—in the country. Bullets a bit loose, .44 I think, but good enough at short range. Six into the chamber and some more in my pocket. Finally, right into his heart. Khatam! Tamam!

I have bid sat sri akal to my London friends. They are nice, simple folk, mostly peddlers of clothes. I feel for them. They came to this country to make some money but it isn't as easy as they thought. But they are warm and friendly and they've been good to me. I ordered food for all of them, even laddoos today. Sweets are auspicious, so I called for laddoos for everyone. They don't really know me, are only aware of me as the man who drops in and out of the Shepherd's Bush gurudwara or turns up occasionally at their dinners. Sometimes in style, on a motorbike or even in a car, wearing a good suit. I'm different from them. Most of them can't even speak straight English but I talk to

goras all the time, some even think I am a prince from Patiala.
The night I brought a white woman to dinner, all the Punjabis
looked at me as if I were God. They know nothing of what I
live for, what I dream of. That's the way I have lived, a stranger
to everyone, here and in America, and in Africa, or Russia, or
Germany. I have played hide-and-seek with life for years, saying
one thing to one man and another to the next. Sometimes, I
even forget my real name, my true identity. It's best like that. In
this business there are no true friends. I can trust nobody. Except
this revolver. Its steel is pure, like my intentions. Its barrel is clean,
like my heart. And its aim will be true, because destiny guides
those whose intentions are pure and hearts clean.

Michael O'Dwyer was as bad as Dyer. Dyer and O'Dwyer!
Motherfuckers! They couldn't find any other name or what?
When Dyer killed hundreds of innocents at Jallianwala Bagh this
O'Dwyer was protecting him. He defended him, approved his
action. Said Shabash! Well done! Taught Punjabis a good lesson!

And for years he dug his iron heel into my people. Whipped
and flogged them, recruited them by force for the war, put them
in jail for no crime, took away their necklaces and their bangles
for the war fund. A pity that Dyer was dead before I could get
to him. I would have given him a proper death—not the old
man's death that he got, drooling in his bed. I would have put
a nice hard bullet through his heart, and I would have done it
standing in front of him. He fancied himself as a tough soldier.
We would have seen then how tough he was.

If he were still alive, it would have been brilliant if he had
turned up tomorrow at Caxton Hall to listen to the speech of
his great protector. I would have got not one but two pigeons
in one day and I, Mohamed Singh Azad, aka Udham Singh,
would have been doubly grateful. Double box of laddoos for
my Punjabi friends.

This Caxton Hall is a good place. All the rich, famous

people come here for weddings, parties, speeches, dances. The
newspapers cover everything that happens here. The shots from
this revolver will echo in not one but two palaces—Westminster
and Buckingham Palace. The newspapers and the radio will do
the rest.

George Pancham was deaf to the bullets that Dyer fired at
Jallianwala Bagh.

But George VI will have no choice.

13 MARCH 1940

I wanted to get out of the flat quickly this morning. I had a bath
and put on my special suit, the blue one. I wore a red tie and hat
and looked at myself in the mirror. Yes, I looked like a proper
London sahib, even though I am dark. Good enough to go to
Caxton Hall and listen to a lecture on Afghanistan. One doesn't
learn all this in a day, not if you are a poor, low-caste orphan. I
came up the hard way and it was not until I reached California
that I learnt how to dress like a sahib, or walk like one. In those
towns, when they were building the railway, I learnt how to
walk tall and straight among white Americans and then vanish
among the brown Indians and Mexicans. That's why the Ghadar
revolutionaries found me useful.

Wearing my overcoat, I stepped out into the light snow
but there was still time before the lecture at Caxton Hall so I
went to Leicester Square. May as well see a good Paul Robeson
picture, I thought. Good stuff, those movies. I know a thing or
two about them, I've acted in some. Ha! Wonder what the boys
at the orphanage would have said to that. Wah, Udham yaar,
acting in an angrezi picture with mems. But the picture was not
to start for a while so I had to give it a miss.

It wasn't yet three when I reached Caxton Hall. I didn't
have a ticket but that wasn't going to stop me. As soon as I saw
the lady, I knew there was a kindness about her. The way she

smiled gently when I greeted her. I raised my hat and asked her if I could accompany her inside on her ticket. She thought for a minute, and then she nodded slightly.

That was all. You have to know how to do these things. Not every Indian selling underwear from the back of an old car or running a samosa-pakora stall in the East End can do this. It has taken twenty years of watching, learning, practice. That's why I know that I can do things that others cannot. Every man in Sunam would be proud of me if they knew.

I followed the lady into the big hall and then I tipped my hat to her in thanks and left her. She was a kind one and I didn't want any trouble for her. I went to the right side of the hall and walked down the gangway, along the wood-panelled wall. The place was getting crowded. They had put in some extra chairs but still some people were standing. I stopped just near the front row and found a good place to lean against the wall. I don't think anybody really noticed me. I have this ability to disappear in open sight.

I looked around. A clock on the wall showed three o'clock. A dais had been set up for the speakers with a large map of Afghanistan on the wall behind them. I recognized Zetland, the secretary of state. Seen many pictures of him in the newspapers. He was the chairman, sitting in the centre, the man who pushed India into World War II without asking anyone. The man next to Zetland started his speech and he wouldn't stop. Thank God, I had enough sweets in my pocket, and I kept popping them into my mouth one after the other otherwise I would have fallen asleep, even standing up.

But the man I had come for was not on the stage. Michael O'Dwyer was right there in the front row, just a few yards from me, one leg crossed over the other. He was listening attentively to the speech, and every once in a while, he would whisper something to his neighbour. Then his turn came to speak and he went up to the dais. He was over seventy and retired but the bastard still spoke as if he were Lieutenant Governor of Punjab. He looked a real proud parrot with his chest all puffed up and his voice going up and down. I could see what a terror he must have been in Punjab, squeezing the poor for their last drop of blood. *Go to the war, give your gold, give your young men. Don't eat anything. We need the food for the war. And don't open your mouths or I will have you whipped, flogged, arrested, exiled, hanged. Don't say the word Ghadar. Or you go to the gallows or to kala pani, or both!*

Yes, that was O'Dwyer. I wanted to kill him right then. But I had to get close. Finally, he finished and came back to his seat and many people clapped. I, too, clapped. No harm clapping, I thought.

At last, the meeting ended. O'Dwyer stood up. That was my moment. I took two steps towards the centre of the hall and fired. Two into O'Dwyer first—he was falling even as I was firing. Then Zetland got two and he too fell. One bullet each at two other gents and then I turned and rushed up the gangway, shouting at people to make way. A woman came in my way and then a man jumped on me from the back, and I fell and the revolver slipped from my hand. How did it matter.... I was not going to run anyway. Several men grabbed me. A police sergeant searched my pockets and took out my knife and the box of revolver ammunition. He also found the loose bullets in my trouser pocket. There was chaos all around. People were picking up empty cartridges and handing them to the sergeant.

An inspector of police came up and looked at me closely.

'You speak English?' he asked.

'Yes,' I told him. 'But it's all over. It's no use.' And my eyes pointed at O'Dwyer's body. Blood all over. Do whatever you want now, I wanted to say. My job is done. This poor orphan has done a big thing, bigger than he could have ever imagined in his wildest dreams.

They took me to another room and kept me there for hours. But I wasn't bothered. Never felt that light and relaxed in years. The inspector and I smoked cigarettes. He made notes of what I said. Another inspector came and put four empty cartridges on the table. Six, I told him, there should be six and showed him six fingers so that he understood. I wasn't there to save bullets, you see. But I was surprised that there was only one dead and I knew who that was. He wasn't going to escape me. He'd had it coming to him a long, long time. Zetland, too, should have died—I had put two right there into his stomach from close up. Actually, the bullets were .44, a bit loose for my revolver, I think.

Sometime in the evening I was taken to Canon Row police station. I was being charged with the murder of Michael O'Dwyer and they wanted to record my statement. Go ahead, I said, write it down but show me what you are writing. I didn't admit to any murder charge. Though I had killed O'Dwyer and I was prepared to hang, I wasn't going to make it easy for them. I wouldn't admit my guilt, like they have never admitted theirs. I have seen people starving in India under British rule. All the money only goes to make big estates in England. Growing things only for England. Indigo, tobacco, cotton…what about food for my people? I had to protest against all that. This was my duty, and I am not sorry. I do not mind the sentence you give me, ten, twenty, or fifty years, or hanging. But I was just protesting, you know. That's what I told them.

15 MARCH 1940

The police asked me my real name! They showed me the national registration card they had found in my pocket when they arrested me. It said Azad Singh. Yes, I said, that was the name I gave to the person who rented me a house in Bournemouth. Then they said my passport says Udham Singh. That, too, is correct. I could give them some more. My poor mother called me Sher Singh—Lion

Lion! The plague took her long ago otherwise she would have seen me being brave as two lions now. When the Alibegh Sant baptized me and my brother, I became Udham. Then I was Ude Singh or Frank Brazil or Mohamed Singh Azad or Bawa Sahib... any religion you want. Many names, many faces, many truths, and half-truths. Many homes too. From the orphanage at Amritsar, to Lahore and London, California, and Europe, railway trains and park benches and prisons. Those who chase a dream, those who are haunted by an obsession can afford no permanent home, no permanent name. I did everything to survive so one day I could fulfil my vow.

M. Singh I told the police: Mohamed Singh, and I showed them the tattoo on my arm. Mohamed Singh Azad was the name under which they had arrested me and I believe that was the name under which the news of the shooting spread across the world on the BBC, German radio, Turkish radio. The news must have reached Sunam, too, and there the old men and the children must have heard it over the radio in the square. They may not have known that this Mohamed Singh Azad was me, the Sunam boy, the younger son of Tehal Singh Kamboj, the boy whom many knew only as the mad wanderer who sometimes turned up without a warning and then vanished without a trace. Sometimes, he returned as a failure like the first time from the war in Basra, at other times a hero, with money in his pocket and a motorbike under him. But perhaps some may have guessed—this is the same Ude, it can be no other. Then they would know that I had always meant what I had said, that I would do something big someday.

But this name does not suit the British government. If they hang me as Mohamed, people would think that they hanged a Muslim man and that would create problems for them. The inspector said we will change your name on the charge sheet to Udham Singh—that makes me a Sikh. They are used to hanging

Sikhs. They hanged my Bhagat and they hanged so many others of the Ghadar. It makes no difference to me now, I said. There is only one place left to go, and that needs no passport.

To the gallows, and then to God.

3 APRIL 1940

A priest comes to see me often. I have not asked for him but he feels responsible for me. He says the big bishop has given him the responsibility of saving the souls of all Indians in London. He's a nice man, the nice kind of Englishman. But he is wasting his time and mine. This life has been well-lived. Who cares about the next? Anyway, I talk to him from time to time. I also talk to the doctor who watches me very closely. I know what that doctor is trying to do—he is trying to see if I am mad. Maybe it will help if I behave as though I am mad. A madman cannot be hanged, I think. But I've been nice to him.

To the priest I said my brother and sister were killed in Amritsar in the shooting and that I saw all sorts of terrible things happening to the people of the city. They will go looking for my brother and sister. Letters will go to India, policemen will search records.... What they do not understand is that for an orphan there are many brothers and sisters.

The only real brother that I had died much before the shooting at Jallianwala Bagh. I missed him a lot when he went away, suddenly, after catching a cold. He wasn't as tough as I was, even though we both were born of the same mother. But his is the face that still comes to me early in the morning, before sunrise. I like that early morning time—amrit-vela, the Sikhs call it—ever since the days at the orphanage when we used to get up and bathe at four in the morning, winter and summer. In the winter the water was not water at all, but thin sheets of ice. It went through my half-asleep body like a knife. We would say our prayers with our teeth chattering and wait our turn to get the hot tea in the mud kulhad.

That I remember well.

Memories before that are like faded old photographs, surrounded by mist. Each separate, floating in the distance. I don't bother about them much. It's all long ago and not important. But sometimes I want to hold on to them when they come and I want to fill in the colours, to remember more....

...A railway crossing in the jungle with a little hut next to it. A train comes in the morning and then again in the opposite direction later in the day. My father waits for it, and when he sees it in the distance, he pulls down the log barrier so that no man or animal comes in its way. The train whistles each time it passes the barrier. The little pieces of coal from the engine fly into my eyes and they itch for a long time and my clothes smell of coal dust. But I wait eagerly every time for that long whistle. It speaks of unknown lands, faraway places....

...When there is no train and everything is quiet the animals come out of the jungle. Once a leopard came for the goat that my father kept for milk. But I picked up my father's axe and ran at the leopard. It took one jump and vanished into the jungle, never to return....

...Sher Singh was my name then. How could a poor leopard stand up to me? My father looked at me and he was proud of me. That is the only clear memory of my father that comes back to me. His beard untied, a flat, pale-yellow turban on his head, his mouth half open in surprise, his eyes full of pride. Then he fell ill, and I don't remember what happened but to this day I can feel the desolation of the terrible night that he died....

The sadhus with whom my brother and I wandered around after that were kind to us. We went from village to village, slept under trees, sat around little fires, and ate what the villagers left in the karmandals of the sadhus. We often met other groups of holy men. One night we stayed with the followers of a Sant.

I remember it clearly since we stayed up all night listening to shabads being sung by his followers. The sadhus thought it best to leave us with the Sant and one of his young followers was very good to us, made sure that we ate well. We also took baptism at that time, though I am not sure I have kept up with all the vows. But then, like Bhagat, my only God is revolution. When we reached Amritsar, the Sant's follower left us at the orphanage.

That orphanage was our home for many years, our only real home. During those years my brother and I learnt to read and write at the Khalsa school. And to pray. Khalsa schools were new then, the Singh Sabha wanted to make sure the Sikh children knew their language, their culture, their religion. I learnt other things—everybody said I was a natural carpenter.

Wonder why I thought of those sadhus today. I used to often dress like a sadhu myself when I came out of prison in India. I was sick and tired of the police following me. I should never have been caught by the police, such stupid guys, I should have been able to fool them. But it was those postcards of naked women that I used to carry with me, just to slip one to someone to get some work done, that put me in their sights. Then they caught me with the guns and the Ghadar papers and put me away for five years and whipped me black and blue. They let me out after four years, the jailors couldn't handle me, and disguising myself as a sadhu—sadhus are safe everywhere—I went to Kashmir. I spent some good days there with that Ghadari boy, Sucha. Helped him get away, too, first to Kabul and then to Germany while I came to England. He thought I was a CID informer at first. That was some joke!

5 APRIL 1940

Again, I refused to eat today. Bhagat Singh and Dutt and others also went on hunger strike in prison. But these jailers will not let me die so easily, they want to keep me alive so they can hang me.

They shove a tube into my throat three times a day, sometimes only twice if I say I am going to vomit, and they put food inside me. I don't fight them here in Brixton. I lie down and let them do what they want. It's going to be a long battle ahead so why fight them now. Feeding me like a royal guest of the bloody royal family. But once they decide to hang me, I will resist them. Every day! I won't make anything easy for these bastards. I know how to survive in prison.

6 APRIL 1940

I have written many letters from prison, including to my friend Shiv Singh Johal. I never address him in a familiar manner, otherwise he'll get into big trouble. I call him Mr Singh or Jahal Singh or something. Jahal is a good name, it means uncivilized. The man is really stupid. He doesn't get the real meaning of what I write in my letters. I ask for books, Gurmukhi books and Urdu books, books of history and Indian newspapers. I tell them that I have plenty of time to study in prison—I am a royal guest. Soon I have to go for a big exam, and get the highest degree one can get: martyrdom for my country. I will also pass the exam that Bhagat Singh, Sukhdev, and Rajguru passed. I am hoping someone will have the sense to understand and hide a small hacksaw in the binding of some old Hindustani book and send it to me. If the book looks really old and dirty it is possible that the guards will not check it properly. Then I can cut my way out of Brixton. But they don't even hand me religious books now. They hate me. I am today the most hated man in the British empire. Very good.

Today I have asked for another book—Waris Shah's *Heer*—the greatest love story of Punjab. That's the book I will take with me to the Old Bailey and take my oath on. People will remember this and think of me not only as a hero but also a lover, a Punjabi Ranjha.

13 APRIL 1940

It is that day again. In Punjab, they will be celebrating Baisakhi. Going to fairs, wearing new clothes, buying things. Girls will want glass bangles. Children will want to eat. Pickpockets will have a great day. The men will drink, sitting in the fields. Punjabis only need an excuse to drink. I can see the bright turbans, yellow, blue, green. If the harvest has been good, there will be money to spend, and the Punjabi never thinks before spending money.

They have forgotten that Baisakhi of twenty-one years ago. Some of them were not even born when Dyer opened fire in Jallianwala Bagh. But every Baisakhi is a black day for me. We should all wear black bands and black turbans. Eternal mourning. Never forget what happened. Do not celebrate. I burn in anger, my heart aches as if it will burst open with the pain. No matter how many years go by, the pain does not lessen, this fire does not die out. This year at least the questioning finger that used to point at me from the sky is no longer there. What are you doing about it, that accusing finger of God used to ask. Why are you still living and not doing what you have to do? Is there nobody who will avenge those poor innocent children who were just sitting with their fathers in Jallianwala Bagh?

I have lived with this horror for so many years. I have thought about it so much that there is no distinction between what I may have seen, or heard, or dreamt. It no longer matters whether I was there or not, whether it was my brother who was shot or some other Punjabi youth, whether I actually poured water into the parched mouths of the dying or whether I wished I had been able to. I have thought so much about it that I have rubbed out all distinctions between the real and the imagined.

Every time someone mentioned Jallianwala Bagh, my entire being was shaken and the blood throbbed in my temples. No matter where in the world I was and no matter what I was doing— working on the Lunatic Line railway or on ships, as a carpenter

or a motor mechanic, Azad or Sher, Udham or Mohamed, the
nightmare of people dying, the whine of bullets, the screams of
the dying never left me. It would come when I least expected
it; I could do nothing about it. I would wake up with the sweat
pouring down my neck and chest and a choking in my throat....
Always on Baisakhi. There is nothing for me to celebrate today.
But, maybe this year, my six bullets at Caxton Hall will have
drowned out the screams.

I only had a pistol with a few bullets. Dyer had fifty soldiers
with guns. If he had a machine gun, he said he would have used
it. If I had a machine gun, I would have used it. So, we are equal.
He did not fire a warning shot over the heads of the crowd at
Jallianwala Bagh. I did not do so in Caxton Hall. Equal again.
He wanted to teach all Punjab a lesson; I have taught all vilayat
a lesson. The people in the Bagh were not the people who had
caused the disturbances three days earlier or burnt down the
bank buildings or chased down that woman missionary. But in
front of me was Michael O'Dwyer himself. The man who had
tortured Punjab and protected Dyer.

So I killed him. At least I had a reason, where Dyer had none.

15 APRIL 1940

They don't allow me any newspapers. I would like to get what I
have read for so many years. *Hindustan Ghadar, Ghadar ki Goonj*....
Each poem, each article preaching revolution was written in
blood, and distributed free to the world. Smuggled out, distributed
house to house at night. I still know many poems by heart.

Ghadar Party birha chukiya Hind azad karawan da
Aao shero Ghadar machaiye mauka nahin khujawan da

Ghadar Party has taken up the mission to free India
Come raise hell, this is not a chance to be missed

They were brave men, generous men, my Ghadar bhais. I am happy I was part of them and helped them move men from Mexico to California and other places. I was of value to them. I was fast and I could be trusted. They did not give up their revolution even though their conspiracy to cause a revolt in the Indian army units had failed. Even after the martial law in Punjab, even after O'Dwyer thought he had finished them, they were active, in many countries, many continents.

4 JUNE 1940

I have been brought to the Old Bailey, the place where all murderers land up for trial. But I am a martyr, not a murderer. I will become a star in the night sky forever, the star of Free India.

My suit, the same blue suit that I had on in Caxton Hall the day I had my sweet revenge, now hangs loose on me. I have lost some twenty, thirty pounds since I was imprisoned. A royal guest losing weight! My fault, they will say. After all, they tried their best to feed me through a tube shoved down my throat.

Thin, yes, but not weak. Weak are the ones who are weak in spirit and that Azad is not. I will fight them with my eyes, my words, my mind, and my soul, right to the end. When one is willing to kiss the hangman's noose there is nothing that anybody can do to him. Even death will come to me respectfully, with her head bowed.

All day, I have listened to the arguments of the lawyers. Often, I wanted to speak, sometimes I wanted to shout. They are going to hang me anyway. Why do we have to go through all this? My lawyers are trying to show that I did not know that Michael O'Dwyer would be there, that if I had wanted to shoot him, I could have done that on earlier occasions. English lawyers on both sides. The Indian lawyer on my side, Menon, has not spoken all day. They are all playing games. Useless questions—how far was this table...who was sitting where...who spoke when...who fell first...who picked up which empty cartridge from where....They also spent a lot of time on my red diary...and wondered why I had written the word 'Action' in it...and why I had the addresses of O'Dwyer and the others in it. What is there to wonder? Ha. The jury won't want to believe what I said in my statement at the police station, that I just went to the hall to protest. They would rather believe what I said to the detective earlier, that more than one man should have died that day.

I answered all their questions, speaking very fast. The judge said I should speak slowly. He could understand only one word in six, he said. That's his bloody problem.

The detective had said in court that I had confessed to him that I had a grudge against O'Dwyer, that he deserved to die, that I wanted to die young and not wait until I was old, and so on. Today, I denied all those statements in the court. I did everything to confuse them, just like I have been confusing so many intelligence men for many years. Not going to make it easy.

I said I knew Michael O'Dwyer. Had first met him when I was in a car outside Kensington Gardens. He came out of the garden with his dog and saw me. Punjabi? he asked. I told him I was a tourist, and he gave me his phone number. Then I met him three or four times and he gave me his country address in Devonshire, and said I should come and have tea with him. I told the court that I went for tea, and I also drove him in my motor car to Brighton and the seaside. My lawyer was happy I said that—it meant that if I really wanted to kill O'Dwyer, I could have done it earlier, just killed him with my hands and run my motor car over him. Stories, all stories—many of them just made up.

I told them how I got the revolver and bullets from a man in Bournemouth. Fifty bullets for five shillings and I shot off a few in the countryside, testing the revolver. That I had needed a revolver since I planned to go by land to India, through Italy and Libya, and then through Palestine, Baghdad, and Afghanistan. That I had also needed a passport. I had heard of Zetland because people told me that he could give me a passport. I said that I went with a loaded revolver to Caxton Hall to protest, knowing that a lot of people interested in India usually went there. I always kept it loaded and had made sure it was loaded that day too. I just raised the revolver, and someone struck my arm and the revolver went off. If my arm had not been struck nobody would have died, I said. They asked me if I had murder in my heart when I went to the meeting. Murder? I? I said I could not even murder a cat, so how could I murder a man? They kept staring at me. They thought I was mad.

5 JUNE 1940

Thank God they gave me a chair today before the questioning started. I had been standing all day yesterday. The prosecution lawyer asked me if I remembered Jallianwala Bagh and if that had made me hate the British. I said I was too young at the time. He asked if I knew that Michael O'Dwyer was the Governor of Punjab at the time. I said I was hardly in India for long, that I was in East Africa. Then he asked me a lot of questions about my revolver and how I ended up shooting O'Dwyer twice in the back from nine inches away.

I dodged all the questions as best as I could. I did not want to make it easy for them. I confused them by saying things that I had denied yesterday. I told them I wanted to die when I was young and not wait till one got old and that I was dying for my country. I told them again someone pushed me forward and then someone pushed down my hand and that was it. I had only come to shoot in the air. To protest.

Then the judge gave a long lecture to the jury. Typical Englishman style, trying to sound fair. Actually, he was telling them that there was no doubt that I was a murderer: I went in with a loaded gun, I fired at people and killed someone. No explanation I had given was good enough. Six bullets don't go off by accident.

The jury went off for an hour or so. I don't know why they needed a full hour. Their mind was already made up. When they came back, they took just one minute to say that they had found me guilty of murder.

The court clerk asked me if I had anything to say before they gave me the death sentence. That was the moment I had been waiting for. Now the truth. No more dodging. No more confusing answers. The full truth. I pulled out the pages I had written down.

Yes, sir, I said, I have a statement. *Down with Britain. Down with British democracies. Read your own history and if you have any human decency about you—you would die of shock.*

The judge shouted that I was trying to make a political speech. He wanted to take my statement and read it himself quietly. But I wanted everybody to hear it, the jury and all, not just the judge. He ordered that nothing I said would be published. But I kept speaking as loudly as I could.

I am not afraid to die. I am proud to die. I want to help my native land, and I hope when I have gone that in my place will come others of my countrymen to drive you dirty dogs out to free the country. You people go to India and when you come back you are given prizes and put into the House of Commons, but when we come to England we are put to death. I do not care anything about it, but when you dirty dogs come to India—the intellectuals they call themselves, the rulers—they are of bastard bloodhound class and they order machine guns to fire on Indian streets without hesitation…mow down thousands of poor women and children…. I have nothing against the public at all. I have more friends in England than I have in India. I have nothing against the public. I have great sympathy with the workers of England, but I am against the dirty British government. Your people are suffering the same as I am suffering through—those dirty dogs and mad beasts—killing, mutilating, and destroying. We know what is going on in India, hundreds of thousands of people being killed by your dirty dogs.

The judge refused to hear any more. His face was red with anger. He shouted that I should put away my papers and he would pass sentence on me.

I carried on without paying any attention to him.

I have to say a lot. You people are dirty. You don't want to hear from us what you are doing in India. Beasts, beasts, beasts. Down with British imperialism, down with dirty British dogs!

The judge then said I would be hanged. Hanged until I was dead.

I shouted: *I don't care about the sentence of death. It does not worry me. I am dying for a purpose. Inquilab! Inquilab! Inquilab!*

I tore my speech into small bits which I threw up in the air. I thumped the railing of the dock, and spat into the court.

7 JUNE 1940

I am no longer the accused, innocent until proven guilty. Instead, I have become the condemned man, waiting to be hanged. I was taken, handcuffed and under heavy escort, not to Brixton where I had been for the last two and a half months but to Pentonville Prison. The Ville they call it, as if it is some fancy palace or hotel. A special place where special royal guests are given special treatment. This is where they hanged and buried the brave Madan Lal Dhingra. They will do the same to me soon. I wish they hang me on the twenty-third of the month. That was the day that they hanged Bhagat Singh. He had said: 'Shoot me if you think I am waging war. Shoot me like they shoot an enemy in war.' But they were cowards so they hanged him in the dark. I wish to die on the same day and meet him; I know he is waiting for me.

9 JUNE 1940

I used to be called No. 1010. Here in the Ville, I am 6828. A special throne is brought for me thrice a day and so many people come to feed me. Real royal treatment. I refuse to eat on my own. I will fast to death. I am not afraid. So, they bring this big throne and put me on it and strap down my arms and legs. Then one big man stands behind me and holds my head and pulls it back and they put a big rubber thing in my mouth so I cannot shut it. They then push a rubber tube down my throat and pour food into my stomach. I fight and I try to throw away the thing in my mouth and push out the tube. This happens at least thrice a day. Many weeks on hunger strike.

10 JUNE 1940

They have to take good care of me. They have to save me for the hangman. If something happens to me, they will be responsible. This nice room all to myself, without any sharp angles, and no glass. They even took away my spectacles so I would not kill myself with them! And they gave me a new set of grey clothes without even one button—so that I don't swallow the button and kill myself. No belt for the trousers and no laces for my slippers, either.

This is how much care they take to keep a man alive. Only so they can kill him themselves.

16 JUNE 1940

Finally, four prayer books arrived from my friend, Shiv Singh, that jahal man, after weeks of waiting. Three are in Urdu and one in Gurmukhi. They have also now agreed to give my spectacles back when I need them to read or write. They have realized that I cannot read, write, and kill myself at the same time with the same pair of spectacles. I hear they have decided to hang me on the twenty-fifth, not the twenty-third, unfortunately. Again, two steps behind my guru, my best friend.

20 JUNE 1940

I am not to be hanged on twenty-fifth, after all. A group has appealed against the sentence. What's the use? These dirty dogs are not going to let me go. And I am not afraid of dying, anyway. I have told my friends before. Do not waste your money. Use it on education. Maybe some money has come from the Stockton community of California even though they don't like the London group. But I am a Ghadar bhagat—so for me they will do everything, even if they don't like each other.

15 JULY 1940

The court was very crowded today though I couldn't see much. A green curtain blocked me off on three sides. I took one look at the three judges. They didn't meet my eye. I sat down and my lawyer told the whole story again. He wanted the judges to turn down the death sentence because he said that the earlier judge had not explained things properly to the jury, that he should have explained that I did everything out of patriotic feeling.

But the chief judge said there was nothing to be done, no grounds to change the verdict. This was all such drama, a very British drama. They must sound as if they are being very fair. Very white, they call it. Bloody dogs. All the time they knew and I knew that they were not going to change anything. I just smiled and walked out of the court with the warders. They are nice chaps, these prison warders. They have become my friends. Human beings are easy to handle. They like being asked about ordinary things, things about themselves. Things about their children, their wives, their difficulties. Everybody has difficulties. When we reached the prison, I played three-handed whist with them for a while. I have become quite an expert at it. I always know what to do when they deal me a widow card.

16 JULY 1940

The warders tell me many things. One of them told me that my lawyer had come to check whether I wanted to appeal to the King for mercy. But the prison chief did not allow him to see me. In any case, I do not want to appeal. But I know what Shiv Singh and the others will do. They will go around and collect signatures and send letters to the British government and ask for mercy. Even that priest who has been coming to see me, Holland, will write letters to the Home Office.

Fools! Signatures do not move this government of killers and murderers, otherwise India would have been free by now. This is a brutal regime. This is terrorism of a hundred and fifty years and I would rather die than live under the misery of these terrorists. This Raj is a gang of devils, bandits, and vultures. Appeals and petitions have no effect on them. Only blood can defeat them, my blood and that of Bhagat Singh and Dhingra and so many others who have come before me. And those who will come after me.

20 JULY 1940

My days are coming to an end. I can feel it in the way the warders treat me now. They are even gentle when they force the pipe down my throat if I don't take my meal tray. They are more patient, as if they are saying to themselves—it's only a matter of a few days more.

I walk every hour in the yard with its high walls. The open sky is blue and clear. It's very beautiful and at times I feel I have not looked at simple things enough in my life. The blue sky or the green leaves or the pretty birds. There was never any time; there was always so much that had to be done.

25 JULY 1940

Hangings are all the same. I have seen many hanged when I was in prison in India. I have always thought I would be happiest if I met this sort of death. It takes only two minutes and off she goes. In this country, hangmen are white-faced, nice-looking, kind-hearted. But they take life just the same. Their Lord Jesus was hanged from a cross with nails in his hands and feet so I say only the good get away with that death.

These white-faced hangmen will come quietly on the morning that is selected by the High Sheriff for Prisoner 6828. I have seen the steps by which they will come. Metal steps covered with a rubber mat so I won't hear their footsteps and become difficult. But I am prepared. My prayer books have helped me to prepare myself. The warders have told me that the hanging will be right here, next door. And there is a patch of land in the prison where I will be buried with all the other brave revolutionaries.

31 JULY 1940

This is the morning that I have been waiting for. I am dressed in civilian clothes for the first time in the past two weeks. The priest has been with me for an hour. He has been talking to me of the God that awaits me on the other side of this journey. But I am only waiting to see Bhagat.

They are now at the door. I didn't hear them come. The rubber covering on the steps took care of that. The door opens—there are several of them but there is only one man who is looking me in the eye. He must be the hangman.

Hold out your arms, he says, and I stretch them forward. I feel nothing, only a very deep calm. He quickly pulls my arms behind my back and ties them at the wrist. The leather of the strap is soft and gentle. They have moved the wardrobe in the room and behind it is a green metal door. It opens and I can see the rope in the next room. This is the rope to which I am to be wed.

Come with me, lad, you'll be all right, says the hangman, and leads me into the other room. I feel the warders gently holding my elbows as I step forward. They don't push me. They don't need to. There is a line made with chalk under the rope before which they make me stand. Another man ties my ankles together with a leather strap. I see the others in the room, standing in a line, looking at me.

The hangman is in front of me. He whips out a white handkerchief from his pocket. No, it's a white sack that he opens out. The sack is over my head even as the priest is saying the prayers. I see nothing more. I feel the noose around my neck, loose at first, and then tight. Then the ground opens under my feet.

I have become immortal.

I have become one with Bhagat Singh.